Des Dillon was born and brought up in the Lanarkshire town of Coatbridge. He has written poetry and fiction, including *Me an Ma Gal*, *The Big Empty*, *Duck* and *Itchycooblue*, and had several of his books adapted for film and television. He has worked as a teacher of English, a creative writing tutor and as a scriptwriter for *High Road*. Des Dillon lives in West Kilbride, and is currently Writer in Residence at Castlemilk.

Return of the Busby Babes

DES DILLON

review

Return
of the
Busby Babes

First published in 2000
by REVIEW

An imprint of Headline Book Publishing

10 9 8 7 6 5 4 3 2

The character of Bailey Bloggs is an invention of the author,
and is not based on any real-life football player, alive or
dead. No disrespect is intended to any real-life football
player. This is a work of fiction intended as a homage
to the spirit of football.

ISBN 0 7427 7173 9

Typeset in Palatino
Designed and Typeset by Ben Cracknell Studios

Printed and bound in Great Britain by
Clays Ltd, St Ives plc

Headline Book Publishing
A division of the Hodder Headline Group
338 Euston Road
London NW1 3BH

www.reviewbooks.co.uk
www.hodderheadline.com

Dedicated to Pat Dillon and Alice Riley – thanks for the stories

And to Edwin Morgan for the soundest advice ever an unpublished writer was given – in a car – somewhere in Glasgow – some years ago:

'Des – you should write stories the way you tell them.'

And I did – and I do – thanks Eddie.

AIRDRIE & COATBRIDGE CYBERTISER

WEDNESDAY, 14 MARCH 2004

ROVERS BRANDED DONKEYS

Albion Rovers slumped to yet another defeat as the crisis looms on at Cliftonville. After the six–nil drubbing at the hands of Forfar Athletic manager Matt Brennan branded his players 'a bunch of donkeys'. This latest result does nothing to offset the imminent liquidation of the club. Brennan also added that – barring a miracle – Albion Rovers will be no more at the end of next season. Branded the worst team in the world . . .

Same day. Wales. Cardiff. An ordinary house. The telly's on. First it's this brass band music. Then it fades away to some guy talking. It sounds like the adverts you used to get at the pictures in the sixties. Black and white. Some guy telling what the government said was good for you. Eat potatoes – that kind of stuff. But then the voice fades and there's this crowd cheering. And there's somebody watching all this.

It's just a guy watching football. Well that's what it looks like. A guy watching some old football game that's been filmed in black and white by Pathé and transferred to disc. For whatever fans might want to buy it. There's a big trade in that now – old games crammed onto a disc. Much like what they done with music in the 1990s. But now it's football – or even ancient rock bands.

The guy watching's about sixty odds. That's what age he is. But good looking. Young looking really. He's probably watching the team he loved as a boy and saying, *I remember the team of fifty eight – they'd tank the arse off of any these young powder puffs you've got playing these days. Won't get out their bed for less than a grand!*

Funny thing is – you'd think he'd be happy watching the team of yesterday. When I was a lad and all that jazz going through his head. Maybe the odd smile at the grace of the players. Or the half cheer at that goal he's half cheered at a million times. Full cheered on the drink with his mates. But there's nothing like that from this guy. He's quiet. And he's staring. And if you look closer his eyes are glassy. Wet. Must have been on the drink last night you might think. Or he's got the cold or something.

But when you see his face you remember something. It's him. That's what you remember. His face – you remember it from somewhere. Now where is that? Where do I know him from?

And when you place him it all becomes apparent. Bailey Bloggs – that's who it is. Not a Busby Babe that you would

3

know. Not really in the squad at all. Just on the far fringe. It's Bailey Bloggs watching the disc. And it's a nineteen fifty-eight Manchester United game. He fingers a lucky medal on his neck. And you can see how his eyes are watery now. He's crying, that's what he's doing. Not out loud. Not so as you'd hear anything. But he's crying with his eyes. There's a wee football game inside his tears. A beautiful game – between eight Bailey Bloggses and eight will-o' the wisp blue lightning figures. And they're winning the figures. The score inside the tear's eight–nil and rising. There's nothing Bailey can do about it. Nothing at all. And it's whatever's on the telly that's causing the tears. The telly's burning like black and white flames.

United's playing Red Star Belgrade and the Busby Babes are whizzing about with skill and elegance. You can see in the subtle changes in Bailey's face what it all means to him. Every frame of the disc's loaded with another million frames in his head. That's twenty-seven frames a second. That's twenty seven million memories a second. That's twenty seven billion emotional changes a second. The sad binary of neurones and the life they repeat in your head.

Bailey Bloggs can't take it any more. *Change,* he says and it clicks to a fly-on-the-wall documentary based in a ladies' toilet in Tottenham Court Road subway. They've tastefully only allowed the frame to be from the waist up when the ladies are sitting down. But still there's a queue outside wanting to appear in the doc. They've come from all over the country to be in it. Abroad even. To pish for fame. It's the busiest bog in London. The world maybe.

Bailey sighs. *Off,* he says. He gets up and walks to the window. There's some snow falling. Easy flakes. Coming down like frozen daisies. Bailey lies back on the couch he's got at the window. He looks up into the downcoming snow. Watching the flakes's soothing. Easy and light they go. Easy and light. With no weight on their pretty little shoulders. No weight at all. They're happy. Joyful like Christmas. Like childhood. It takes his bad memories away. Concentrate. Concentrate on the snow. Avoid the darkness that lies behind. Stay out of the caverns. He tries to follow one. Head up. Pick one. There – there – that one there swirling down. He fixes his gaze. Fixes focus. He follows it from the tops of the trees. Another one as big reaches out and joins it. They say there's no two snowflakes the same. But these two are the same. Swear. They look exactly the same size and shape. So they join. And like a miniature bra – a bra for fairies maybe – they fall side by side to the ground.

Scotland. Coatbridge. An ordinary house. Mary Maglone's lying looking at the snow. She's got a couch at the window too. And there's two flakes an inch apart from each other. And they're moving closer and closer.

And when they join she smiles. And when she smiles they float in and draw their new edge down the surface of the window pane. It's a whisper. A whisper so light and airy only somebody special can hear it. Only somebody a bit off the wall can understand snow language. Somebody a bit different from the rest of us. Mary smiles again. But her eyes are closed and she's smiling at a picture in her head. The whispers are telling her things. And she's listening and watching. Watching two other snowflakes falling. Somewhere else. In somebody else's sky. And a voice using more breath than vocal cords *Baaaaaaaailey Blogggggggggs, Bailey Bloggs*, it's saying.

On the floor beside her's the newspaper.

ROVERS BRANDED DONKEYS

Albion Rovers slumped to yet another defeat as the crisis looms on at Cliftonville. After the six–nil drubbing at the hands of Forfar Athletic manager Matt Brennan branded his players 'a bunch of donkeys'. This latest result does nothing to offset the imminent liquidation of the club. Brennan also added that – barring a miracle – Albion Rovers will be no more at the end of next season. Branded the worst team in the world…

But he can't concentrate on the snow, Bailey Bloggs. He'd hear the secret whispers too if he'd only listen. *Mary Maglone*, they'd be saying. *Mary Maglone*.

But every time it asks him to listen he feels a void inside or beside him or behind him – he can't tell. But it frightens him anyway, the void, and he pulls back. Pulls back from the future. Pulls into the present. And when he's standing in the present he can't hold it. He can't hold his mind in the present moment. He starts falling. Falling into the past. Into the pictures he's trying to get rid of. The images he doesn't want.

He's back in the airport. Belgrade. There was a long delay. Why was that? That's right – Digger Berry's lost his passport. He was like a wee boy going about. Five feet five of stress and energy. He smiles for a minute Bailey Bloggs. Then it drops. It goes away.

You can't get out of them kind of countries without your passport. It's a laugh – they've got to unload all the baggage again to look for Digger's. And there it is in his suitcase.

They're up in the air. The Captain announces a fuel stopover at Munich. Nobody thinks a thing. Nothing. Once they're settled there's two card schools on the go.

Bump bump it lands. The plane tears down through the snow. Twenty minutes it's only going to take so they've to stay on the plane then it's a short hop back to Manchester.

Coatbridge. Years ago. Barney Wheelan came to Celtic from some boghopper team in Donegal. He's steadily drunk his way down over the years and now he's with the Rovers. Monthly contract. But you know what they say – unlucky with money – lucky in love.

So he's just started with Albion Rovers and he's at this Labour Party dance. It's Bring Your Own Drink. Eddie Duncan and his wife Rena's there. So's Flannagin. He sees her across the floor. Usual stuff. Eyes meet and all that. Beautiful. Long red curly hair, brown eyes, body . . . wow.

She's got this long red Spanish dress. Curls falling over like decorations and her eyes shining in her white skin. She's buying bingo tickets. She smiles over. Somebody sparks a match and it flares in her eye. Barney winks. She winks back. Big Eddie whispers in his ear.

Her name's Carol.

Carol is it? Barney goes, and forms the name on his lips a few times.

It's well into the night and Barney's sitting on this table smoking a joint and crashing another can. His feet are rocking on a chair. ♪♪ *Take It to the Limit* is on and people are up doing moonies. Flannagin's got Rena up. But Eddie thinks nothing of it. It's the Labour Party. They all dance with each other's wives. That's the way it is.

Barney looks round the place. It reminds him of the village dances in Donegal. All round the hall people are dotted in chairs dropping tears in their drink. Glass crunching under every table. It's them shaky pop-up tables and red plastic chairs. Ashtrays are overflowing and fag ends are waterfalling onto Formica surfaces smeared with beer and Buckfast. They hadn't invented Buckie Turbo yet.

That's the stage the night's at.

An old woman's screaming at her man's ear.

He's sleeping – pissed but she can't see his eyes. In the corner Flannagin's shoving his hand up Rena's frock and she's rubbing off his leg. Barney looks about for big Eddie. But he's not there. He goes to do something. To say something. But fuck it. What's it got to do with him anyway?

The white flesh between her black stockings and red knickers's glowing in ultraviolet light. Barney's right in there staring at Flannagin's hand all over Rena's arse. He's got two fingers under the knicker elastic, his thumbs pressing her thigh. Barney can see the bare skin on her cheek through the tent shaped gap. He's engrossed in that when he feels something's not right. That intuition drunks have got. The sense that's something's about to happen. Something violent.

He looks round. There's nothing. It's all the same as it was a minute ago. Then Carol comes bouncing in the hall. Her mouth's opening and shutting and her face is scrunching up and down like a walrus. You can tell she's screaming but you can't hear the noise for the music.

Big Eddie's getting kilt out there!

she's shouting.

Barney gets the drift when Carol's about ten feet away. His face changes and he starts moving. Carol slows on a turn cos she sees he's coming. It's like one of them dreams when you're trying to run and the harder you try the slower you go.

Barney jumps off the table and cos his feet are on the chair it flips up. At the same time he slips on the beer and falls forwards. The sharp edge of the chair leg fucks him right in the eye. He gets to his feet. But he can't see out his right eye. It's throbbing. He charges out the hall holding it with one hand. His good eye's swivelling like a lopsided Cyclops.

Coatbridge. Mary Maglone gets up and looks out her window. She can see Rovers park. She's a fan. Albion Rovers. You'd think in the year 2004 there'd be no more of them mucky pitched football parks. But there is. Albion Rovers. Nine miles east of Glasgow. It's all pies and greyhounds. Outside it's red and tangerine. Well it would be if it wasn't for the brown patches of rust eating through. Four winos shelter beneath sheets of bent-over corrugated steel. Every now and then a slob goes through the main gate. Which is a hole really. Carrying a training bag. The winos shout abuse and depending on who it is they get the fingers, a brick lobbed, or ignored.

Inside there's nothing but a baldy pitch and concrete steps for the crowd that never comes. There's a stand. It's wood and it shakes from side to side any time there's enough supporters. It could limp on another three or four years. The worst soccer team in Britain. The worst ground in the universe. Every league needs a worst team – who'd hold the structure up? They're to be liquidated at the end of next season if things don't pick up. There's little chance of that.

And if that's bad enough. But there's another threat. A threat that should shut the Rovers down well before next season. Albion Rovers. Finished.

Back in Cardiff, Bailey Bloggs's jammed in his memories. Stuck where he doesn't want to be. He tries looking out at the snow again but it's no use. There's not enough gravity in that thinking to drag him out of where his mind is.

Bailey Bloggs's back on the plane. It's refuelling. Two o'clock. It's bitter cold outside. The snow's coming down in sheets. White's all there is out there. White white white. Judder. Jolt. The plane starts moving. That's what it is. It starts moving and all the faces are bright and the card school's going good guns and there's jokes and laughing. And crack. Life everywhere. All over the place. Everywhere you look. Except out there in the snow. It's nothing. Nothing forever. For all he knows there might be nothing out there beyond the blizzard. Nothing at all. Then in the distance he thinks he sees something. Figures. Footballers in fact. But they're glowing like they're made out of blue light. Bailey doesn't remember that memory. That's not usually in it when he re-lives that day. He can't think where it might be coming from. He ignores it. He pushes it away. Comes into the present again. Cancels it out. That's not part of the thing. Not part of it at all. When it's gone he falls back through his neurones again. And soon he's back in the plane and when he's looking out at the snow – the figures are gone.

But there's a funny noise off the engines. Bailey looks about. Jerking his head this way and that to see if there's any-body else scared. Some eyes are darting about and knuckles tightening but nothing much really. Most's carrying on with the laughter and banter. The plane taxis back to the start and waits. There's tension but nobody's letting on really.

Two thirty-four the plane has another go. The engines

start roaring up and the torque tug tug tugs the

plane into motion. Forty seconds seems like nothing but it's a lot when you're soaring along the runway in a blizzard. Specially when the runway feels like a cobbled street. Take off's aborted. Even people that never seemed that bothered's nervous now. Laughing at crap jokes. Talking non stop and not really listening to what other people's saying.

Albion Rovers football ground. And the thing that's a threat to it's spread about like dread. A shadow that's got other darker shadows in it moving about. A panther with scorpions on its back. To see it right you'd need to be up in a plane or a helicopter.

From the air you'd see hundreds of square miles of blackened land surrounding the park. And a few council houses here and there. Four in a block. And there's all sorts of diggers and shovels and piling machines. It's the landscape of a hostile planet and all the wee aliens are moving about in yellow and orange. And the beams of light from giant machines search for intruders at night. It's a development. The biggest leisure retail and residential development Lanarkshire's ever seen. It's all American and Japanese money. The optical processor industry is booming here. There's rumour of Lanarkshire being re-named The Valley Of Light. At the far edge there's a massive concrete and steel tower. It could be an airport traffic control tower but it's not. It's the boardroom of the giant corporation.

If you stared you'd see a shadow at the window. Charlie Flannagin. He's smoking a cigar and surveying the scene. He stands to make millions on the deal. He's doing the leg work for the real money men. They hide away in a big house in Glasgow. Flannagin's making sure nothing stands in the way. In their way. Nothing. He stares at Rovers' ground as he spits the end of his cigar into a bucket. He's the Great White Hunter and he's loading his gun to level the sights. And Rovers are an old sick elephant with yellow tusks and wrinkled skin. And limping on slow to the graveyard. But it's not going to even have the dignity of getting to the elephants' graveyard. Flannagin's going to shoot it down in mid amble. Dead. Drops to its front knees. A loud trumpet in the air. Down to the back knees. Another shot rings out and it rolls onto its side letting out a last sigh of breath. He slots the cigar in his mouth like a shotgun cartridge and looks at the model of the site.

There's a link to the motorways and the main rail lines. But the main thing is the link to the new Zoomph MAPTT. The Magnetic Air Pressure Tube Train. It gets to Paris in an hour. No one knows but Flannagin and The Board. Rovers Park stands on the only geologically sound site for exit and entry from underground. The formation of the rock and a geological anomaly means that chance has plucked it from obscurity. And chance has attracted the money. The narrow eyes of power. The obliteration of Rovers Park means instant access to the optical microprocessor industry that Lanarkshire's world famous for. A monopoly on the European market. But Rovers don't know; if they did they could sell up and move on – millions. The Board has decided to keep the information top secret. Possession of an entry and exit point for the Zoomph MAPTT would mean Power. Power even they have only dreamt about. There's a special carbo crystal in the warrens of old coal mines below Lanarkshire. It was worthless years ago – people used to burn it in their fires. Dross they called it. Now – the Board uses it at the very heart of their Optical Processors. It's got the quickest light conductor in the world. It re-directs laser light at a perfect right angle – 90°. The Board owns all the mines. You can see why they want to hold onto the Zoomph MAPTT.

But there probably won't be a problem. Cos Rovers are so much in debt the bank's decided to liquidate them at the end of next season. And they've never won a thing in their hundred-year history. Not one fuckin iota. By the time a year passes Rovers'll be no more than four winos drinking under white concrete and shining new steel-titanium superstructures.

Barney Wheelan charges out the hall holding his burst eye with one hand. His good eye's swivelling like a lopsided Cyclops.

People are screaming when he gets to the lounge. Barney thinks they're scared of him. But they're screaming at the blood running down his face. He spots this wriggling pyramid of bodies. He grabs a lump of hair and starts melting right hooks in.

No no he's only trying to help Eddie! somebody's shouting.

Barney drops him screaming on the floor and grabs the next cunt. Under the pile of bodies you can hear Eddie shouting, *Tell them to get off me or I'll break your fuckin arm.*

But boots and punches are avalanching in still. Eddie can hardly breathe under the pressure. He's suffocating. Barney hears this dull crack under the bodies and a scream. Eddie's broke the guy's arm. Carol appears. She's batting the eyelashes like a Spanish dancer. She smiles and tilts her head. Her eyes are glowing. Barney winks with his good eye, punching cunts all the time.

KRASHSHSH

This bottle crashes over his head. All this glass showers down. A million Carols are glaring in the fragments. They're jaggy teardrops spinning through the air. Some woman's screaming. Barney's dizzy. Carol's spinning. Her face changes. Mad crazy. She flies at the guy with the neck of the bottle in his hand. **Slash Slash** she goes with the talons and stands back hands on her hips. There's blood under her nails and her mouth's red and sneering. She grins – waiting.

The dizziness is away now and Barney can see clear. The guy slaps the blood on his face and looks at his fingers.

Ya fuckin slut!!! he goes and grabs Carol by the dress. It splits up the seam and he rips it right off.

There she is in her underwear. Barney'll remember the moment the rest of his life. Red stockings and suspenders – white bra – white knickers. He'll remember her red hair through the silk. Carol takes one look at the guy and out it comes:

YAAA BAAAASTAAAAAAAARD!

She launches in with kicks and scratches and punches. The fight's still going on. Every cunt's fighting now. It's your duty. Carol's in her knickers and everything slows down. For a second men master the art of fighting and staring.

Carol picks the dress up and wraps it round herself. The fight gets back into full swing. Two guys in hospital. A cracked rib for Eddie, a fucked up eye, a split head and a limp for Barney. All that's up with Carol is her lost dignity and the stitches up the side of her dress.

The drone as the plane engines rev up.

Hope he's not going to try again, Bailey hears from the card school. And that's what's going through everybody's mind. There's a letting out of pressure as the plane taxis back to the terminus. Thank fuck. Everybody troops off laughing. Mostly bravado. Some's quiet. It's funny how you remember the wee things. Bailey remembers Harry Gregg buying a packet of Players. A packet of Players for fucksakes. That's a laugh considering. Harry gives one to Blanchflower. It's the trivial remarks that stick out in the end. Take on more meaning. Blanchflower goes, *Looks like we might be going back via the hook of Holland. Should get a few beers there. Party time!*

And he rubs his hands together and the air's coming out his mouth in clouds. And it's cold. So fuckin cold. And Big Duncan. Aw – the big man – he sent his landlady a telegram.

```
ALL FLIGHTS CANCELLED - STOP - FLYING
       TOMORROW - STOP - DUNCAN.
```

Next thing Jackie's nipping his fag and they're all heading back on the plane.

I hope me coffee cups are not cracked – that's like a cobbled street that runway, he goes.

The cups. That's it. The cups Red Star presented the team with. Coffee cups. The things you remember. A set of cups and saucers for fucksakes. It's behind Jackie's ear the nipped fag. Bailey can smell snuffed tobacco all the way up to the plane. And the cold stab of the air makes his eyes water. The snow's not that deep. Just over the soles of your boots. Bits of it are being swirled about. Whirlpools they look like. Like they could suck you into another world. But that's daft. It's tarmac under there.

Once they're on and in their seats the plane starts moving. The boys – the ones that aren't scared and the ones that are kidding on they're not scared – they start singing.

♪♪*Give us a chance you miserable swine miserable swine miserable swine . . .*

Give us a chance you miserable swine . . .

But Bailey knows there's something wrong. The steward – he's strapped into his seat and he's not smiling. He's definitely not smiling. His eyes are locked on the back of the plane. Like he's seen something. Something terrible. But the lads keep singing. Bailey feels like telling them to shut up.

Shut the fuck up, he wants to shout. But he can't. He's drawn to the worry on the steward's face. Bailey sinks down in his seat. Then somebody shouts, *Stop the plane!*

Bailey's relieved. The plane slows down. Comes to a halt on the runway. Bailey's waiting on it turning and taxiing back. But it doesn't. It just sits there. Waiting. Purring. And all about's swirling snow. And through the snow's dark.

But it's not stopped to abandon the flight. It's to get Alf Clark. When he gets on the lads give him a right roasting. Specially Roger Byrne. Alf gets in his seat with a happy grin hanging off his face.

It's Coatbridge town hall. Shining marble floors and wood panelled walls. Flannagin's rubber soles squeak along the corridors. You'd think there was a hamster tied to the sole of each shoe.

Morning Charlie – hello Mr Flannagin! is all you can hear as he walks along. He chaps on Lang's door. Nothing. Looks left at a couple of office babes slinking into the hologram terminal. One leans forward six inches exactly, holds her right hand up and waves.

Hi Charlie – going to Stars at the weekend?

Be there probably doll, he shouts trying to puzzle out where he's met her. Dyed blonde hair big tits? He can't think – there's millions of them.

Her giggles are still travelling round the corridors when her long legs disappear. Flannagin looks right. Nothing. He chaps the door harder. Nothing. Makes a funnel with his hands and tries to see through the frosted glass. But he can't. It's like trying to see through a block of ice. He tries the handle soft. Locked. He checks about again before pulling this key out his pocket and opening the door.

So he's in. He clicks the door shut with the palm of his hand. Ci-lick it says. And the smell of wood polish and office supplies accentuates the silence. He goes straight to the bottom drawer of a filing cabinet and gets the drink. Pours a whisky and sits in the swivel chair. And he fixes his tie and coughs a couple of times before making a few phone calls.

Yes.

Wnabzbzbz nnnanana naanmnm

No Boss.

Wnabzbzbz nnnanana naanmnm

Everything's going to be alright Boss.

Wnabzbzbz nnnanana naanmnm

What?

Wnabzbzbz nnnanana naanmnm

What? Well it wouldn't go amiss.

Wnabzbzbz nnnanana naanmnm
Say fifteen grand?

Wnabzbzbz nnnanana naanmnm

OK. Ten. Ten grand.

The call's over. He pours another bigger drink. Pottering about at the photos on the desk. Looking in drawers for anything he might use as leverage later. Knickers, a VirtualTrip helmet – gives a five minute full-blown acid trip by a combination of stroboscopic images and acupressure. They've been banned from all business premises – production had fallen thirty per cent. It was nearly as bad as Lemmings 2001 – Tony Blair has criminalised that game and all its merchandise.

So Flannagin's still sitting there when the keys go in the lock. The door swings open and Lang comes in backwards. He doesn't see Flannagin till he's took his jacket off. He shites himself.

What the fuck are you doing here Charlie?

He looks about.

How'd you get in?

Flannagin swings a wee key in the air, takes his feet off the table and gets up. Lang checks outside the door before he speaks.

I said to keep the visits down.

Don't worry Tony we can say it's a Masonic thing.

Masonic. Fuckin Masonic? That's worse.

Lang shuts the door and pours a drink. Flannagin pings his glass a couple of times for a refill. Lang slugs his whisky. But it's only halfway down when Flannagin slaps a wad of notes on the desk.

Ten grand, he goes.

Lang whips open a drawer and sweeps the money into it with the glass still in his hand. He fumbles for the key and locks the door.

What the fuck are you doing? Are you trying to get us lifted? Walls have ears for fucksakes.

What and eyes too?

Lang drops the blinds. *Maybe I should pull out of this. Give you all the money back.*

Flannagin laughs.

It's not too late, Lang goes. *It's all still here.*

Flannagin thinks for a moment. *Look you probably won't need to do anything. It's a back up, Compulsory Purchase Order. Just in case they win the league.*

Rovers? says Lang. *Rovers?*

They look at each other. A shoulder goes. Another shoulder. They both burst out laughing.

Or the fuckin cup, goes Lang. *In case they win the cup!*

But he goes quiet again. The grin wipes itself slowly off his face.

What's up? says Flannagin.

Proby – the motorway contractor – M8 tunnel?

What about him?

He's giving me a lot more than your lot for a CPO.

Flannagin stares at him.

How much then?

Another ten, says Lang.

Ten for fucksakes?

Ten – and that's it done – no problem.

Flannagin stares at him and lifts the phone.

Bailey's still in nineteen fifty-eight. He's oblivious to the snow outside now. His window sill's a Christmas card. All it needs is a wee robin and a sprig of holly. He's back in the plane. The plane that once he's in he can never get off till the whole scenario plays again. Till it's all over and the immense burden of guilt overpowers him and he passes out.

The plane gets off again. Roger Byrne's face's contorted with fear. It makes Bailey feel better cos he's not the only one that's shit scared. So he laughs a bit Bailey. Through his teeth. More out of nerves than anything. But the pressure's building up. You can feel it in there. Like the pressure's pressing the words back into people's mouths. Down past their voicebox and into their lungs. And the words press through the lung wall membrane. And into the bloodstream. On up to the brain and they fizzle out in the neurones that gave birth to them. And laughter. It's shoving that back too. Soon there's nothing but the bumping wheels on the ground and the roaring engines. It's like that for a while. Somebody starts sniggering. A manic snigger. Next thing Johnny Berry

shouts, *We're all going to get fuckin killed here, what are you laughing at?*

Billy Wheelan shouts up the plane, *Well, if anything happens I'm ready to die.* And you can't tell if he's serious or kidding. Or maybe half-kidding. You just can't tell. So he goes to laugh Bailey – but he can't. He's thinking about dying. The whole plane's thinking about it.

And that thought makes the plane go silent for a while. Bailey settles on the word *die.* The easy way Billy said it. Like it was part of life. Like the darkness behind the snow's as much part of snow as the snow itself. White and black.

23

Opposites attract. Life and Death. Nothing drastic. Like you just moved from this life into another one. No problem. Easy osey over.

Speed's picking up. Snow's coming out from the wheels like comets. Like there's three white comets racing the plane down the runway. And they'll never quite overtake it. Out the window Bailey sees places he's never seen the first two times. Must be another runway, he's thinking when -

Lift.

The plane starts to

There's   a   hellish

screeeeeeech

And then

BANG

NMOD ƎⱭISⱭ∩

Then the plane's going round and round. They're all trapped in a mad washing machine. Tumble. Weightless. Face floating above. Twice the weight. Bodies thumping to the floor. Weightless again. But no noise. Can't hear a thing. The sound's been left behind and it can't catch up till the plane stops tumbling.

The Labour Party dance. When Barney met Carol. The fight's over. Two guys in hospital. Eddie's got a cracked rib. Barney's got a fucked up eye, a split head and a limp. Carol's dignity's damaged and the stitches up the side of her dress. They're walking up to Eddie's house. Rena's been lost in the process. But if they were watching they'd have seen her sneaking away during the fight – with Flannagin. But they're walking up the road and they're singing.

There's eyes at every window. Eddie's got an arm round Carol and so's Barney. Carol's swearing away to herself. The blood's caked on Barney's face and the rush of victory's coursing through his veins with the drink. He starts singing ♪♪ 'Somewhere Over the Rainbow'. Carol joins in.

Carol's got a Super Lager in one hand and she's holding her seam together with the other. It's like a sleazy *Wizard of Oz* and she's Dorothy. They skip up the maze of broken slabs echoing into closes. That's the point where Barney falls in love. And so does Carol. So does Carol.

Coatbridge. In Kirkwood there's boarded up windows. Hundreds of wanes running about. Burnt out cars and stray dogs. There's a massive red brick building. It's a cube really. Flat roof. In the middle of one wall there's a door. Solid steel. Above it it says

> **BOOKMAKERS. INTERNET FACILITIES. FAR EAST NIGHT BETTING. OPTICAL LINK. VIRTUAL ANYTHING. TWO FOR ONE MON–FRI.**

On another wall there's a door the exact same.

MACKENZIES it says above that.

LICENSED TO SELL ALCOHOL. CLASS A B & C DRUGS.

Fifty young team go by singing into the doorway. Like the doorway's the enemy.

♪♪ *For it's a grand old team to play for*
For it's a grand old team to know
For if
You know
The history
It's enough to make your heart grow
    Oh oh oh oh
We don't care what Sky television says
What the hell do we care
For we only know that there's going to be a show
And the Glasgow Celtic will be there
PLC!

GOD BLESS TV!

They start singing it all over again. And they fade into the distance on the way to catch the train into Parkhead. Inside the pub Duncan Edwards can hear the songs. He's been a big Celtic fan all his life. His pal got signed up for them when he was wee. Pat the Leg they call him. Best player in the whole town. He's dead now. Eddie's dreaming. It's him in the Celtic jersey. European cup final or something. Last minute and it's *Edwards – Edwards – still Edwards – oh he's out free – Edwards – Edwards – edddddddddwaaaaaards –*

goaaaaaaaaaaaaaaaaaaaaaaaaaaaaaaaaal!!!!!!!!

Eddie! Rena shouts. She's wanting to know what he wants. He lifts his glass for the same. Rena's got her elbows on the bar and she's leaning over so her high heels are lifting off the ground. And her feet are lifting out the back of the shoes. The guys at the Hologram jukebox can see the flesh at the top of her stockings. And the wee holes on her heels where they've wore away. She twists her head round like a yoga instructor, sees them, smiles and lifts a bit more till she's got no weight on her feet at all. She flicks her long blond hair at them and looks into the bar. Into the mirrors behind the bottles of whisky and Buckie Turbo. She's checking her red lips loving the heat of their eyes drilling lines up and down the length of her legs. Wishing it was their lips – all kissing her at once.

The guys stop staring when big Eddie gets up to go to the bog. He knocks his chair over and bumps into people and tables all the way.

Is he drunk? one of the guys asks Rena.

No – he's just a clumsy big cunt, she goes.

They laugh. And there's something else about him too. The back of his neck's all pitted and burnt. Red. Like he's had an accident years ago.

Look at that eejit, Rena says to Alice behind the bar. She leans over and whispers a loud secret in Alice's ear. *It's a wonder he can ever get it in me.*

The boys at the jukebox's eyes light up. *Good job God gave us runways.* Rena goes and pats her legs. And they lick their lips. The toilet door squeaks shut and one of the team moves next to Rena.

Four lager Alice.

Rena's kidding on he's not there. But his outer thigh's pressing against hers. She's making no attempt to move. They flirt with each other a bit in the mirror while the pints are getting poured.

Big Eddie still playing?

Aye, she goes, *when he gets a game.*

She turns a bit to the man and some of her hair lands on his shoulder. He can smell the perfume and that dusty talcum smell you get. She doesn't try to remove her hair. Neither does he.

Four lager, says Alice.

As he reaches for the lager he runs the length of his left forearm down her right tit. She presses in rather than away.

He's playing Saturday, she goes. *I'll be in here.*

She waltzes over the jukie an sticks on 'I Love to Love You Baby'. Donna Summer. Banned from broadcast by Tony Blair's Unsuitable Act 2001. All the banned records have found a new lease of life in hologram jukeboxes up and down the country. Even Bill Clinton's new duet with Madonna's banned. Whirr – click: Donna Summer appears on top of a table – ebony thighs shining in the neon like sexy stone. ♪♪ *Who-ahhh*, she sings starting off in mid orgasm.

Eddie comes back out the toilet. *Diarrhoea*, he says, and points to his arse.

Eddie's sitting in the class. He's thirteen. He's came in late. He's muttered something about having to run for his Maw's messages and the teacher just goes, *Aye – right – right – sit down Duncan. Sit down.*

So he's sat there and he's breathing fast. He's red. His hair's damp with sweat. Stuck to his forehead in miniature ropes. The voice of the teacher's soothing in its normality. Eddie's staring dead ahead. There's nothing in his mind. Nothing at all. He can't afford to let anything in. In case it all comes back. He thinks he's good at blocking it out. But it's the shock. He doesn't realise that. The shock's keeping it all out.

The door goes. It's Linda Harkins with a note. The whole school's to go to assembly. Eddie's heart jumps. He knows what it is.

There's turmoil inside Bailey's head. Mayhem. The plane skids off the runway, through a fence and across a road. The left wing smashes into a house. It rips open like tinfoil. Then it's yanked off along with half the tail. The cockpit hits a tree and crushes like a bean tin. The right side of the fuselage slides and smashes into a garage. The truck inside explodes. The slates soar up into the air like a sudden flock of starlings. Fireball. The roof disintegrates and the slates shower down on the still moving plane. The plane grinds to a stop in sleet and sludge. The fireball dies.

There's silence.

A long silence.

Only the creak of wrenched metal and the thrizz of snow on the quiet roof. It's pitch black. Blood's running down Bailey's face. He thinks he's in hell. Death at least anyway. He's scared. There's that much pain. Everywhere. There's blood. A lot of blood. He does nothing for ages. But it's not ages. It's only a couple of seconds. A snowflake falls on his lip. He licks it. The cold taste is still with him after years and years. An ice cube in a drink or whatever and he's back there. The tiny coldness of the flake brings him to his senses. There's no telling how the mind works in catastrophe. No telling at all. He looks up and there's fire above him. And light. He's still alive.

I'm not dead. I'm not dead, he's saying but he can't remember if he said it out loud or into himself. And he can't believe it. He can't believe he's alive. There's fire above. Got to get out. He gets outside.

There's Harry Gregg, stuck through the roof of the aeroplane like a mad tank commander in the midst of battle.

Absurd. Over to the right Bert Whalley's lying with not a mark on him in the snow. Dead. His eyes are wide open. Harry kicks his way out. He slides down onto the ground. In the distance there's five people running through the snow. Jim Thain – think that's who it is – aye that's it Jim Thain – he comes round the crushed cockpit with a fire extinguisher,

Run ya stupid bastard! Run!

he yells and bolts the course.

There's all this hissing and moaning then Harry's ears prick up. There's a wane crying. A bloody kid in there somewhere. He shouts to Jim Thain,

Come back, there's people alive in here!

But he's halfway in the plane anyhow when he shouts that. Bailey Bloggs can see everything from where he's lying. Harry scrambles about over bodies and what not. Stuff you can't bring into pictures in your head. Won't.

Ah ha! He finds the carry cot. He tugs the sheets and blankets out. It's empty. It's fuckin empty. Then there's the crying again.

Under a chair. Under a chair. He grabs the wane, jumps out the plane and runs. You never know when it'll blow up. He looks like a rugby player that's got loose with the ball. Fifty odd yards he goes in seconds. Gives the wane to the Radio Operator who's bewildered in a field and runs back. Right in the plane he goes. He tries to get Ray Wood out but he's jammed. Same with Albert Scanlon. Harry jumps out and bolts round the back of what used to be the front section. Bobby Charlton and Denis Violet's lying there. And here's the mad thing. Harry thinks the two of them are dead but he picks them up anyway. Where the fuck he gets the strength who knows? But he picks them up by their waistbands and drags them out. He trails them through the snow. Flops them down in the middle of the field. The bit of the plane Harry came out of's exploding and exploding. The fuselage jumps up at every bang like a man being shot. Every flash is followed by a soft thud and a rush of air.

But Harry runs back anyway. There's no fear. He's way beyond fear. He's in Action. Next thing he finds Matt Busby. He's propped up on his elbows. One of his ankles's turned the wrong way.

My chest. My legs! he's saying. He doesn't know who he's saying it to. He senses a presence.

Jackie Blanchflower's shouting about a broken back. Roger Byrne's lying across his legs. Harry notices Jackie's right arm's hanging off. There's that much blood it's not scary anymore. He takes off his tie and makes a tourniquet but he goes too tight and the tie breaks. *Fuck fuck fuck!* he says looking about for something else. There's this stewardess. Dazed. Doesn't know where she is. The plane starts exploding again.

For fucksakes, will you give me something to tie his arm with?

But she stares. And stares. She's like a mannequin. There's sirens and spinning lights. All sorts of people start appearing. This guy's got a long needle and a medical bag. The plane explodes again and throws Harry on his arse. But that's not what shocks Harry. What shocks him most is he turns and there's Bobby and Denis. He thought they were ghosts. Bailey remembers getting took away and there was snow landing on his face. Other people on stretchers too. They looked dead. There's blue lights and flashing lights and the explosions. And snow landing on his face. Snow landing on his face.

Coatbridge. Old Monkland. Four-high veranda flats. Bogging. It's like Beirut. Some windows are boarded up with wood and some's boarded up with steel. There's some buildings in the middle of being knocked down. And there's these wee pockets of nice housing here and there about the place.

There's a few women in a lane. Their wanes wind in and out their legs trying to get attention. But they're getting none. Cos the women are looking up at the top flat. There's shouting and smashing up there. And the odd thing flies over the veranda. Pot. Cup. Shoe. Some of the shouting's definitely a woman from Coatbridge. *Ya Baaaaaaastard,* she's shouting. The women nod. They know the score. Been there before. Manys a time. Manys a time right enough. But the other shouting's got an Irish accent. Barney Wheelan it sounds like.

That's terrible that, says one woman.

So it is Masie. Terrible. What's this place coming to I don't know.

A dog pishes up against this old drunk lying on the path. The women don't notice – they're stretching their necks. The wanes spit on the dog and when that doesn't work they chuck some stones. But the dog's still not for moving. Till this right ugly wane scuds it on the arse with a halfer. Then it's offski. Leaning back over its shoulder to memorise the ugly half-brick chucker. The women are taking in a live soap opera.

It's that Irish fella. The footballer.

Is that who it is?

The smashing gets louder till there's a sudden stop. Then a slamming door and an almighty crash. A soup plate maybe smashing off the front door. There's footsteps. Somebody coming down the close. At speed.

Barney Wheelan comes flying out with his jacket in his hand and his shoes half on. He comes up the path stamping into his shoes. Trying to wriggle the folded-over heels straight up. Carol's up on the veranda now with her arms folded like

Maw Broon. He looks up. The women kid on they're not looking. But they are. They're looking alright. The wanes are looking now and all. Even the old drunk's got one eye open. Even the arse-whacked dog's stopped at a distance.

You are a fuckin maniac. D'you know that? A fuckin maniac, shouts Barney. But Carol's not like the madwoman she was in the house. She's the picture of control. By this time she's lit a fag and she's drawing on it long.

Aye – and you're a fuckin alky, she says. But she talks. She doesn't shout. Behind the lowness of her voice's the energy of a nuclear fission. The old drunk's nodding away. He recognises the very situation. That's exactly him ten years ago. All the eyes are squinting on Barney. He doesn't like it. Not one bit does he like it. He's down tying his laces. So he cranes up and looks like he's in some hellish praying position. This is his prayer.

Alky? Alky? I'm no a fuckin alky. He starts walking away. *Just cos I like a pint?*

That's your war cry – she starts doing him – *I just like a wee pint hen . . . hic . . .*

The women like that and start laughing. So does the drunk. The wanes laugh too but they don't know what they're laughing at really. The dog wonders if it could maybe take a bite out Barney. Barney gives them all a black look and staggers off down Kellock. The thing they notice most about him is the scar round about his right eye. You can tell he's been in the wars at one time or another.

Three kids appear on the veranda. They're in some nick. Look like a good feed'd kill them. They're crushing round their Maw's legs and she's blowing smoke over the scheme. The wanes are caged behind the bars of the veranda. And you can't tell if the bars are there to keep the world safe from them or to keep them safe from the world. When you look into their eyes it could be any of the two. Any of the two it could be.

Barney storms straight to the pub.

Munich. A crushed plane lies in bits. There's snow. And after Bailey's took to hospital there's something weird happens. A big wind blows up. From high above looking down there's bits of wreckage. Lights. Red and blue lights – spinning. Ambulances going everywhere. A stream of people and equipment moving from the terminus to the plane. From the plane to the terminus. And fire. Explosions whoomphing and lighting the place up. Then the black hole they leave behind. But there's something else and all. Something strange. Seven lights. Blue – a white electric blue. And they're moving. And if you watched for a while you'd see they're acting in a pattern. They're coming together in a circle then moving out again randomly. Coming together in a circle and moving about. It could be anything. There's a lot of things could explain it. A machine. The reflection of one of the blue spinning ambulance lights. Something to do with it refracting off helicopter rotors hovering overhead. OK there's ways to explain it within the boundaries of the laws of physics.

But it'd be hard to explain this: the lights shoot up in the air. One German medic looks up. He wrings his eyes. Blinks. He looks up again. The seven lights have shapes. Like men. Phantoms. The medic tugs the nurse. She ignores him. He tugs her again. She sighs and looks up – to shut him up more than anything. They're the only two to witness seven spirits floating in the sky above the plane. And even through the snow their light is incandescent. But it's not a light that blinds. You can look straight at it. And more amazing than that – they're playing football. The ball – a simple sphere of light – whooshes to one player. His gravity bends the ball round his body and catapults it across to another. When one of them kicks the ball the contact flares it up a lucid blue and red – it cools to blue-white as it moves through the void between them. They're passing the ball about and moving away. Jogging sprinting and dribbling away out to the east.

The medic and the nurse never mention it again. They put it down to fatigue. It's a secret they'll never raise again. Like they've had a fling at a Christmas party.

So seven spirits float up from the airport and across the land. Seven footballers. Seven Busby Babes. Roger Byrne. Tommy Taylor. David Pegg. Bill Whelan. Eddie Coleman. Mark Jones. Geoff Bent.

They play ethereal football. Passing the ball in the eerie quiet above the storm clouds. The ball hovers and wishhh – it zooms like a meteor from player to player. The high wind blows them on and on. Over towards Salzburg. Up and up. Shouting for the ball in a soundless language. Moving with unprecedented grace. Giant hills appear in the distance. And the wind's dropping. And they're losing altitude. But it's not just the wind. There's something else. Something pulling them down. A kind of gravity. Down towards the mountain. Towards this flat bit on the mountainside.

The seven descend onto it. They kick the ball about. The ball swooshes in curves of light from one foot to the next. Like a loose electron going from atom to atom bending through the magnetic field of each one. As they play they sink further and further into the snow. It's late afternoon. It's getting dark on the hills.

Overhead a pilot remarks to his co-pilot about strange lights on the mountain. The co-pilot leans over. Far below there's seven blue lights moving beneath a gauze of snow. Like kids playing beneath a white blanket with torches. They've learned to shrug stuff off over the years. There's a lot of uncanny lights in the skies.

And if you walked up to the mountain you'd see spotlights like stage lights. But no beam. No beam coming through the air and landing in a flat pool of light on the surface of the snow. This is another light from another place. And if you sat and watched the magic dance all night long you'd notice a slowing down till they come to a stop. Seven lights buzzing. Perfect circles somewhere under the snow. And they're in a perfect circle.

Or they would be if there was one more. The seven have arranged themselves so that one more light'll make the perfect circle. There's a space for the eighth. A space for one more light.

And if you waited. Two weeks later the spirit of Duncan Edwards'd come jogging across the sky to join his mates.

Roger! Tommy! He'd be shouting into silence. *Billy – Mark – are you there?*

It's after the Labour Party dance. Carol's got a SuperLager in one hand and she's holding her seam together with the other. It's like a sleazy *Wizard of Oz* and she's Dorothy. They skip up the maze of broken slabs echoing into closes. That's the point where Barney falls in love. And so does Carol. So does Carol.

And five weeks later they're married. Brian Rogers's got a caravan in St Andrews. He gives them it for their honeymoon. Wedding present.

They get to the caravan, unload all the stuff out the car and sit down shattered. Barney catches glimpses of her unawares. Every time he remember she's his wife this rush goes through him.

I'll away and lie down for an hour, she goes.

I'm coming too!

Well! Carol opens the room where the bed is and all these millions of balloons come tumbling out like giant pool balls. Only silent. They burst out laughing – holding each other up.

That bastard Brian must have been up and done that, Barney says.

Aww, goes Carol, *is that no nice?*

They get the gear off anyway and get squeaking in among the balloons.

POP SIGH MOAN SIGH POP MOAN POP MOAN POP SIGH

The next day Barney goes down the beach and Carol's tidying the caravan. There's a path out Kinkell Braes Caravan Park down onto the beach. He's looking in rock pools for crabs and anything trapped in the retreating tide.

Next thing there's this big daft-looking bird. It's flapping but it's not going nowhere. Like there's no air round its body for the wings to dig into. Vacuum. It's trying to fly in outer space. Barney's walking towards it and it's watching him and flapping faster. He can see its wee beady eye peeling and unpeeling in fear.

Coatbridge. It's one of them wee schemes that's sprung up the last twenty years on sites that used to be factories or railway land. Most of the Optical Processor factories are small. To look at that is. A building about the size of a football field. But they go on for hundreds of feet underground. That's where the raw materials are. These wee houses are made out of tan coloured bricks and wee white windows with hundreds of wee squares in them. Maybe a bullseye glass in one pane. And English architecture in Scotland. Two worlds merging.

In one house the curtains are Hollywood Pink. An American car sits in the driveway. Pink. Well – hangs over each side of the driveway in fact. A Cadillac. The driveways were built for a British car and a very slim person. Carol gets out the car by shoving back the soft-top, climbing the window and walking along the bonnet. She's dainty as a sparrow.

Inside Brian Rogers shuffles up the hall. It's your usual. One kind of wallpaper on the bottom. Rag-rolling on the top and a dado rail. Cornice and a few B&Q paintings. It's oil paintings they do in the store for you. You might want a Hockney pool and behind it a Van Gogh cornfield with peacocks instead of crows. You thinks that's crazy? That's what Carol's got in the hall. But it's all different when Brian comes into the living room. It's the nineteen fifties. Elvis statue. Buddy Holly photos in silver frames. Rockabilly paraphernalia. 'That'll Be The Day' plays loud.

Brian shakes his head. He walks over and clicks it off.

Hoy you! a woman shouts from the scullery. *Put that back on!*

He puts it back on and turns it down. Donna comes in. She's in American late fifties gear. She turns it back up. Brian puts his face in his hands.

Oh what's wrong with my wee Teddy Bear – notsy like the music?

41

It's fuckin shite.

He sits down and flicks the paper open. She kisses him on the top of the head. Same time she's lifting her skirt up. She flashes the sussies and all the tackle at him.

But you like these, she goes.

C'mere!

Brian grabs her and tips her onto the floor.

Do-on't Brian – we've got to visit Jean the night.

Plenty time, he grunts.

I don't want to be all sticky.

Jean won't notice. She doesn't even know what world she's in.

Another song comes on. It's *The Best Fifties Album In The World $EVER$ Volume Sixteen.* Ricky Vallance's writhing about mangled up in his crushed racing car. Brian and Donna bang away to the morbid lyrics.

Cardiff. Bailey Bloggs's lying on a leather couch. A black one with all the wee buttons tugging the leather. The psychologist's nodding away.

Mm mm yes. Mm mm carry on, he's going. Picking his nails.

. . . me – why was it me and not – say big Duncan? That's what I keep saying. Keep asking myself.

There's a tear in Bailey's eye. There's a pause and it's just cars going by outside. But a silence in the room. And if you took away the two men breathing and the occasional creak of the leather you could hear it. If you listened really hard you could hear it. The tiny rushing inside the turbulence of the tear as it rolls down Bailey's cheek. And there's different types of tears. The tears of anguish and regret are filled with churning water – like Bailey's. The tears of sadness – they're filled with dark waters. And the tears of joy? On a really good day a school of porpoises breaks the surface.

The shrink breaks the silence with, *And how have you done with the focusing?*

Bailey doesn't answer.

The thing about Neuro-Linguistic Programming is it takes time. Repetition Bailey. Repetition. Have you been doing it daily as well as during the . . . attacks?

Bailey still can't answer.

Yes – well – repetition – that's the key. Let's try the Swish Pattern now.

But Bailey's mind's somewhere else.

. . . the prime of their lives, he goes distant, *with all that talent?*

The psychologist leans forward, *We can't bring the dead back*, he says, *now we've been over this ground Bailey.*

Brian Rogers's never going to do nothing wrong in his life. He's going to walk the straight and narrow. Like Alf Tupper Tough of the Track – in the comics. You can't get out of line is what he's thinking. If you get out of line you're fucked. And he's young. He's about seven. But that's the thinking he's got.

And he's thinking that cos he's took a drink of his Da's Ginger Beer. He's walking along the lobby and there it is shining like a rocket in Da's room. It used to be Maw's room. But it's Da's room now. It used to smell of talcum and milk. Now it's stale beer and tobacco. There's a lot of Auntie smell in there now. And the smell of creaking springs and grunting. And the smell of shame. And the smell of other kids looking at you on the streets. Their mothers pulling them away. The smell of knowing things before you know what they are. Feeling the meaning before you know the words. But the ginger beer's glowing like a chalice.

He crawls in and cracks the lid open. Kshshsh it says to the darkness. The darkness says nothing back. It watches. I am the darkness it's saying. And I'm watching you. It used to be Jesus that watched. But now it's the space under the bed. Or the bust bulb in the bog. Or the loft.

It's the middle of the day but the curtains are still shut. His Da's been down the park drinking wine since eight. He could see him from the window if he opened the curtains. Standing laughing at shite jokes with these other men. They've not got a full set of teeth between them. And a couple of the Aunties are there. Talking like witches.

Glug glug. He takes a couple of slugs. It burns the back of his throat. That's what he's thinking. He's thinking it's mental that you drink something and you've got to drink water after it. He screws the lid back and sits it exactly where it was. At reaching distance if you were a man and you were lying in the bed with a hangover. Probably never notice it his Da. He's that drunk all the time he never notices nothing. He's been like that since Maw floated up to the sky.

It's a flat in the town centre. Modern and sparse. Like the kind you see on perfume adverts. The kind that's got its kitchen out B&Q. The kitchen with red doors and stainless-steel cooker washing machine and fridge. You can hardly see the joints in things. Like the whole room's made out of the same sheet of metal. A guy's kitchen. Where fuck all ever gets cooked cleaned or bought unless there's a bird visiting.

Through in the bedroom Jimbo sits up in bed. Black satin sheets – they're that cool every guy that lives on his own's got them. Jimbo's bird's got a face on her like a bulldog licking the pish off a jaggy nettle. Super huff. Her arms are folded that tight you'd think they've fell out with Jimbo and all. Or she's scared to let them go in case they run away. And if you think her face's bad you should see Jimbo's. His is like the mongrel that was licking the balls of the bulldog that was licking the pish of a jaggy nettle. You'd expect them to bark at each other. But they talk.

OK OK – it happens more than that, Jimbo goes, *but it's just stress the doctor said. Stress.*

He leans over to kiss her but she flicks the covers up, gets out and slides into her knickers. The white lacy ones that are that sexy every bird in the country wears them.

I've had enough of this Jimbo, she goes.

Jimbo struggles out from under the covers. She's flinging her clothes on. Jimbo does the palm out pleading bit.

I'll get help.

His bird twists her face at him.

Hmm – you're beyond help. I'd get a better shag at a pensioners' outing, she goes.

Jimbo's stunned to a lump of wood.

B . . . b . . . b . . . he says.

B . . . b . . . b . . . she says back taking the cunt out him – wiggling her pinky.

I'll get Viagra – the Torque five hundreds!

But that's a mistake. Jimbo's a bit inexperienced with

women. That's the wrong thing to say.

Viagra? Viagra!? You need Viagra to get a hard on with me? And not just ordinary Viagra. No – you need Viagra Torque. No fuckin thanks. And not just Viagra Torque – but Torque five hundred! No – I'll get somecunt that can give me something. A man. Somecunt with a DICK!

But it's not you, he says, *I'd be the same with any bird.*

So I heard, she says. *You're the laughing stock of the place.*

She holds her hand up with her palm facing the ground. She wiggles her bent pinky at him again.

Wiggle wiggle, she goes, *wiggle wiggle – that's you. I'll be telling all my pals. The ones that don't know already that is. I should have took a photograph!*

She whips her car keys out her handbag and storms out. Her vicious laugh's trailing behind like a black and red ribbon. It's cut off by the door. All Jimbo can hear is a muffled version of it going down out the close and starting a car. Then the car – a SheJag – thrusts itself into the night.

It's the honeymoon. Barney's on the beach watching this big bird. It's flapping but it's not going nowhere. Like it's trying to fly in space. Barney's walking towards it and it's looking at him and flapping harder. He can see its wee beady eye.

Oh fuck, it's saying, *here's a mad cunt coming.*

It's getting bigger and bigger as he's getting nearer. That's when he remembers what it is. A Cormorant. A big brown Cormorant. You get hundreds of them back home. Like Herons but not as graceful. Like Herons full of smack. He remembers chasing them along the shore in Donegal. For a minute he gets a fright when he remembers how long and far his journey's been. And how downwards. He takes the full force of it on the heart. It's like a mini heart attack. But he blocks it out and shoves it to the side. He makes off towards the bird again.

It's gave up on the flapping now and it's running like fuck along the rocks to get away. Its flippers are slapping from one rock to the next. Barney keeps thinking of this lank secretary that worked in the ferry office at Bundoran. The Cormorant thinks it's fly dodging side to side but it's running into this wee cul-de-sac of rocks.

Bang! It slaps off a cliff and turns shaking its head from side to side. Once it's re-focused it stands right up and spreads out its wings to frighten Barney.

Oh ho I'm scared, he goes and starts towards it slow. Spreading his arms out.

It lets out this squawk and drops the wings. Gives in. Gives in easy. Barney's thinking if he gave in so easy he'd be fucked years ago. He feels like booting its arse for giving in so easy. Then he thinks that maybe that's what he's done. It's not been a long hard struggle at all. That's just the way his head's telling it to him. He's gave up. With the drink and that. He's gave up years ago. Suddenly the rush and recede of the sea's in his ears. He turns and it goes out for miles. And there's nothing on it. Not even a wee boat. Or a sail to mark the length and breadth of the thing.

Then he remembers the other name for Cormorants. A Shag. A fuckin Shag. That's a good detour to stop thinking. Who in their right mind's going to call a bird a Shag?

I don't know who's in charge of names but he should be shot, Barney says to the bird.

It looks at him like it understands. Its head's nodding up and down like yes. But it's fear and exhaustion.

He gets an idea. Bursts out laughing. The sea rushes in and out. He laughs again. The Shag looks at him puzzled. Barney moves towards it.

Here wee burdy – come to your uncle Barney.

It's going backwards till it's practically breaking its tail feathers off the rocks behind. Barney grabs it and it flops. Even a caught sparrow struggles like fuck at every chink of light. But this big bastard's got a dose of the poor me's. Suffering from bird depression. Probably brought on cos it can't fly. Impotent in the wing department. Pals have probably flew off to Blackpool or Saltcoats. Or Airdrie.

Barney decides to sing to it. Maybe cheer it up a bit. He launches into the 'Ugly Duckling' song:

He moves closer.

His shadow falls on it.

He sticks his left arm out.

He sticks his right arm out.

QUACK! he yells.

Barney grabs the fucker and it lets out this tiny squeak. A squick really. It's going to get out of town now alright.

Outside Albion Rovers' ground a gaggle of supporters sing 'We Shall Not Be Moved' to some building workers. The workers are chipping wee stones at them. The supporters are ducking behind the soaring retaining wall. It stops feet away from the corrugated perimeter fence of the ground. Ping ping the stones are going.

You are are going nowhere. Ping. *In the League and all.* And now that they've got them pinned down the workers start doing a wee routine all about Rovers. Every time a tangerine tammy sticks its head up another stone or four-inch nail shooms and pings off the reinforcing bar that's rising into the sky from the restrictive concrete. Like it wants to escape. Like if it wasn't for the concrete it'd make it all the way to Heaven. The heavy weight of the concrete's dragging it down. And as far as that part of the construction goes – that's the way the steel'll be till Rovers are shut down. They can't continue here till they can move their machines into where the pitch is. They need to tunnel down to the geological anomaly that makes Rovers' ground a very special place.

The workers are doing their Albion Rovers routine.

Hello is that Albion Rovers?

Yes.

Could you tell me what time's the game at?

What time d'you want it to be at sir?

Boom boom tsh! says one of the workers.

The workers laugh like fuck. The supporters sing louder.

♪♪ *We're on our way to Hea-a-ven we shall not be moved.*

The workers fling more nails. One of the supporters sticks his head up. Whoom – a scaffolding coupling clangs its way through the puzzle of steel and just misses his head. The supporters shut their gubs.

Hello is that Albion Rovers?

Yes.

49

What time's the game at?
Come up early and you'll get a game.
Boom boom tsh!

♪♪ *We're on our way to Hea-a-ven we shall not*
    be moved.

One of the supporters can't take it. He jumps up and lobs
the scaffolding coupling at the workers. He's a soldier in a
trench. He flings it and crouches back down. There's a pause.
Then a rain of nails shower down on him. When it's finished
another supporter jumps up.

We'll win the fuckin League this year – fat cunts! he goes.

They crouch down for another shower. Nothing. Just this
laughing. The supporters stick their heads up. No nails. No
nothing. Just four jolly workers and their laughing's shaking
the whole scaffold so that the yellow wedges keeping it
together're working their way out. The fattest guy's on one
knee and pointing.

Where are you going to put the trophy? We're going right
through there with this wall.

We'll fight to the finish!
Flattened, this other one's going. *Fuckin flattened. Hee hee hee!*
No cunt's flattening us. We're unflattenable.
They might put a wee plaque on the line. The home of Albion
Rovers – the best laugh in Scotland.

Some players start to arrive.

There's your heroes. Get to fuck. Away and worship.

The supporters come out from behind the wall. And the
workers sing them away with their new wee song.

♪♪ *We're on our way to flattened we shall not be*
    there
    On our way to flattened we shall not be there
    By next week next month or next ye-ee-ar
    We shall not be there.

The supporters give them the fingers. Edward Duncan arrives and signs a few autographs. Three old grannies come up and ogle at him. He signs their knitting patterns. Knitting's back in a big way. A team from Bearsden won the world speed-knitting championships in 2002. When the women fold away their patterns the four nail marked supporters get round Eddie and gab about the usual stuff.

D'you think we'll do alright this season Eddie?

Is it true about the liquidation? And all this they're going. Eddie's trying to get away from them as polite as he can. *See the manager's* all he says to them. *See the manager – he'll tell you everything. The whole shebang.*

A taxi draws up. Barney Wheelan's in there pished out his head. The door flies open but nothing happens. Everybody's looking but there's only this black hole and the driver in the front looking dead ahead. He doesn't want to know. He's got that same look on his face as when you've got your dog out for a walk and it starts doing a shite. And you look at something up a tree or in the sky. Anything. Like the dog's not yours. But it is yours cos it's on a leash and you're holding one end. That's what the driver's like. Like the back half of the taxi's not his. Somebody welded it on as he was passing.

There's a grunt. An arm comes out the black hole. It's a magic trick. *Ooh*, says one of the old women, *Ooh*.

It puts a hand on the ground the arm. Barney's weight passes over the top of the arm so it's the ground and the taxi holding him up. He's a bridge for no reason. He looks up at the gathering supporters. Using only one of his eyes. His mouth's hanging open. Slabbers are hanging down like stalactites. He grins and his head flops. But that doesn't stop him shouting the odds at the driver. You can't understand a word he's saying – it's gobbledygook. But it's gobbledygook with an Irish accent. O'gobbledygook.

By this time big Eddie's stumbled over and paid the fare.

Dropping a few coins on the way. Barney's still a bridge for no reason. But the half of him held up with the arm's sinking down and down. His left shoulder's nearly on his hand.

The driver takes the cash and drives off. He doesn't look back at all. Smooth acceleration and he's away. What happens to Barney is – he swivels round through about seventy degrees on the palm of his hand. Drizzzzzz is the noise his hand's making on the ground. Wee bits of glass and grit are forcing their way into his skin. Once the taxi's four feet away the other half of his body slumps out and bumps onto the ground with a helluva skelp. The driver gets out and slams the door – gets back in and roars off. Barney's still on the ground singing 'The Irish Rover' up to the bit where the ship struck a rock and it's a shock – when it spins round a couple of million times and they all drown except Barney and his dog.

♪♪ *Then the ship struck a rock*
Oh Lord what a right cunt of a shock
The bulkhead was turned right o-o-ver
Turned nine times around
And the poor old dog was drowned
In the hold of the Irish Ro-o-ver

But it must make him seasick cos

RAGHGHGH!

he boaks all over himself.

Oohghghg! everybody says moving away. Looking at the pool of sick like a portal into Hell's just opened.

Big Eddie stumbles Barney to his feet and hobbles him into the ground. Not before dragging Barney's feet through the sick. There's a big crowd today. About fifty. And they're watching the fun and nodding.

Fuckin drunk again that Barney. Will he never learn? One of them goes.

That's the Irish for you, says his pal. *Alkies.*

Behind them a clapped out Cadillac draws up. Elvis is blaring out the mucky half open windows. ♪♪ *Oh well a well a hoola hoo hoola hoola hoo*, or something.

It's Brian Rogers. The car's hardly stopped and he kisses his wife and gets out. He strides into the ground without looking back. Head down. The car's pink. Apart from the rust maps all over it. It looks like the topography of The Planet Pink somewhere in deep space. Brian signs two autographs and goes in. The workers are singing 'Teddy Bear' to the car. The car backfires in answer.

Jimbo arrives. He's dejected. Hardly anybody notices him going in.

Then the swelling crowd – seventy now at least – part like the Red Sea.

Here's Matt – here's Matt the Survivor, they're going, *somebody ask him about shutting down. Ask him if we're shutting down at the end of next season.*

But there's something weird. It's weird cos the passage they've made for him doesn't go through the gate. It goes right up to this wee wall. A wee wall about arse height. Matt the Survivor walks up the gap shaking hands and signing autographs. Questions are coming at him from all angles.

Is it true we're getting shut down Matt?

Are we bankrupt right enough Matt?

You're a survivor Matt – we'll survive this!

No comment. No comment, he keeps repeating.

He's got a Dalwhinnie whisky bag in his hand. Sometimes a wane'll hold it while he signs. Sometimes it's scrunched between his legs.

I'll hold the Padre Matt, the wane'd go.

Sometimes he grips it in his teeth. He reaches the wall and

the massive crowd – now eighty – fall silent. The workers are leaning over high above wondering what the fuck's going on. Matt loosens the strings on the bag. One of the workers shouts on his mates.

Hey Joe what the fuck's happening here – c'mere – shout on Dan.

He starts pulling something out. The worker can't quite see what it is. Then something mad. At the same time everybody in the crowd whips out a MILLENNIUM MART USA bag. The workers are flinging puzzled eyebrows at each other. Matt's got the thing out the bag. It's red and white. He leans over and sits it on the wall. It's only when he kneels down the workers see what it is. A wee Padre Pio statue. The crowd know exactly what it is cos they kneel down same time as him. They place their carrier bags on the ground and kneel on them. Matt blesses himself. So do the crowd. The workers have got a what the fuck's this all about look. Matt starts praying.

Awaken us Padre Pio to Glory
Dispel the darkness of defeat
Destroy the heaviness of foot
Give the lank of limb and fat of gut
   gentleness of touch
Encourage a sense of adventure
Bring us an awareness of space
Awaken our jinkiness
   and Padre Pio make us slinky
Glory be to you for ever more
   and the greatest gift of all holy benefactor
Padre Pio give us a goal.

The crowd bless themselves and start singing,

♪♪ *Padre Pio give us a goal.*

The workers don't know to laugh or send for the men in white coats so they're stuck in critic limbo. Matt puts the statue back in the bag and goes in to the slaps on the back of the support.

You're the Survivor Matt – nothing'll shut us down. Nothing.

It's the boat to Arranmore. An open boat. They've been away to the harvest and this is them coming home. It's dark. And the sea's rough. It's that cold if you take a sharp breath up the nostrils it's like a punch in the face. But they've seen rougher seas than this so they go out. The Rutland channel's never worried them that much. But when they pass out the rocks into the channel it strikes them how rough it really is. There's fear but they keep on laughing and joking. There's wee screams and giggles as the boat's pushed suddenly up – or when it falls into a trough. Nobody cracks a light about how dangerous it is. But there's a big wave coming at them. It's came round the island from the Atlantic. The place both tails of the wave is going to meet is right where they are.

When the boat flips over they cling to the upturned hull. Matt can't remember how many. Nobody's crying. You'd think they would be but they're not. It's like they're taking a rest in a field. Under a tree in a storm. There's some laughing. Nerves. Mostly it's silence. Now and then the cry for help comes from somebody out in the sea. Or half a cry as they sink in a trough and their voice is snipped off by the rough edge of a wave. Then there's another voice behind Matt saying, *I said it was too much – I said it was too choppy now didn't I Mathew? Didn't I?*

But Matt can't answer. He knows all the things that are going on round about. All the things in the black sea that sometimes throws up some white froth just so as you know it's there. And he's meant to be off to Scotland in a week. To Aberdeen. To play. It looks like it's all over now.

The voice comes again and Matt still can't answer. His eyes are locked out of focus out there in the dark that's above and below. Everywhere.

Every ten yards the boat rolls and somebody else slides into the sea. They don't scream. Johnny Quinn slides down. And he's looking up at Matt. His nails are splintering one by one and his palms are squeaking on the wood. As he gets faster and loses his grip completely he's got a cross between a grin and a smile. Then there's a shlip and he's gone. Under the sea.

Sometimes the prow dips into the water and when it comes back up somebody else's gone. Lassies and all. There's two huddling and clinging onto the rudder. Lorna and Angela Harkins. The boat sinks and rises and they're gone. Just the shining side of the boat. When the water runs off Matt's face he's got his arm linked through the rudder. The two lassies are gone. Then he starts to notice the cold. Ice's building up on his cuffs. His clothes are cold cardboard.

Every now and then the clouds part and the moon comes out. And he can see black shapes on the hull. Then it's gone and it's him and the sound of the odd movement. It's getting colder. After a while he tries to move his arm from the rudder. But it's locked with cold. It's calm for a minute and another gust comes tumbling in. When the stern goes under he holds his breath. It seems he's under for ages. He's just about to give up. Give in to the sweetness of dying. And he's about to spurt out bubbles of air and draw in water when the boat rises again. He moves from one darkness into a lesser darkness. And compared to the sea the air feels warm for a second. He breathes again.

One by one they slip in.

Throughout the night.

Then it's only Matt, his cousin Paul and his brother Luke lying flat on the upturned hull. Ice is on his eyelashes now and everything looks like it's snowing. And rainbows. Every time the clouds part. There's kaleidoscopes of rainbows when he looks up towards the moon.

Matt thinks he sees a snowy field of land to his left. He spins round and there's only the darkness and the heaving sea. That's when he remembers the scapula. With his hand that's not locked round the rudder he fumbles it out from under his heavy jumper. It's Padre Pio. He kisses it.

Padre Pio save us from this mess. Amen. That's all he says. Normally prayers'd be long-drawn-out affairs. Rosaries. But this is small. But it's big. It's got the size of ten rosaries compressed into one line. That's the most powerful prayer he's ever said.

But his mind's leaving him. He looks to his right and sees another snowy field.

Luke where's all the snow? he goes.

Ya daft cunt, it's your eyes, Luke says.

Matt's eyes are all dusted with the night. And so are Luke's. Distant lights reflect so Luke's eyes are crusted with emeralds and diamonds and all sorts of rich gems.

They don't seem to be going anywhere. Arranmore gets closer then all the distance in the world's between them again.

We'd be better trying to reach the stars, Paul says.

Matt watches the lights of Arranmore go out one by one until – blackness. Then, through the roar of the sea songs come pouring over the waves. Raglin Road. And fires on the beach. The other boats back from the harvest. He tries to yell. It comes out but there's nothing travelling. The sea crushes it. And Paul's delirious now.

Is it our stop yet? he keeps saying. He thinks he's on a train.

He's fucked, Paul, that's the way the rest went before they slid in. He thinks he's on a fuckin train.

And he's describing stuff out the window. Stuff on the main line from Derry.

My there's two pretty looking lassies there! he goes, swinging his head. And Matt and Luke agree with everything he says. He's that happy. Looks like nothing could upset him.

Hey there's another three. Man would you not look at that there – ain't she something! Paul goes at these other three mirages.

Aye the one on the right now she's the one for me! Matt says.

He laughs at that Paul. Like a drunk man in the pub he laughs. *The fat one Matthew? The fat one? You're not after the fat one for fucksakes. You can have her all to yerself.*

I like the fat ones, Matt says.

And Paul laughs. And he keeps laughing and looking at the girls who are walking somewhere out on the waves. And when they disappear behind a hedge he looks disappointed. But then the waves shove them back over a crest and he's happy.

I've had nothing to eat since we left Derry, Matt, he says, *I'm starving.*

Och we'll be pulling in soon sure and we'll have a right nosh up.

At O Malley's, says Luke.

O Malley's? No way – we'll be going to Maloney's – now there's the place for us, Matt goes, *steak sausage egg and chips.*

Maloney's, says Paul, *fuckin Maloney's – we're moving in the right circles now Matt – aye we're the boys for Maloney's alright.*

Paul conks out. So it's quiet for a while. Matt's holding him by the scruff of his jacket. He can see he's still alive cos every time he breathes out the thin layer of ice below his nose melts in the heat. Then it forms. Then it melts. But it's been a long time. And Matt and Luke's surprised when the sun comes up. There's bodies floating distant in the sea. And there's a boat coming out from the Rosses. Out from Burtonport. When they see it they cry. And the tears are little spheres of ice clinking off the upturned boat. And inside the ice? Life itself.

So when he's warm in the hospital bed in Dunloe he looks left. There's Luke sweet as a baby. And to the right there's Paul sat up in bed.

Alright Matt ya fucker, goes Luke.

Are we three lucky bastards or what? says Paul.

Matt stares at one then the other.

It's only us Matt for fucksakes, Luke goes – and he's smiling like a birthday cake. *It's only us that's left.*

Matt stares. He's trying to get his mouth to work.

Me you and Paul. That's all – the rest are all . . . and he breaks down. His shoulders first. Then his eyes run. Then shuddering. Then it comes out in sobs.

Matt's head's a lot worse than he thinks. All he can say over and over's: *It was Padre Pio. He saved us. Padre Pio. Me and my brother and Paul. It was Padre Pio.*

The nurses arrive. He feels a jag in the arse. He's out. The last thing he hears before he goes is Paul asking him, *Hey Matt were we in Maloney's last night? Only I can still taste steak on my lips.*

No wonder Matt was praying before he went into the ground. It can't be easy being the manager of the worst team in Britain. Rovers are bottom of the Third Division. They've been beat in friendlies with school teams.

The crowd's all in. It's mostly old unemployed steelworkers. It's all young lassies that work in the Optical Microprocessor industry. The unemployed here are them that can't afford to go and see Celtic or Rangers in the NEW TV League.

Today it's East Fife they're playing. But there's one supporter that's different. Mary Maglone. Not cos she's one of about ten women that go to see the Rovers every week. No. She sticks out cos she looks like a lost hippy. A new age chick that's aged quick. And there's something else you need to know about Mary Maglone. She's psychic. Or more precise, she's a medium. She talks to dead folk.

That should set her up nice for watching the Rovers, says Barney about her. *They're like death warmed up anyhow.*

So Mary Maglone's scary. Everybody says she's a witch. It's the long sticky out grey hair and the red lipstick and the wrinkly face that does it. But her eyes? Her eyes are blue. Clear as a bell. She's got a bit to herself on the terraces. But that's nothing new. So's everybody.

Mary's been feeling strange for days. But she's not sure what it is. There's a fuzziness of messages. It's like radio hiss. A firewall. She knows there's something happening but she doesn't think it's got anything to do with the Wee Rovers. Then she puzzles over a feeling. A sensation that you or me might not get. Not your run-of-the-mill feeling. Something different. Something strange. She senses something lighter than air. She looks up. Like she's looking for shapes in the clouds. And she'll swear if you ask her that a wee blue light twinked as she looked. Blinked and shot off beyond the top of the stands. A wee blue star on a recce mission. Then sleet starts falling. She smiles as snowflakes land on her face.

Smiles like she's been told a good joke but she's not letting on what it is. Then – one of them sugary sweet shots you get in a film by a bad director. She lets one fall on her tongue. First its frostiness grips her – a million microscopic hooks of frost. She couldn't peel it off if she tried. She tastes it. And whoom – she's in a plane and there's silence and bodies and flames and people groaning. And whoom – she's back out again. Looking at the flakes falling. Shaking with fear.

The flakes are dotted about the ground as the teams come out with their arms wrapped round their bodies and breath coming out like cattle.

The game starts to a roar. Well a rirr really. There's no East Fife fans at all hardly. Twenty maybe at the other end of the pitch and that's only cos East Fife are giving away a free ticket to the Time Capsule to every supporter. You need to show your East Fife season ticket. Swimming and ice skating and a free ride on the underground Heritage Roller Coaster that takes you on a heart-stopping rib-tickling ride through the underworld of pit shafts and mine workings. The Bellies of Hell it's called. Or a slide down Britain's highest water flume. Two hundred feet up in a glass elevator with your swimming costume on. And the rain and sleet bouncing off the glass. It's not heated so it gets colder as you go up. And down you go – it's a vertical drop at first. It angles slow over a long distance and bends at the end so you surge into the water near horizontal. If you get it wrong you skim across the surface of the pool like an epileptic fit. At the beginning it's you rushing down through the warm air rushing up.

But there's no warm air on the Rovers pitch today. Rovers boot the ball about the mud. It's like the Somme round about the two goalmouths. A battlefield with no bullets. East Fife look like the better team early on. It's one of them games where the sound of the ball'd give you a headache. And the crunching tackles'd make you think you've broke your armchair leg. Only that could never happen here. Cos Rovers have never been on the telly. Not unless they were walking past a crime scene or something. Or *You've Been Framed And Digitised 2004*.

The game's brutal. Fuckin brutal. Barney vomits after every run. He's parked mini-pizzas all over the field. He's stinking of sour drink. Big Eddie's tripping over everybody if he's not tripping them up.

The only good player's Jimbo. He's a miracle at running and dribbling. If you never knew about him you'd be wanting to know what such a good player's doing with this bunch of turkeys. But every time he strikes the ball it zooms off at a crazy angle. It looks like it's remote control and there's some sicko whirring it off in the wrong direction every time. Jimbo can't pass or shoot.

The workers overlooking the park are having a great time. They're ripping the pish out Jimbo.

Hey Pele, they're shouting, *good job you're not in charge of the EuroTrident missiles!*

And it puts Jimbo off cos he looks up, loses his feet and crashes into the greyhound stalls. The greyhounds escape and run up the visitors' end of the pitch. The workers crease themselves.

Eight greyhounds sit facing the visitors. Staring. Oblivious to the game behind. We soon find out why. The visitors start buying Rovers pies. They take one bite and fling them on the pitch. The greyhounds scoff the lot.

But it's the same old story. East Fife four – Albion Rovers nil. Away at the back of the terrace is Flannagin. He's grinning as the players walk off the pitch dejected. Flannagin writes something in his wee book and folds it. He slides it into the inside pocket of his black coat. But his smugness is soon smudged cos there's this trickling noise. He looks up to see if it's coming off the broke guttering.

No.

What about the edge of the corrugated walls? Nothing. Then out of focus away to the left in his line of vision there's a brown slur. He whips the head round and there's a greyhound. Benny its name is. It's got its lips drew back over its teeth. It's got the leg up and it's pishing on his briefcase. You'd think he'd go mental and scream at the thing. But not him. Not Flannagin. He's got his own ways of dealing with problems. He lets it finish its pish. The only reaction from him's sliding his cigar case out his pocket. He takes one out and clicks it shut. Lights it.

The last yellow dribbles are falling off Benny's dick. Steam's rising off the bag and the puddle's waterfalling down two steps of terrace. The smell's like boiled dog. Flannagin takes a long draw and blows a cloud of smoke. But the line of smoke's cut off cos he turns ninety degrees and the smoke looks like a ghost's blew it out.

Benny's starting to walk away. And its first two steps are bowley cos it's trying to shoogle its dick back into position.

WHAM

Flannagin boots it hard on the balls as it walks away. Everybody in the place turns round at the

YELP!

But all they see's Flannagin carrying his bag with a MILLENNIUM MART USA bag round the handle. There's a couple of puffs of smoke behind him. Isolated in the air. Like baby clouds looking for a sky and maybe a big mammie cloud. Flannagin's got the bag outstretched like it's a shitty nappy he's carrying. And there's Benny dragging itself away with its front paws cos its back legs are twined round each other in a knot of pain. Like pleated hair.

It's the honeymoon. Barney's on the beach trying to catch the cormorant. He walks up to it trapped in a cul de sac of rocks. Barney's singing to it. He sticks his left arm out.

He sticks his right arm out.

 *QUACK!* *he yells*

He grabs the Cormorant and it lets out this tiny squeak.

It's going to get out of town now alright.

He sings to it all the way up the caravan. But every time he tries to look it in the face it twists its head away in disgust.

Well! There are some people and some birds don't know they're fuckin born. There's millions of things you can do if you're a Shag and can't fly, Barney's saying:

Paddle.

Float and let the waves push you up the sky a bit and drop you down again.

Peck.

Look for crabs in rock pools.

Squawk as loud as you like.

Annoy dogs.

Get a Bird Shag and Shag her.

Use your wings as sails.

Peck the eyes out wee other burds that can't fly.

Catch a train to London under a seat.

Pick your feathers.

Sneak into the Queen's garden party and eat the cucumber sandwiches.

Sit in a cage in a pet shop and see if any cunt'll buy you.

Fly past film sets and get in movies.

Fall in love with a hat.

Look up skirts at knickers.

Look in the swimming pool windae.
Tap your beak on glass.
Jump out and frighten passing wanes.
Make feet prints in the sand.
Jump out and frighten old pensioners.
Strut right in a cafe and ask for a cone in burdy language . . . a ninety-nine.

Sit in among the soup tins in MILLENNIUM MART USA's and frighten cunts.

Fuck. He could go on and on. This turkey can do anything except fly but it gives up and lets Barney catch it. No way he's letting it go to waste. Till it learns to fly or they invent flychairs, this fucker better get a life.

He decides to give it a life.

He sneaks back up the caravan and there's Carol cleaning the windows. She doesn't see him. She's got denim shorts on and her crotch's bumping off the glass now and then.

Pause. Stare.

But there's more important things to do. He sneaks round the blind side. She's singing away to 'Wannabe' by the Spice girls. She was at the Spice concert in Rovers ground in 2002. Barney slips the Shag in the door and presses his back against the caravan. Shoulders are going up and down. Carol's facing down to sea and scrubbing and humming. The mad Cormorant's probably bewildered looking at the cooker, the fridge, the telly. Stuff it's never seen before. Ceramic birds on the wall. And wee animal ornaments. Maybe it's thinking about taking a bite out the brass fish on the window ledge. That'd be a laugh. Clunk'd be the noise off its beak.

And *Aw ya fucker,* is what it'd say in birdie language.

AAARGHGHGHGHGHGHGHG!!!

The door opens. Carol comes flying out. Fuck. She could

67

give the Shag flying lessons. She's running around the caravan flapping her arms. Next thing the Shag flops out the door like an extra from a Laurel and Hardy film. Barney bursts out laughing. Carol sees him. She glances at Barney. She glances at the Shag.

You bastard, she goes, and comes at him half-angry half-laughing. Starts punching soft lumps out him. Barney's that weak with laughing she gets one on his beak and it starts bleeding. Then it's all;

Oh are you alright – I'm sorry, oh Barney – I'm sorry, oh I'm sorry . . . and pulling her jumper up to wipe it. The Shag figures this is a good time to fuck off. It's running east flapping like fuck and not getting a millimetre off the ground. It keeps turning back to check Barney's not coming after it. It runs right off the cliff.

It's all going well next couple of days. They're thinking they've made it. Found the love of their lives. Down the beach holding hands. Carol's all over him like a cheap suit. Cuddling and kissing every minute. They're in bed five times a day. Magic.

That's how the Muttoes Lane incident comes as a bit of a shock.

Cardiff. Bailey Bloggs comes out a shop. It's a disc shop. A bit run down. Seedy almost. He's got a disc in a brown paper bag. He sees some people coming and he stuffs it inside his jacket.

Morning Bailey, says this woman with her wane.

Morning Gladys.

Hi there Mr Bloggs, says her wee lassie.

Hi lass, Bailey goes and moves on. It's cold so he looks like he's holding his arms tight to his body for heat.

He gets home and shoves it in the player. He's got the curtains shut and the phone off the hook. The disc starts. It's another Busby Babes job. The very stuff his Psychologist's told him not to watch. The very stuff that's driving him down and down. And he knows not to watch it. He's like a man trying to stop drinking. But keeps lifting it up again.

Don't do it Bailey – you don't deserve this, he's saying to himself. But he can't resist it. There's some kind of freedom from the pain while he's watching it. It's a bit like when you probe a rotten tooth with a toothpick – while you're doing it the pain's bearable. It's only when you try to ignore it it's insufferable. Bailey can't stop feeling the pain. He's addicted to sorrow.

It's Eddie at school years ago. In the assembly hall the classes line up in their rows. Father Boyle's pacing about the stage. Eddie knows what it is. Rumours are rippling through the crowd like breezes. Half of the school's wondering what's happening and the other half's filling up with guilt. Riley stands and stares till they're quiet.

Silence and stillness.

Except for Eddie Duncan's **heart** beat **beat beating in his chest**. He'd swear the lassie next to him's looking to see what the thumping is.

Riley walks to the front. The only noise is his shoes and the creaking stage. The smell of school varnish and dinner halls. Riley coughs and tap taps the microphone. Eddie's looking at Riley like he's a killer coming at him.

I have some sad news. Very sad news. A boy has been hit by a locomotive, says Riley.

There's a gasp – a murmur then everybody's looking about for who's not there. Riley stares again and the murmur reduces to a mirmir. Then a mir. Then a m, then nothing.

He's critically ill, says Riley, *and you boy –* he points *– if all you can do is whisper in your sidekick's ear you can see me in my office after this assembly.*

Riley presses silence on the culprit.

Father Boyle? he goes. Up steps the Priest and blesses himself. There's a rush of wind as the whole hall does father son holy ghost. They get into a big rosary session.

It's Glasgow. Pollockshields. A big – big house on the corner.
Sandstone. Bay windows manicured gardens the whole
fuckin bit. Nice wee trees. A million at least it's worth.
There's a plush office in there. A massive office. With
controlled Aromatherapy Air Conditioning. Flannagin's
walking about the room cos he can never sit down. Up and
down. Up and down. He can never sit down thinking about
the money he's going to make. His bag's over near the
radiator.

In the middle of the office's a model of the Leisure and
Retail complex. It's like something out a movie. White's the
dominant colour. With pastel-coloured stonework here and
there. And greenery. Trees and plants. And wee people
walking about. If you saw them through a magnifying glass
they'd all be in their twenties with short efficient skirts and
blue business suits. WCS's on their wrists. But there's the
odd woman with a go chair and happy looking students in
full colour to make it look like a real planet. The students
can't wait to get a job and get a Watchstrap Communications
System. PC and mobile phone the size of a watch. All voice
activated. It's not a wee screen. That's what you'd think – a
screen the size of a watch what fuckin use is that? But it
actually uses the same technology they invented for bar
codes and projects the image onto the rods and cones of your
eyes. Doesn't matter what angle you're at. And it can't
accidentally go in somebody else's eyes either cos it's RC'd –
Retina Coded. So it looks like a bunch of maddies going
about talking to their wrists. Ten years ago they'd have
locked you up for that.

When you look at the whole set up you just know we're
entering a new era. The human race that is. A new era of
glass and steel and trees sticking up out slabbed concourses
and piazzas. And heading south out this edifice is the
Zoomph MAPTT – Magnetic Air Pressure Tube Train. Going
down easy at an angle into the Persian carpet. Under the

table's a cutaway of the unique geology needed for the Zoomph MAPTT – Magnetic Air Pressure Tube Train. And above that – like a beggar at the banquet – Rovers Park. All this to be built in a place where the housing used to lean cheek to jowl with steel furnaces and pit shafts. Black skies and flames. Hell. That's what it was like.

No wonder nobody was that bothered when they shut the steel works down, big Eddie says all the time. *Who the fuck'd want to work in a place like that?*

Or the mines. Fuck the mines, Barney'd go if he was sober.

Never mind the end of next season. Flannagin's telling them by his calculations and the four–nil defeat today Rovers'll not last three more games. The crowd's falling ten per cent every week. The overdraft'll be called in. There's this guy sitting at the table. Well – there's six guys at the table but this guy's sucking the energy out them all. He's powerful. You'd expect *Carmina Burana* to come out his mouth instead of words.

♪♪ *Da da da da!*

Even clearing his throat he silences the place. It looks like even the wee people in the model are stood still and listening too.

Figures figures, he says, *he gives me figures.*

Flannagin drops his head more than the rest in the room.

Don't give me figures – we're already three weeks behind schedule . . .

A guy jumps out a chair and lays all these building site plans on a table.

Programme Boss, he goes. But he's waved away.

. . . no further behind I want to fall . . . You tell me there will be no Rovers. You deliver no Rovers. But he stops talking cos he's sniffing the air.

What's that?

What's what sir? goes some arselicker.

That smell.

They all start hamster impersonations. Turning their heads this way and that. If their noses were bigger they'd be sword-fencing.

Sniff sniff. Sniff sniff, they're going.

Flannagin's the only one not sniffing cos he can see out the side of his eye the steam rising from the briefcase. The sycophantic cunt – the one with the wee moustache and the hair combed over the side of his baldy head – he's walking about bent over like a Jap apologising. He's sniffing away. Flannagin's a bit embarrassed as moustache reaches his crotch tilting his head towards it a bit and sniffing. He passes and stops at the bag.

Jesus – what's in there Flannagin? he goes, *the players' knickers?*

All Flannagin can do is mumble about a dog – a grey-hound. At the same time he's registering that the wee cunt with the moustache'll be getting it soon as he figures a way. Done right in. Flannagin's hand's going in and out of a fist.

Lang wants more, Flannagin says to the Boss.

Moustache – Kelvin that's his name – walks past Flannagin smiling and shaking his head. The whole room's silent.

But this is the last payment. Guaranteed result, Flannagin goes.

The Boss sighs – nods – and Kelvin gets a wad of notes out a drawer. Then he stares right in Flannagin's eyes like he's *The Omen.*

Let Lang know what we can do for him if he doesn't deliver. Or if the price goes up again, he goes.

And he means it. He really means it. You can tell just by Flannagin's reaction never mind the rest of the guys in the room curling into their own bodies like burning shoes. Flannagin lifts the money and starts walking to the door. As an afterthought – and he can't tell where it's came from – he turns.

He says the only problem he'd have is if Rovers won the Scottish Cup or something like that, Flannagin goes.

The whole room bursts out laughing.

Flannagin's just started work. Tennant's Steelwork. He's fifteen years old. He's got his big dark blue overalls turned up at the bottom. Him and his mate Peter. They get put on working with the Bam. The Bam's the most feared man in Tennant's. Everybody's shit scared of him. He does what he wants. Even the management never challenge him. He can take afternoons off and get paid. No questions.

He's a Proddy the Bam. But he's a good Proddy. Goes to church and all that. Prays every day. And if there's one thing the Bam hates it's swearing.

He terrorises Flannagin and Peter. Has them running about like headless chickens. And he stands amidst the sparks and metal glowing like white sun and laughs. And sometimes the red of the cooling steel shines on the inside of his tongue like he's on fire. Like his insides are made out of flame. And his skin. His skin's just the cool membrane that covers his insides of fire. And brimstone. And apocalyptic laughter. The laughter moves through the steelwork and fills the black spaces where light can never reach.

The Book of Revelation. That's the Bam's favourite. We're all going to die in fire and molten rock. Specially the Papes. The Catholics. But he's not saying that stuff about the Papes out of bigotry. He believes it. He truly believes it.

And the Bam asks Flannagin and Peter this riddle.

You die. And you get to this room. There's two doors in the room. And there's a figure guarding each door. One door goes to Heaven. The other door goes to Hell. You've got to ask one question and one question only. How do you make sure you get into Heaven?

Ask what one's the door into Heaven, goes Flannagin.

Aye – but there's a problem. Cos one door's guarded by God – who always tells the truth. And the other door's guarded by the Devil who always tells lies.

Well – just ask God what's the door into Heaven? says Peter.

Ah! But there's another problem so there is. The two figures

75

*guarding the doors. Even though one's God and one's the Devil –
they look the exact same so you can't tell what one's God and what
one's the Devil.*

Flannagin goes, *Just ask any one what's the door into Heaven.*

*But the Devil always tells lies. So if you ask him he'll send you
through the door into Hell.*

Flannagin thinks for a minute.

Feel the doors.

Eh? the Bam says.

Feel the doors and the one that's hot's the one into Hell.

But the Bam comes back with another answer.

*You're not allowed to touch anything. You can only ask one
question and that's that.*

So that's it. Every few days Flannagin or Peter come in
with an answer to the riddle but the Bam laughs at them.
The whole work's been working on that riddle since years
before Flannagin and Peter. Nobody's ever got it. And now
it's revived in the two new boys they're all at it again. The
Bam loves it.

How are you going to get into Heaven, he goes, *if you can't
work out the one question you've got to ask?*

Then, this day, out the blue he starts a swear box. He's
welded it together like a wee church. A slot in the top and
there's no way in. A church that only takes money. You can't
even get in to pray. The Church of Honesty it should be
called. And there's no way out if you're a coin trapped in the
inner darkness. The Bam's going to burn a hole in it at
Christmas and give it to charity. So right through September
and October Flannagin and Peter's shoving coins in this box
out of fear for the Bam. But Flannagin's met a bird and he
wants to get her something good for Christmas. Something
expensive. It's a coat she likes in the Co-op. Every couple of
days the Bam taps the box with a pin hammer and listens to
the mounting coins. He smiles.

So this day he taps it with the hammer and he turns and smiles at Flannagin.

The wee black wanes'll get a good feed this year, he goes. And he smiles and the deep blue arc of the electric furnace makes the Bam's teeth look like a sea. And Flannagin thinks it's a blue wave coming at him. And the white tips of his bottom teeth are the frills of the wave.

What you staring at ya pup? says the Bam.

Your teeth – they look like the Sea of Galilee! He can't think why he says that. He's not religious. The Bam curves his hand at his ear to hear.

What? he goes.

Your teeth – cos of the arc. They look like Galilee – the Sea.

But the Bam still can't hear him. He crushes one side of his face at Flannagin. So Flannagin shouts it out.

Your teeth – in the blue arc off the furnace – they look like the Sea of fuckin Galilee.

That's it. The Bam points at the box.

And make that two for taking the Lord's name in vain, he goes.

I never.

You did ya punk.

I only said the Sea of Galilee.

That's as good as blasphemy.

Aw get yerself to fuck, Flannagin says.

Three.

Fuck off.

Four, says the Bam but he's getting angry.

The machines and furnaces in the work are slowing down and dimming cos the Bam's draining them of their energy to fuel his anger. Flannagin screams,

Fuck fuck bastard shit praise the fuckin Lord . . . I'm putting fuck all else in your wee holy box ya fat cunt,

Critical mass. The Bam goes ballistic. He flies at Flannagin with his arms straight down at each side like sledgehammers. And he's tilted forwards so there's no way he could stop if he wanted. The whole work's watching. Flannagin's going backwards. But he trips over his turnups and bangs into a steel column. The Bam's nearly on him. There's these hook things on the wall. They're like a brace and bit that you turn to twist wires together.

Flannagin grapples a wire twisting hook from the wall and swings it without looking. Next thing there's silence. Flannagin's got his eyes shut waiting for the sledgehammer blows to come in but there's none. The whole work breathes in. Flannagin opens his eyes. There's the Bam standing with this hook through his cheek. He's running about taking the weight of it with his hands in case it rips right through. He's a crazy fish on the end of a line of fear. Flannagin's the fisherman working his way backwards – away from his catch. A couple of the men try to hold the Bam and guide him to first aid. But he shakes them off and walks away with the blood running down the steel hook.

After visiting the big house in Pollockshields Flannagin's in Mackenzie's. He's sitting with Rena. Having a right old laugh. He's telling her about the greyhound. How he felt the insole of his shoe connecting with the softness of its balls and then crushing into bone.

And the yelp – the yelp – that was the best bit. Oh man. The yelp! There's tears coming down his face with laughter.

He stands up to demonstrate the kick. But he tells her nothing about the incident in the Boss's. When he's booted the dog ten times or more he goes to the Hologram jukebox. Sticks on the Eagles. 'Best of My Love'. Up they pop on the table with the Arizona desert stretching right out behind them to the toilet doors. Him and Rena move to a darker corner. Nobody's even bothering with what they're up to. This is the kind of place where an atom bomb might get a reaction. But nipping about? Shagging another man's wife? That's standard issue that so it is. Standard issue.

♪♪ 'The Best of My Love' is belting out the jukebox and Flannagin's holding Rena's hand.

What they're talking about in the corner is Spain. She's got his hand now and she's stroking the back of it. They've just got to wait for the downfall of the Rovers and they're off. That's when he'll get his money. And her. She's got a stake in it too. She gets a bookies pen and starts adding up how much they're going to make on the back of a fag packet. His re-mortgaged house plus all her insurance policies and the long-term account Eddie's had for years. The one she persuaded Eddie to put into a joint account and then a year later persuaded him to allow single signature withdrawals. *It's too much hassle the two of us having to go down every time*, she told the big man. All that's in the pot. And when it's all over they'll have near half a million quid.

Money turns me on, says Rena. And she draws Flannagin's hand up the inside of her thigh, *Turns me right on.*

Me too, goes Flannagin.

No – I mean money turns me right on.

She grabs his hand and shoves it on her pussy. He looks about. Coast's clear. He bumps the gums on her. But Rena's up and fixing her skirt.

What? he goes.

She walks into the women's bog. *C'mon Charlie,* she goes.

Last thing's his eyes glinting in the dull back end of the pub before disappearing into the women's bog. By this time Bachman Turner Overdrive's crushing out the jukebox. A whole seventies disco appears around the table next to the jukebox.

It's the honeymoon. The caravan after the Cormorant thing. They're thinking they've made it. Found the love of their lives. Carol's all over him like a cheap suit. Cuddling and kissing every minute. They're in bed five times a day. Magic.

That's how the Muttoes Lane incident comes as a bit of a shock.

They're walking about St Andrews and the sun's out. You can taste the sea and the whole town's moving slow and easy. Great day. Carol's in sky blue. Her hair's really red. She smells fresh. The odd white cloud's puffing by minding it's own business. Barney's holding her hand. Every time he stops at a shop window she shunts into him gently and kisses the back of his neck. People on the streets are saying,

Look at that young couple so much in love George.

And George slides his arm round Mildred's waist and they remember being in love. Barney and Carol are infecting the whole town. Smiles are floating around like flocks of white birds.

Lucky really – the Muttoes Lane incident – cos this day St Andrews is in danger of engulfing itself in love and shrinking away to the size of a pinhead never to be heard of again.

They're strolling along North Street and Barney spots this street sign.

MUTTOES LANE

He's one for saying things before his head's checked in for breakfast. Carol's drinking Lucozade. The sun's shining through the bottle and turning her skin a happy colour.

People are nodding good morning as they pass and Barney says, *Look Carol – that's where you should live!*

Eh? she goes. The Lucozade bottle balanced perfectly at her lips.

Over there . . . that's where you should move to.

She looks for what he's on about.

What are you on about? she goes, and takes another slug.

Muttoes Lane! says Barney, and points, *that's where you should live.*

She looks at the street sign. She looks at him. This Cormorant flies across the inside of her eyes and they narrow.

Barney look at her. She looks at the street sign. He looks at the street sign. **MUTTOES LANE** it says. Never forget it cos . . .

ZZZZZIIING

KRASHSSH

TINKLE

TINKLE

She fucks him over the head with the bottle. The whole loving street unlocks arms and turns. The blood's running down his head and people are coming to his rescue. Looks like a mixture of Doctors and Nosey Bastards. St Andrews is like that. Carol's storming off. There's droplets of blood spattered on her sky-blue dress.

Barney's thinking in his zingery it's rose petals flung up against the sky. The Doctors and Nosey Bastards are right next to him. He puts his palms up so cunts'll leave him alone.

They leave him

alone.

Barney stems the blood with this white T-shirt and walks out to the quiet streets near the sea. His head's killing him. He gets in the bogs down the harbour and cleans up. Head cuts look a lot worse than they really are cos they bleed like fuck.

He parts his hair in the mirror. It's only two cuts – one an inch but not deep and this other fucker – a wee hole really. This bit of glass is glinting in it. He prises it out with two matchsticks. Sore as fuck.

When he comes out he flings the T-shirt in the sea and walks back to Kinkell Braes. He look like any other tourist. Shirt off in the sun. But that's not what he is. He's a man with a ruined honeymoon.

Carol's in the car with the stuff loaded and her arms folded. Honeymoon comes to an end early. Silence all the way home. Barney can still see rose petals scattered across the sky of her breasts. Fuckin cow.

Albion Rovers. Matt's got the players all gathered together for a talk about the future of the club.

Right lads, he says, *the bank's been on the blower. We need to get some dough in the next three weeks or they're moving in quicker than we thought.*

The players go through their pockets but Matt stops them.

No. No – that's no use. It wouldn't even matter if we done without wages the rest of the month. It's ten grand we need to keep them off our backs.

The players slump. Big Eddie's got tears running down his cheeks. Barney takes a slug of Buckie Turbo. Even Benny's ears go down.

But there is a way, goes Matt through the silence. All the ears prick up again.

Is there? all their eyes seem to be saying. Like wanes with no presents at Christmas.

If we win the Lanarkshire Cup! Matt says and he says it like the punch line of a good joke. He's got his palms out like it's obvious. But they don't seem to get it. He can't make it out.

No presents right enough. All the ears go down again. So Matt tries again. With some more good news.

There's a holiday to Salzburg this year for the winners. Skiing. Airdrie Travel are giving it.

Normally football players have it written in their contracts that they can't go near skis. But this is Albion Rovers.

Will I rush out and buy my skis the now? says Barney. That gets a bit of a laugh. A few grunts just.

That's what's up with you lot. Faith. You guys have got none.

At that Matt whips out the Padre Pio and gets praying. Where he's sat the statue a shaft of light's coming in and shimmering it in a haze.

The dressing room's one big moan and they all shuffle out leaving Matt and Benny kneeling in the holy glow of the statue. For a second the glow is electric blue. But Matt's got his eyes closed.

Coatbridge. Mary Maglone comes out a shop. It's a disc shop. A bit run down. One of the windows has got a big crack running down the length of it. It's taped up with duct tape. The other one's boarded up with cheap wood. Mary's got a disc. It's *The Busby Babes*. She doesn't know why she bought it. She went in to get *It's A Wonderful Life* but something drew her to the sport shelf. And she's thinking what's she doing at the sports shelf when it's a romance she's wanting? But before she knows it she's paid for it and she's out the shop. Weird.

She goes home and watches it. And she's getting déjà vu all the time. Like she knows these guys. But she doesn't. There's surge after surge running through her body as she watches. Now why is that?

Up on the hills above Salzburg the eight lights buzz and glow in the snow all night. And if you checked the time you'd see they're at their brightest when Mary Maglone's getting her surges beside her disc player.

Brian Rogers Da's drunk the same way he's been since his wife died. He's thundering about up the stairs. In his room. They're all watching *Doctor Who* on the fucked-up old telly that's too wrecked to sell. The Da comes thumping down the stairs. Into the room. A day's drinking's wrote across his face like a script for a horror film. His teeth are yellow. His lips and gums are bleached pink with alcohol.

Right cunts – line up!

And there's no talking. No looks. It's like an army. Brian, his two brothers and Janice his sister run into line and spring to attention. It's another doing but they don't have a clue what it's for. He dished out the beatings when the Maw was still alive but now he's a wild savage. The children in the line are hoping they're not the one he's after this time. On the telly the Daleks are exterminating a few soldiers. Brian'd rather be there. He'd rather be in the world of the Daleks. And running away from them. At least he'd have a chance. He'd be able to hide maybe. And anyway Daleks can't get up and down stairs. But Das can. And right at that bit where he's starting to think it might be the drinker of the Ginger Beer his Da's after the drunken sod whips the very same bottle from out under his coat.

It's Albion Rovers' dressing room.

It's a miracle. It's a miracle, Matt's shouting. He's kissing the statue and running round the dressing room. *A fuckin miracle. Thank you Lord. Thank you Padre Pio.*

The players are sitting with the strips on staring at him like he's mad.

We're in the final, he's shouting. *The final. Us – the Wee Rovers. Who'd have thought we'd get past Motherwell? They're the best team in Lanarkshire. I said it didn't I. Didn't I? Faith. You need faith.*

Big Eddie jumps up and shouts *Yes*, he shouts, *fuckin yes boss – that's all we needed – faith.*

Sit down for fucksakes Eddie before you trip over something, goes Barney.

Eddie sits down. Embarrassed.

Barney starts getting his tracksuit on. *There's nothing special about getting to a final cos the other team never fuckin turned up.*

Matt stares at him. And stares. And stares. *That doesn't matter. We're in the final. There's Padre Pio to thank for that. Fuck – it's all the more a miracle that we never even had to play a game.*

Barney laughs. *We've got The New All Europe and Africa Trophy to thank for that boss. They're hardly going to play us when they can be in Barcelona!*

Aye – and who made sure they got drew on the same night to play? Padre Pio – that's who! goes Matt.

Barney puts his hand on Matt's shoulder. *You're some man boss so you are. Some fuckin man right enough. You should be*

Matt the Believer not Matt the Survivor.

Barney pulls the strides on and shoves his feet in his shoes.

I'm off for a beer. See you later, he goes.

He kneels and does a mock prayer to Padre Pio on the way by. *And may the road rise up to meet me and may I be cured of my swallowing the drink – Amen.*

As Barney leaves Matt shouts after him. *That's right Barney – you could do with laying off the drink for a couple of weeks – we've got Airdrie in the final you know. We could beat them.*

He turns to the players. *Nat right lads? Airdrie? No problem?*

But it's just a whole set of blank stares coming back at him. The only hopeful face's the plastic smile of the holy statue.

It's years after the honeymoon. Barney and Carol have settled into wars and silences. Violence and separations.

Twelve's a good number. Like a dozen red roses. You see it in films – he brings a dozen red roses and next scene the roses are on the silk sheets. And you know they'll be in there grinding away soon.

But that's another movie. Kid on people. This is real. Barney and Carol. This's the daffodil day. He's woke up down the glen again. In a bin bag – again. He can't remember how he got there. But he doesn't need to remember. He knows. He knows from the past. From all the other times they've went out for the night – came home and fought and he's grabbed a bin liner and a couple of fags and high-tailed it down the glen.

So he's woke up. Lit a fag and smoked it. And he's searched his pockets and found no money. So he can't get drink. So he's got to go home. How to get back in's the next thing. Then he sees the yellow splodges in the distance. Moving about a foot above the green. His eyes are not working right yet. When they are he sees it's daffodils.

He picks twelve daffodils and makes his way back to the scheme. When he reaches the motorway he's froze by the gale force of passing cars and lorries. And he's a pretty sight on the edge of the M8. Something out the Hillbillies. Unshaved. Bloodshot eyes. Hair like fibre-optics. Scarred down the right side of his face. Big long scabs. Probably Carol that done that. Crusted blood. He runs his fingers over the scars. The braille telling the story of last night's violence. Cars are slowing and looking. Not cos of the blood. Cos of this big bunch of daffodils. A fluorescent yellow against the exhaust stained sides of the motorway. He finds a gap and loups across the road into the scheme.

It's the day of the Airdrie game. It's the Police Station. Barney's in the nick. Lifted for drunk and disorderly. He's shouting up the cells.

I'm in the Cup Final the day – bastards. You better let me out or there'll be trouble.

The Desk Sergeant shakes his head and talkshouts down the cell block.

I've heard it all now Barney. It's usually weddings or funerals or important hospital appointments. But a final?

Aye – I'm in the Lanarkshire Cup Final.

The what? shouts the Sergeant, *say that again!*

By this time he's got the whole nick listening. All the other lifted guys are pressed up to the Police–Client Interface.

The Lanarkshire Cup – Rovers are in the final.

Aye and I've got a speed knitting competition the night, the Sergeant says. Everybody laughs and gets on with their work.

The Desk Sergeant makes a cup of tea and stops listening to Barney. He's kicking the door and hammering it with his fists.

PLEASE DO NOT VANDALISE THE CELLS the

Cyber Guard's going. It's a female voice.

Aw fuck up you electronic tart, Barney shouts.

TRY TO MAKE YOUR STAY WITH US AS COMFORTABLE AS POSSIBLE. IF YOU REQUIRE A DEEP

Des Dillon

RELAXATION AUDIO SAY YES AFTER THE TONE.

Barney goes ballistic.

CALM DOWN MISTER Wheelan SIR. YOU HAVE TEN SECONDS TO CALM DOWN THEN I'M AFRAID I'LL HAVE TO SUMMON A GUARD. NOW DEEP BREATHS. ONE . . . TWO . . .

I'll give you deep breaths – I'll rip your fuckin wires out . . .

He's just finishing his tea the Desk Sergeant when in comes Matt. He's carrying the Dalwhinnie bag. He convinces the Sergeant to let the player out by showing him a photo of the whole team.

That's him there. He's a key player.

The Sergeant walks down and peers through Police–Client Interface.

*

Hey, says the Sergeant as Barney's leaving.

Barney turns.

You'd be better off staying in here than playing with that mob of yours against Airdrie. Less humiliating. Albion Rovers for fucksakes! Don't make me laugh. They couldn't beat Casey's drum.

Barney tilts his head to the one side, grins and walks out the door backwards.

See you next week, shouts the Sergeant through the closed door.

So it's the Airdrie game. Matt's done his thing with the Padre Pio statue at the wee wall. The crowd's in. The players are on the park. The crowd's singing.

> ♪♪ *Padre Pio give us a goal give us a goal give us a goal*
>
> *Padre Pio give us a goal give us a goal give us a goal*
>
> *Padre Pio give us a goal give us a goal give us a goal*
>
> *Padre Pio give us a goal give us a goal give us a goal*

Mary Maglone looks smug. More smug than a Rovers fan should ever look. And it's even worse cos Airdrie are all over them. Matt's stroking the Dalwhinnie bag cos we're well into the first half and there's no scoring. Not that Rovers have put up a game or anything. Fuck – that's a laugh. They're shite. Worse than shite in fact.

It's just that nothing's going right for Airdrie. They're having that much bad luck Barney starts thinking that maybe the stuff with the statue's working right enough.

It's all in Rovers' half of the pitch the game. The ball hits the post. Comes back out to this Airdrie player running in.

WHAMMMMMS off the crossbar. Airdrie have tried everything. Then it's a good move – pass – back heels the whole bit. Good positioning. There's an Airdrie player right through the eleven-man Rovers defence. Five minutes to half time. BANG the ball soaaaaaaaaaaaaaaaaaars in a Pele curve towards the top right-hand corner. The Airdrie fans cheer. But it hits the inside of the post. Hits the underside of the bar and flies out. They gasp. It hits the Rovers goalie's arse. The cheer starts up again. It's on its way in.

And that's what it would have done if it wasn't for Benny the Greyhound walking along the goal-line. Benny yelps as the ball scuds his arse. He twists ninety degrees exactly with the force and continues walking. Towards the centre circle.

It's a second or two before he wonders how come all the things he's looking at now are nothing like the things he was looking at a minute ago. The crowd start cheering.

Benny, Benny, save us a goal! they're going.

All the Airdrie players surround the Ref. Surely it's a penalty or something? A dog saving the ball for fucksakes. But the Ref waves them away. Rovers players have all piled on top of Benny. All you can see is his wee pointed head sticking out. And he'd go ***Ooomph!*** if he could but he can't even breathe out under the weight of the players.

Flannagin's there. He's got his book out but it's flopped forwards in disbelief. He's biting his lip. The crowd are singing and dancing. Airdrie are at the shoulder-shrugging stage. The Ref looks at his watch and blows the whistle. Half time nil–nil.

In the dressing room Airdrie eat oranges and drink cans of Lucozade Body Rhythm Isotonic. There's a big portable screen. It's a roll-it-up job. Photo-reactive synthetic silk. It's all the rage now. Like a cinema under your arm. The manager's got it hanging from the wall. And he replays sections of the game to the players. He's going through the strategy. They're all eyes and ears. Point point he's going. How to get a goal.

Better in the first five minutes. It's only a matter of time, he's going.

But it's a different story in the Rovers' dressing room. They're munching into pies and slugging cans of beer. Some of them's sparked up fags. Or a joint it looks like away at the back. They're coughing like old men. Matt's giving them the pep talk. He's drawing on an old blackboard. But there's nobody listening.

We're nearly there boys. Get a goal right away then – forty-five minutes and we're OK.

But there's nothing. Not a peep. And they're knackered.

Their shoulders are leaning forward that much they're nearly touching in the middle of their chests. Nobody's taking a blind bit of notice. The only one that's watching is Benny. He's got his tongue out and he's breathing happy dog breaths. He's been clapped more in the last half hour than his whole life before it. Matt looks at the blank faces of the players and decides to go for another approach.

Do you want to keep your jobs or not?

Some look up. The ones that are lying down's ears twitch.

One goal and we're all still in a job. And there's the Airdrie Travel skiing holiday in Salzburg.

You never said it was skiing, says Eddie.

I did – skiing I said but none of you were listening.

They all look a bit more interested. Benny's the happiest dog alive. He's alternating between eating pies and licking his balls. Pegg Davidson looks at Benny licking its balls.

I wish I could do that, he says.

The players snigger. Barney's a master of timing. When the whole team's watching the greyhound licking its balls. That second after Pegg cracked his joke Barney comes away with, *Fling it a biscuit and it might let you!*

The laughter that roars out the place puts the Airdrie manager off. The players lose a wee bit of confidence. What's the Rovers got to be so happy about. They can't understand it. It's like in the Desert War. The Americans done a mock retreat. The Arab Nations thought they were winning. But that was what America wanted them to think. Every time the Arabs came across an abandoned American camp it was full of grub and drink and drugs and the paraphernalia of prostitution. They were being demoralised bit by bit. And the Americans kept retreating. So by the time the Arabs chased the Americans all the way to the Med things were grim. Soldiers were deserting left right and centre. The Americans launched a massive offensive and the Arabs surrendered. Only a hundred people got killed in that war.

The art of fighting without fighting they call it – from the Tao of Bruce Lee. A famous philosopher.

Even with a demoralised Airdrie the second half takes place in Rovers' penalty box. Airdrie try everything but running into the net with the ball balanced on their heads. By this time Flannagin's furious. He's right down on the touchline shouting.

C'mon to fuck Airdrie – how can you let a bunch of donkeys like this hold you?

The Ref gets fed up with him. It's chest to chest. The Ref's face is red but Flannagin's is redder. Both men's arms are straight with balled up fists at the end. They're like two cartoon characters. Flannagin won't give up. He gets a red card. The Ref thinks he's the Airdrie manager. But he's still not for moving Flannagin. No sir. He's shouting the odds at the Airdrie players when the Ref nods to two Police. And he's still shouting and bawling when the Police drag him away backwards up the terraces and make him stand in the damp shade and dripping rain.

One or two snowflakes are falling. Mary Maglone catches one and watches it melt on her hand. And she can see pictures forming in it as it melts. Strange pictures. It looks like men running. But then it's water. A cold puddle where the life line meets the love line. She goes to rub her hands together and in a flash she sees a face. She sees it. It's gone. But she doesn't recognise it. It's Bailey Bloggs.

Into injury time and still no goals. The Airdrie players are right round the Rovers' goal – in an arc. It's shootie in. But the ball can't make its way through. Off the park the Airdrie manager's got Benny tied to the leg of the bench. But Benny's that excited about the attention he got he wants back on the park. He knows it's something to do with the park. Something to do with the ball. If he gets the ball he'll get claps and pies. So he tugs.

And he tugs.

And he tugs.

Next thing the bench is up in the air. Everybody turns to the yell of the Airdrie manager as he falls backwards with his arms flung up. He hits the ground with a helluva skelp. The whole ground's watching. The players have turned away from the goal. Except Jimbo that is. It's only a second they've all been looking away for. But that lapse is fatal. There's Jimbo halfway up the park. It's only the Airdrie goalie between him and glory.

He's that far away all the Rovers and Airdrie players can do is gape in amazement. He gets to the penalty box. It's him and the goalie.

Jimbo jooks to the left.

So does the goalie.

                                        Jimbo jooks to the right.

                                        So does the goalie.

Jimbo blooters the ball. The goalie dives and misses. The ball comes back off the post. Jimbo boots it again. It scuds back off the bar this time. Jimbo's nervous. He's got the ball at his feet but doesn't know what to do. He turns to the players away at the other end like they're going to tell him. By this time the goalie's up and running at him. Jimbo goes to shoot again. He sees the white goalmouth and the red net waving in the wind.

Then

BLACKNESS

The goalie flattens him. Roars from the crowd and the

players. A whistle. **Penalty!**

Jimbo lines up to take it. Flannagin's up behind the goal now moving about. He's standing still – then running three yards to the right. Then he's hopping back on his hunkers going *Ooh ooh*, like a monkey. Then he's still. Then it's star jumps. But Jimbo's not watching him. He's too nervous to get put off.

Jimbo bangs it. It curves round the goal and whacks Flannagin on the jaw. Flannagin's out like a light. The Airdrie supporters laugh and laugh. They point at Jimbo and rub their bellies. Airdrie players are running up the pitch to try for a last minute goal. Rovers players are too fat and unfit to catch them. Flannagin's being carried away on a stretcher. The Airdrie Goalie boots the ball up. But it's a mis-kick. Jimbo's just getting up off the ground where he's been lying dejected. The ball hits him on the arse and skids into the back of the net. There's a whistle. Jimbo's wondering what all the cheering's about. Flannagin falls off the stretcher as the bearers twist round quick to see what the commotion is. He's lying down the steps of the terrace. Carpet shaped.

Jimbo still doesn't know what's going on when the players mob him. He's flattened on the ground. There's bits of grass tickling his nose and muck in his mouth. It's only his head sticking out and Benny's licking his face like it's a dog lollipop.

Soon as the players stand up it's the final whistle.

They don't take it that bad the Airdrie players. They shake

the hands and swap jerseys. Some of them's laughing. It's been a farce really. They'll get over it. Put it down to experience.

Barney's standing by the side of the M8. His face is some
mess. He's holding a bunch of daffodils for Carol. A
fluorescent yellow against the exhaust-stained sides of the
motorway. He finds a gap and loups across the road into the
scheme.

He chaps the door and she opens it, glances at the daffodils,
and walks away. The door's wide to the wall. There's the
smell of disinfectant and furniture polish.

Hi Marie, he goes. It's Carol's sister.

What the hell happened to your face? she goes.

Carol draws Barney a tell her fuck all look.

Fight.

Fight? Where?

Galleria.

You shouldn't go in that pub. Was it a tumbler?

Carol springs at the daffodils and goes away to stick them
in a vase. Barney's staring out the window.

That's a bath running for you, Carol shouts.

Right.

You been down that Estate sleeping again? goes Marie.

Carol appears. She's got Barney's clean pants, socks, white
T-shirt, jeans, jumper and towel all stacked in one hand.

The bath's great. A warm bath's like a womb to Barney
when he's coming off drink. Some scabs fall off his face
leaving deep red gouges with pink edges. It must have been
Carol's nails right enough.

When he's finished he goes in the living room. It's like a
showroom it's that shiny. This black and white film comes
on. Carol and Marie's in the scullery drinking cider. Barney
gets a joint together and relaxes feeling sick and happy. Carol
comes in now and again wearing black silk French knickers
under white ski-pants.

Where's the wanes? Barney goes.

My Maw's got them.

So Barney knows Carol's planning going out. The guy in the film is going on about thirty-nine steps and getting chased all over the mountains.

Ticket for Dumfries please, goes Hanna Banana.

The Lanarkshire Cup's an old dented thing. In dire need of a tin of Brasso. You wouldn't notice a searchlight shining on it never mind seeing your reflection in it. The *Coatbridge and Airdrie Cybertizer*'s there. The team line up like the dirty dozen on the pitch. There's the cup in front of them and Benny's the new mascot. A dog with a scarf.

So all over Lanarkshire the next day the dirty dozen grin out from the breakfast table. There's hardly anybody can believe it. Hardly anybody that is except Mary Maglone.

All over her walls are photos and trinkets of the Rovers. Years gone past and all. She pins the colour Cup Special up and goes into another wee room. A room with stars and moons painted on the door. Gold and silver. Inside this room's different. Everything in it's white. If you half shut your eyes you'd hardly be able to make out the lines and edges of the box shape. Like being trapped under snow. There's a window too but the frame's pure white and there's a white blind pulled down over it. There's sun outside. A square of white light delineates itself on the white floor. The only thing that isn't white's the ouija board on top of the table. Mary sits down and starts chanting.

We're in a plane. The players are drunk and singing. They can't believe their luck. Some of them's never been on a plane before. It's exciting.

They hit a bit of turbulence. A laugh goes up. There's all the roller coaster jokes. But there's nerves. Real nerves. The turbulence gets worse. They joke less. Matt's got the statue out.

This is your Captain speaking. We've come into a bit of air turbulence. Nothing to worry about. Air Traffic control tell me it's clear five minutes ahead.

The

      plane

           drops

                fifty

                    feet.

Christ! It's all seat belts and clinging onto the armrests. White faces. Matt catches Padre Pio as it flies up in the air. No Smoking. Fasten Your Seatbelts. More panic.

Your Captain again. We're coming in to land at Salzburg. With the turbulence and cross-winds we may experience some buffeting.

The plane comes in to land but it's getting shook from

side

                                        to side

so he aborts. He goes round in a long sweep over the city. Out the window the wisps of clouds clear now and then and there's lights in rows and spirals far below. Life. And that's what Eddie's thinking. Life down there in the streets and us up here in the plane getting bumped about. And all the players are wondering if they're going to make it on to the ground safe. The plane comes round again. This time there's no message from the Captain. There's no noise other than wind and engine noise cos they're coming in. They're a tube of tension with wings. Down.

Down.

Down.

The clouds clear. And there it is. The runway. Long straight lines of shining stars. But it's moving about

side   to   side

like water in a bucket.

Down.

Down.

Down.

Bump.

We're on the runway. But it's not over yet. The weather's bad. There's a skim of icy water on the tar. The plane's screaming and the brakes are locking. The wheels are screeching but it veers off the runway. And it's heading for some buildings. Heading for some buildings. Buildings, Eddie's thinking. And he's not the only one.

Oh my fuck it's heading for them buildings! says Barney. But he says it to himself. And he blesses himself. But he won't remember it. It's automatic.

This is the way the Busby Babes went! Brian shouts.

The rest of the players are stretching their faces over their skulls and hunching their shoulders – waiting for impact.

The plane tears through a fence. There's a fuel dump just ahead. But the wheels are on grass now. The wheels dig into the grass. Biting. The mud and turf gathers up the stalks of the undercarriage. Slow and slow. The plane slows down. Right down. The undercarriage is bending back with the strain.

Snap.

And one of the wheels folds. By this time the plane's that slow the left wing bounce bounce bounces a few times off the ground and the plane swings round in an arc like a slow compass and comes to a halt. There's a

silence

and then the cheer goes up. Matt gives his Padre Pio a kiss and shoves it back in the bag. The Captain comes in. And even though they think it's his fault the players clap and cheer him on.

On you go the Captain. On you go, says Brian Rogers. *On you fuckin go my man.*

But the elation only lasts about a minute. Soon as it fades they're all chalk white with shock. The Pilot's opening the doors and letting the emergency chutes down. Emergency vehicles are rushing to the scene. There's eight guys recorded on the medical list who suffered mild shock.

Brian Rogers. Taylor Thomas. Pegg Davidson. Barnie Wheelan. Cole Edwards. Jonesy Mark. Brent Geogh. Edward Duncan.

It's Eddie Duncan's school. It's the assembly hall. The big
rosary session. All through the prayers the only thing going
through Eddie's head's,

a boy has been hit by a locomotive
a boy has been hit by a locomotive
a boy has been hit by a locomotive

And he keeps thinking of this other boy. Not Pat. Not his
pal Pat. Not Pat the best footballer in the school. It's not him
that's been hit by the train, Eddie keeps saying over and over
in himself. It's another boy. Eddie pushes Pat's face out his
head and imagines another boy.

It's a wee boy skipping up to school. His schoolbag's
slung over his shoulder. He's singing. Maybe a Human
League. Or a Madonna. Or Boy George. One of them other
songs you sing when there's nobody there. 'Karma
Chameleon'. Aye that's it. It's a wee boy singing 'Karma
Chameleon'. Eddie sings inside his head. His mouth's still
forming the words of the Hail Marys but in his head he's
singing to keep the horrible pictures of Pat out.

They pray till they're dry in the mouth and get sent home
early.

Do not go near the railway.
Anyone found near British Rail
property will be dealt with severely,

Riley shouts over and over as they're pushing out the swing
doors.

But all the way home they're buzzing about it. Just at the
Clock Bar where you can walk up the side of the wall onto
the main line. Tam McGowan says *C'mon we'll go over the
British and see if we can see anything.*

A team of them make their way along the railway watching for trains. Tam McGowan turns back and wonders why Eddie's not coming. He's usually first there. He sees Eddie walking off in the other direction. Tam shrugs and leads the team to the cordoned off area of the line. He slides up but there's nobody there. No Police. No nothing. Just the tape they put round the place. He waves the rest of the gang up. There's all these yellow marks the Police have made.

They all stop on the line staring at the blood like it's a book they can't read. It's smattered on the stones and smeared up the side of the track. It's funny how black blood looks. You always imagine it to be red. It's red in the films. But on the lines it's thick like jelly. And it's dark red. So dark red it's black where there's no light shining on it.

Eight guys are treated for mild shock.

Brian Rogers. Taylor Thomas. Pegg Davidson. Barnie Wheelan. Cole Edwards. Jonesy Mark. Brent Geogh. Edward Duncan.

And it's the same eight that's geared up three days later with all the kit. They're climbing to the top of a steep run. Ski suits goggles the whole bit. The skies are clear. The sun's even out. But they've ignored an avalanche warning. The reason they're all there on the hill is a woman. Ingrid. The barmaid in the lodge. Usual. Long blond hair and blue eyes.

My name eez Eengreed, she goes and they all copy her and laugh.

But they can't decide who she fancies.

I like famous football teemz, she goes. *Albeeon Roverz you are you? I no know you name before? How why?*

The only thing certain is they all fancy Ingrid. Whoever wins the race's got the right to chat her up without interference.

Up and up they go. Using the upskiing parachutes. That's weird. You get your kit on and this wee harness that goes to the front. Then you let the canopy fall and you lift these wee strings so it fills with wind. Up they go. They're headed for the start of a race. The race of a lifetime down the hill. They line up at the top. Fold away the wee parachutes. They're like jolly SAS men going into action.

Get fuckin back, goes Jonesy, *it's got to be a straight . . .*

Go! Barney shouts, and they're all off. Jonesy's three seconds behind. There's bursts of ice snow and flurries of powder. The SAS going down the hill. Watch out baddies here we come. Swish. Swish. Whooah!!! Over mounds. They're not that good and the hill's too fast. They're out of control. But they seem to like it. Faster and faster they go. Steeper and steeper. Sometimes they're lifted that high and squinty you'd think there's no way they're going to land safe. They're up in the air like crazy propellers.

Pegg Davidson hits this rock that's sticking up at an angle out the mountain. It's like one of them car rolling escapades on a film. One minute he's gliding down the hill tucked in like a professional next thing whooosh he's tumbling through the air. Then he's back on the ground with a crisp thud and getting ahead of the rest. Down they go.

Down

                                and down

Through the trees and out the other end. Brent Geogh looks behind and counts the others. He laughs. Indestructible. They're getting cocky now skiing in and out each other like dancers. Swishing snow in each other's faces.

But it's all pointless anyhow. No way Ingrid fancies any of that motley crew. It's young Jimbo she's into. No sooner have the Coatbridge downhill ski champions left and she's over at his table with a couple of drinks.

You arr not to go ski no?

Jimbo shakes his head.

You are not palls wit all Roverz yes?

Jimbo shakes his head.

You a not got tongue yes?

Aye, says Jimbo.

He shows her his tongue and she laughs. It's a long time since he's had a happy reaction from a bird so he does it again. She laughs again. She flicks hers out. He flicks his. They laugh. And she's a touchy bird. She keeps laying her hand on his upper arm when she's talking. Then maybe his leg. And she's right into his space. So close he can feel her breath on his face. It turns him on a bit. He can feel something stirring down there. Maybe that's what it's been all along, he's thinking. Maybe it's just been the right woman that needed to come along?

They get on great guns, her and him. Great guns. And so while the mad bastards are skiing down the hill for the rights to the maiden Jimbo's getting invited into Ingrid's bedroom. You can see the stress on his face. He's at the door and looks like half of him wants to go in and half of him doesn't. Ingrid can't understand it. In they go anyway and she turns the key in the lock. She closes the curtains and turns to face him. She gets the kit off and sits on the bed. She's got a great body. Ten out of ten at least. Jimbo's in there.

Barney's in the living room just after his bath. The wanes are at Carol's Maw's. He gets a joint together and relaxes. Carol and Marie's in the scullery drinking. Hanna Banana's going on about thirty-nine steps and getting chased all over the mountains.

Ticket for Dumfries please, goes Banana.

*

Barney . . . Barney . . .

It's Carol shaking him in the dark. His arm's numb with pins and needles.

Eh?

Alright if I go out with Marie the night. My Maw's got the wane.

Eh?

Just the pub. We've been cleaning this house all day?

Eh . . . aye . . . Barney says without thinking and falls asleep again.

Barney . . . Barney . . .

It's Carol shaking him again.

She's done right up. Stunning. Jealousy rages through his veins like the bends. She smells great and Barney's collected this massive hard on from some dream. He wants to shag her.

That's us away, she goes and kisses the good bit of his cheek. But she's thinking about going out and her face is already pulling away when her lips meet his skin.

Chiri, Marie shouts safe in the lobby. Carol keeps talking so he can't object.

There's Buckfast and cans in the fridge and I went over to Skin's and got a gram. It's that tin foil on the coffee jar. Keep a bit for us, she goes.

He can't get quite wakened and jealousy's killing him. He shoves the hand on her crotch and she pulls back like a complete stranger.

Beep Beep. Taxi's in the car park. Carol and Marie slip away.

Barney sneaks to the window and sees them running with arms folded across their tits and shining in the night like high-class prostitutes.

It feels like death as the taxi speeds away with the driver's jaw opening and shutting. The black between his jaws's the chasm where Barney's jealousy's echoing.

He gets to the pine-scented scullery and the two-hundred watt bulb's like a knockout punch. A pint of water, six paracetamol. He skins three joints. Carol's stripped three fags and left them and some loose skins. His heart warms a bit.

He snuggles in to Saturday night telly with the drink and the joints. But the telly's all babes in discos getting chatted up and birds getting shagged while their men's sitting watching the telly.

ZZZZZZZZZZZZZZZZZZZZZZZZZZZZZZZZZZZZZZZZZZZ

He wakes up and the place is quiet. There's hardly any cars whizzing by on the motorway. It's late but the clock's in the scullery. Eventually he staggers in and it's four in the fuckin morning.

He goes to the bedroom.

Carol's not in bed.

All the jealousy comes rushing in. He goes to the window. Every car that comes along pushes adrenaline in his heart.

There's the odd fight and breaking glass and running footsteps and then silence. It's getting light. Then this taxi stops. There's a load of people in it but he can't make out who they are. Carol gets out laughing and joking like it's a good time. A fuckin real good time. The dancing finishes at two. The taxi reverses root toot tooting its horn. She looks up and starts running with the same fuckin cross-armed run she done when she left.

She comes in.

On the mountain the eight ski downhill. But there's something not right. There's a feeling of oddness behind them. There's a slight tremor working up through the skis. A change in the speed of the air. There's the impact of the wind on their faces as they rush down. But there's this other wind coming from behind too. And it's got bits of ice in it. First thing Jonesy Mark notices the tiny pieces of ice flying past his ears. He nods to Pegg Davidson. One by one they turn round to the horror of a white rumble up there on the ridge. And it's coming down. It's rushing down on them.

Ski, ski like fuck! shouts Barney.

And they're off. But everything's blue in front and everything's white behind. White and getting whiter. Bullhorning round them. Taylor Thomas is just thinking it's surround-sound Dolby stereo – the things that go through your head. They can feel it up through the skis. See it out on the periphery of their vision. If it meets at the front they'll be skiing down in the centre of a tornado. The eye of the storm. Or the calm before the final storm.

Jimbo's in bed with Ingrid. It's the calm after the calm. The two of them's lying looking at the ceiling. Wood. Pine it is. And there's as many knots as you need to count to make the time go by. To force whatever it is you want to force – out your head.

Eventually Ingrid breaks the silence.

Eez eet me? She whips the covers off to show Jimbo her world-class international body. Jimbo goes bright red. He shakes his head.

I not sexee enough? You want I wear strange clothes – yes? Wellingtons?

Jimbo goes redder again. He shakes his head

What ees it then?

Jimbo takes a breath and starts telling her this story.

When I was eighteen I played for Scotland in the World Cup.

You Woreeld Cup?

Under twenty-ones, he goes. *Young.*

He puts his hand out the size of a young boy. She gets it and nods.

I took a penalty. We'd've won the game if I scored. I took it and missed.

She cuddles into him.

Oh my poor wee – ees it wee?

Jimbo nods. *Wee – aye.*

My poor wee Jeembo. You meesed the ball. But that's OK that's the past eh? No?

It's not just that.

Just that?

Ever since that I've . . . I . . .

He can't say it but he lifts the covers and points at his limp dick.

I can't . . .

Ah, goes Ingrid, *hard on, that why Jimbo not get hard on. I see. I see.*

She flings the arms round him and rocks him gentle from side to side.

Jeembo no hard on, she keeps going. *Jeembo no hard on.*

Shh! Don't say that out this room, he says, *to my mates!*

She kisses him.

Eengrid no say. Eengrid fix you.

She slides down and starts giving him a blow job. He smiles and closes his eyes. After a minute there's no reaction so Ingrid slides back up.

Poor Jeembo, she says, *poor Jeembo.*

The avalanche is moving at twice the speed they're moving at. And they're in a gully. The outer edges of its bullhorn are in front of them now. They try to ski for the opening. The ground shakes more and more. It's like snow at first. Light snow. Then heavy. Then a blizzard. Soon each skier can only see his own hands. It's the end. It's really the end. It feels like death. Weird. Cole Edwards stops and crouches down. He's gave up. He lets the snow pile over him. It's so loud it's quiet. Then it's like somebody kicking you full force on the back. Like on the pitch when you're not expecting it. Then you're up in the air. Then there's soft falling.

Then white. All white.

Then black.

A compression immeasurable. Grade by grade it gathers. Just when you think the last weight's been washed over you another weight pressures on. Layers of snow. Layers of ice. Then nothing moves. There's nothing. No breathing in and no breathing out. It's not sore. There's no pain. It's like absolute peace. Like high bells ringing. Like you imagined it at primary school. The roaring stops and you're buried so deep in the snow there's only darkness. Ten feet above you's the blinding white of the snow. But here it's a cold tomb. It's even shaped itself round your fingers.

Brian's Da's terrorising them into admitting who drank the Ginger Beer.

Who the fuck drunk this then? he

goes, pressing the bottle at them.

Nobody says a word.

I said who was at this Ginger Beer?

He's holding it up like a trophy he's won.

Not me . . . nope . . . I never . . . that's what you'd hear if you were passing the living room door. But you'd feel gravity tighten too. Right at the spot where Brian's feet touch the ground. You'd feel gravity tighten there and draw all the strength out him. He's a weakness standing there. Adrenaline's dissolving his will to stay conscious. The whole room's spinning. And his Da's grinning. Cos he can sense the terror. Smell it. He smiles the Da. Smiles along the row of trembling figures. He walks to Patrick.

Was it you? Shake of the head. SLAP! There's tiny rays of light coming from Patrick's cheek. The Da moves to Johnny. The end of the line's Brian followed by Jean.

Somecunt better own up cos it's two slaps the next time – and

then the belt. Was it you? Johnny shakes his head. SLAP!

Was it you? Brian denies it. His Da's eyes are right in his. But he gets his slap anyway Brian and the Da moves onto Jean. And she gets it as hard as the boys. But she takes it better. Her head tilts to the side quick and her hair falls down to one side. She straightens it up and stares straight ahead. She's thirteen and a half.

The Da goes along the line again giving two slaps this time. And it's four slaps really cos each one's twice as hard as the ones he started with.

Come on, he's going. *I fuckin hate a liar. That's the worst thing*

I hate. If whoever done it owns up I'll stop.

Silence.

Brian almost takes a step forwards. His heart and his mind's done it. But his body doesn't move. It doesn't even move enough to be a flinch. Nobody even notices. Far as they're all concerned he never moved. Nobody moved.

The Da stares at them. He starts unbuckling the big leather belt. It's a brass buckle and that's what he hits you with. On the bare arse. And you bled for days. Every time the skin stretched it cracked open.

The belt hisses through the trouser loops. He wraps one end round his fist and leaves the brass buckle shining like fear. The whole line takes gulps.

Right this is your last fuckin chance. If whoever it was owns up that's the end of the matter. He's staring right in Patrick's eyes.

Silence.

Rovers are trapped under the avalanche. Back in Coatbridge Mary Maglone stops chopping onions at the sink. She is still. She goes outside. She looks over towards Rovers' ground. Watching flakes of snow swirl and swirl down out the dark sky. To look at her you'd think she was watching notes of music coming down in a symphony. She smiles but there's tears in her eyes.

Barney's at the window watching for Carol. This taxi stops. There's a load of people in it. Carol gets out laughing and joking. The taxi reverses tooting its horn. She looks up and starts running with the same fuckin cross-armed run she done when she left.

She comes in.

Some home after the pub that, Barney goes.

She tilts her whole body to one side, leans against the wall and blows some smoke out.

Eh? she goes cheeky as fuck.

I thought you were only going to the pub?

So? Marie asked me to go to Stars and I went. Something wrong with that?

Fuckin plenty if you say you're only going to the pub and then you don't come fuckin home.

She tries to brush past. He grabs her.

Your fuckin hand off me.

Where were you? he goes but it's through his teeth now.

I told you. I went to Stars with Marie.

Stars shuts at two.

So?

Well – it's five in the fuckin morning.

She looks at her watch.

Quarter past four actually.

Well where have you actually been for two and a quarter hours.

Talking.

Talking? Talking to who?

Marie's pals.

Where?

Let me go to bed.

Where were you talking to Marie's pals?

Outside Stars.

For two hours?

You get drunk and you get talking . . .

Was there any guys there?

Eh?

You fuckin heard.

Course there was guys – it's not only women that go to the dancing.

So you're outside Stars chatting up guys two hours?

Was I fuck. I was talking to Marie's pal Silvia and there was guys there – that's – what the fuck am I explaining myself to you for? Where were you last night.

You fuckin know where I was.

Away with some hoor more like.

Barney grabs her by the jaw and he presses her head against the wall.

Let be go ya phuckin cleep.

He chucks her in the bedroom.

I'm feart to touch you in case I catch something ya fuckin slut.

On the mountain it's a perfect white out. The wind's stopped and the air's settled. Nothing moves except for some inquisitive birds. They're landing and approaching some strange-coloured snow. Eight circles of blue-white light. But they seem ill at ease cos every time they get near to the spots they jump back. Like the pigeons in George Square when a wane tries to catch them.

After a while the light's going down. The birds are on the ground with their heads puffed into their chests. They're all looking in the one direction. Watching. There's eight luminous circles in the snow. They're blue. But not a cold blue. Not the blue of ice. Or the blue of sky. Or the metaphorical blue of depression. Or the blue of paint. This blue's the bluest of ice-blues. And it's moving. The blue's moving – or is it the snow? It's hard to tell. But it must be the blue cos it's only within each circle the excitation. The ripples are starting dead centre and moving out to the edges. Like a stone's been dropped in. Lapping on the shores of snow. That's it. That's what it is. That's what Blue it is. It's the blue of the sea off a South Pacific island. And if you just look at the edges of the blue the snow looks like white sands. Miniature beaches on the arc of every circle of light.

The light gets more intense. It's not just the fading light of day. The actual blue is gathering electricity. Luminosity.

Getting brighter.

And brighter.

And in the middle of each circle appears an ultraviolet buzz. Like a welder's torch. Utraviolet with white hot in the middle. And that's getting brighter.

Brighter.

And brighter. So bright you know something's going to happen. And it does. The snow bulges up in ripples. Wee curves. Then more. It rises at eight spots. Up and up. Till it's the height of a man. The height of a footballer.

Eight ghostly figures re-form out of the snow. They're see-through. Malleable. Like liquid metal – only cold. They look like they're made out of snow. A mixture of snow and blue ice and mercury. The birds rise in a sudden umbrella. They flap off landing at a safer tree. The figures form. And form. And form. For seconds they look solid. Real men stood up there on the precipice. Ordinary men. But there's one thing. They're all wearing football strips. Manchester United. But ancient. Long flapping shorts and strange v-neck shirts.

Roger Byrne. Tommy Taylor. David Pegg. Bill Whelan. Eddie Coleman. Mark Jones. Geoff Bent. Duncan Edwards. They're looking at each other as amazed as the birds. They never expected to be ghosts. They never expected to be trapped in snow. They never expected to be released and standing in minus fifteen with shorts on. They're shivering till they realise they're not cold. They're warm. And they're talking. But the birds don't understand a word. And neither would you cos it's the other language. You'd need a medium to understand them.

Next thing they bunch together. They're discussing tactics. The blue buzzes and buzzes. The light's so intense. From the air you'd think it was a UFO.

Something strange on the hills Air Traffic Control. Can't make it out. Could be a crash.

The huddle opens up like an electric flower. A great blue lotus. Petals leaning away from each other. They look like a high-speed gas flame on a cooker. Then there's white shafts of light going up to Heaven and down to the centre of the earth. And yellow. Yellow light glowing like Easter. And red. There's a loud electric crack. They shoot off at ferocious speeds. The way you see UFOs in rough home-filmed discs.

In and out each other they're going. Whizzing round the place leaving a trail of spirit. The trails form into what looks like an intricate Celtic knot. God's dance troupe dancing on the side of a mountain.

They stop. Hovering twenty feet above the snow. Taut with energy. Then, one at a time, they snap free and wumph into the snow.

Sheew sheewwwww they go. Thump! And a powder of snow dusts up and floats to the ground again.

Soon only eight fluorescent circles of light are left on the surface. Glowing. Glowing harder and harder. So hard each one's a nuclear pile at critical mass. It's going to go. It's going to go. That's what it's like. There's a Heavenly radiance about the whole place. Surely you can see the light right across the countryside? Then the Heavenly light fades. It fades so far – then darkness like somebody clicked the light out.

For a few seconds the birds can only hear each other whistle while their eyes adjust to the natural dark blue of night-time snow.

Ingrid's striking all sorts of sexy poses for Jimbo. The blanket's going up and down in a nice wee rhythm. He's trying his hardest but he can't get it up. She's got the kit on – all the tackle. She's bent over near the door with her arse pointing at the bed.

You want mee Jeembo. Eh? You want Eengrid vom thee back yes? She's giving it all that stuff when the door bursts open. It's Matt and Padre Pio. Ingrid looks up into Matt's eyes without straightening up. Matt looks at her and looks at Jimbo. Padre Pio closes his plaster eyes in disgust. Matt stuffs the statue up his jumper. Ingrid runs into the bog.

What the fuck is it Matt? says Jimbo trying to milk the macho-ness out the situation. Make Matt think he's been at it all night with Ingrid. Giving it to her from all angles. Then maybe a wee floor show. All the stuff a man that can get a hard on would do.

Matt's apologetic. His head's everywhere. But everywhere he rests his eyes is a pair of French knickers or a red frilly bra or a dildo or something. Ingrid's just coming back out the bog when Matt can get himself together enough to speak.

There's been an accident, he goes, *in the snow.*

A what? says Jimbo.

An avalanche.

Barney flings Carol into the bedroom by the hair. Carol gets up and slams the door humming some stupid song. Barney can hear the bed springs going. Squeak squeak they're going. In rhythm. Like she's getting shagged in there. She's trying to do his head in.

Rage gets him. He runs in and tips the fuckin bed up.

YA BAAAAASTAAAARD! she goes, and he gets her by the hair.

Who is he eh?

There's no cunt.

Who the fuck is he?

Leave me Barney.

Tell me who he is so I can rip his fuckin head off.

I want you out my house.

He lets her go and she falls in a pile. Crying.

Oh! So it's the fuckin war cry now? Barney's doing her voice: *I want you out my hou – ouse.*

She springs up. *That's right I want you out my house.* **NOW!!!**

Silence.

He walks in the living room. He's on the couch smoking when she bursts in like a mad witch.

Out.

Fuck off.

Get out.

Get yerself to fuck.

I'll phone the Polis.

Phone the fuckin Polis. I'll kill them too.

Big fuckin hardman.

Hard enough.

I *want* you OUT!!!!*!*

Fuck   *off!*

She sees he's not moving so she tries her brainwashing technique. She sits right beside him on the couch, talking in his ear. Barney smokes away like she doesn't exist.

I don't like you. D'you know that? I don't fuckin like you. You make me sick. You're twisted. You're fuckin twisted, you're twisted as fuck so you are, you're twisted, you're fuckin twisted. You're twisted. You're twisted. You're twisted. You're twisted. You're twisted. You're twisted. You're twisted. You're twisted. You're twisted. You're twisted. You're twisted. You're twisted. Your head's twisted. Ya twisted bastard.

Is there a fly in here? Barney goes, and

smokes the joint. He's smoking it fast and strong. It's making him dizzy. But it's taking the pain away. The jealousy. She looks in his ear cos he's not even turning round. She's got this rant off to a fine art and she adds to it all the time.

And you're sick.

I never knew some cunt switched the telly on.

You're sick.

Who let Granny Harvey in here?

You're sick. D'you know that?

Phew! – has a pig shat in here?

I don't fuckin like you. You make me sick.

Fuck! I can hear the Banshee.

You're sick. You're fuckin sick You're sick. You're sick. You're sick. You're sick.

I can smell fish. Is this the Pittenweem fish

filleters' night out?

You're sick. You're sick. You're sick. You're sick. You're sick.
You're sick. You're sick. You're sick.

I didn't know they let orang-utans in here.

Ya twisted and sick prick.

*Must have left that window open. Some big
stupid looking fuckin crow's got in here and it's
bumping its beak at me and I don't speak
croweese.*

But Carol's already flapping out the room.

SLAM

The bedroom door. Barney's mellow with dope anyway.
Good job. He lies back and thinks of daffodils and Donegal
and whatever it is at the other side of the forest he can never
find.

And this is the way they'll go on. Something's got to give.
Something's got to change.

It's night back on the mountain. The spot where the ghosts appeared is quiet. The same place the Rovers players are buried. It's sleepy hollow. The birds have fell asleep. Only the light dusting of flakes moves round in little eddies over the surface. Rising – catching the light like glitter – and falling in millions of microscopic clicks again. But one bird opens its eyes. There's a thrumming in the distance. Louder it gets. Louder and louder until whooosh right over the top of them – a helicopter. It's there black and frightening in the sky for a moment and then it's gone behind the ridge. It sees nothing cos there's nothing there to see. It's just another bank of fallen snow. It's duh duh duh duh is fading in the distance when a shaft of ice-blue light shoots from the ground and fires up through the night. It explodes silently into a great white star eight hundred feet up.

There's an immense light source. The shadow of the chopper's moving along the face of the mountain in front. It's one sunny day in the middle of the night. Inside the copter the Co-Pilot taps the Pilot.

One eighty, he says. *Light source.*

The pilot turns the machine through a wide arc. It takes a full minute to get through a hundred and eighty degrees and come to stillness. There – off in the rises and falls in a cup between two ridges is a thin tube of light. Like metal. Straight up in the air. And there's a strange emanation coming from where it stops abruptly in the sky. A light like a giant welder's torch.

The Co-Pilot punches out the rough co-ordinates on the GMP and transmits them. As he does the light withdraws sharp and is gone. The sky's much darker in the immediate absence. Much darker. There's a black bar of darkness where the light used to be. And a faint infra-red aftermath. The copter stays still for a full minute to regain composure and then moves carefully. Edging its way towards the co-ordinates. Slow and unsure.

On the ground the Search Team have received the transmission. But they were heading in that direction anyhow. Cos as they angled their way up the steep slope the light shot up in the sky five miles into the hills. Like something holy. They were mesmerised. No one in the Team or the Police or the locals had ever seen anything like it. Nothing like it at all. The hundred-strong party stood transfixed. The intense light came in wide sheets through the trees and flooded under their legs and off the edge of the hill. It had the feeling of wind but not the pressure. The movement of water but not the noise. Bright but didn't affect the vision. You could still look directly at the shaft where the light was emanating from and see it clear. No haze. Just the shaft and the beautiful welder's star hanging there in the night sky. The shaft was lighting up the area without the waves of light being connected to the source. It defied sense. In fact it defied science. Totally. There's something wrong. Something not right here at all. The crowd stayed still twenty seconds after the light disappeared. Nobody said a thing. Nothing. It was all stop. Then a silent decision to move on and up into where the light was. Stepping forward in awe. Upwards in reverence.

Searchbeams are swinging about. They're like a machine. A set of giant paintbrushes painting the mountain white. Cos the ground before them's black. Then the fuzzy light at the head of the beams turns it grey. Then it's a flashing white as the beams move over it. But at the same time there must be another brush behind them. Soon as they've moved over the snow it's black again behind them. But there's something beautiful about that cos it seems they're leaving no footprints. There's virgin snow to the front lit up. But where the feet have trod there's nothing to see. Nothing in the absolute black they're leaving behind as they move. And move. And move.

The birds on the hill hear the returning helicopter. But more alarming to them's the barking dogs coming up towards them. The birds chatter at each other. Then, when the noise overhead's growing and the light from the copter's approaching they hear people. That's when they take to the trees. Then it's shouting voices. Torchlight through the trees.

Soon, high above, a powerful beam of light shines down. The Search Team must be close cos there's the unmistakable sound of crackling radios. And if you knew the Team you'd be able to make out individual voices. Even exactly what they were saying.

It all happens at once for the birds. The copter comes in and lands sending the snow upwards so as it seems like it's snowing on the underside of the trees. Imagine painting a tree – then you go to put some lines of thick white on for snow. But do it on the underneaths. The parts of the tree that snow'd hit and land on if it was coming up instead of down. Do that and you'll see how weird the world looked for the birds that night. The birds of the mountain are used to a slow and unchanging world. Birth to death the snow never moves. But this day is a strange day for the birds. Strange day.

And it's a strange day for the Team too cos that's what they see when they come over the ridge sweeping the snow with their lights. The trees with the upside down snow. The birds watching in eerie stillness. The place is lit up with the copter crew. The Search Team run towards the copter. At the head of the race is Jimbo and Ingrid.

It's on the way home from the Assembly Hall. Eddie's left his pals and went the other way; they're all up the railway. Eddie Duncan's walking home. There's a feeling in his gut like a fire made out the black bits between flames. He's still forcing himself to think of a wee boy. A poor wee boy he doesn't know. Trapped under a train. Getting dragged past his own house. And all the places he knows really well are whizzing past and bumping up and down. And he's screaming but there's nobody can hear him. All the things that looked dead ordinary a minute ago look crazy strange now. Crazy strange. And he can't feel a thing. Only motion.

But Eddie can't keep it out any more. He collapses on the ground. And he's crying. He doesn't care who sees him. This old woman goes by.

Are you alright son?

He keeps on crying.

Are you lost?

Eddie looks up.

My pal got hit by a train, he goes.

And the old woman's already heard it on the streets and on the news. She reaches out and rubs his head.

Just you cry son. There's nothing wrong with that. Nothing wrong with it at all, she goes.

And after a while she walks away and leaves him. But that wee touch on the head's what does it. It goes flooding out and the horrible images come flooding in.

Rescue workers are digging in the snow. They're working like fuck at first. Throwing snow over their shoulders that fast it looks like bed sheets. Right at the front's the Rovers guys. And right at the front of them's Jimbo and Ingrid.

Over by the trees Matt's got the statue out and he's on his knees praying. People's running past him laying cables and passing tools and machinery. There's another helicopter up there now. But Matt prays on. He wouldn't be much good anyway at the digging.

A couple of reporters have came up on the other helicopter. There's a telly camera and he's in front with the microphone.

There's little hope of finding any of these players alive, he's saying and then the camera pans the workers digging. It pans past Jimbo to some Police. But it pans back sharp cos Jimbo shouts. *There's something here.*

Something here. Shh.

The helicopters have done a better job than the diggers – unbeknownst to them they've moved five or six feet of snow – so that's how Jimbo's got down to something quick. The rotors are switched off and the crowd waits on things getting quieter and quieter. Soon they're sitting like big crazy flowers on the hillside. Nothing's moving. Jimbo can hear his own heart. He drags some more snow away. He leans into the hole and blows.

It's a hand, he shouts. *It's a fuckin hand!*

The whole hillside takes in breath and falls silent. Jimbo gets his glove off. He shoves his hand into the hand sticking out. Like he's shaking it. Like he's shaking hands with the world. Maybe the world's other hand's sticking out somewhere round India way. Who knows? There's some crazy things go through your head at times like these.

People's got their heads down. Specially the Rescue Workers. The TV camera's zoomed right in. The hand's like marble. Jimbo squeezes it. It squeezes back. It squeezes back for fucksakes – Jimbo starts crying. The rest of the crowd think he's accepted the death of his teammates.

It squeezed me – it fuckin squeezed me, he says to himself. He turns to the crowd with a big smile on him.

He's alive! He's fuckin alive! shouts Jimbo. The

tears are tripping him. They're running out his eyes and they're ice by the time they reach his chin. But they've got dolphins in them the tears. Dolphins frozen in joy. Jimbo sticks his two outstretched hands in the air.

There's some cunt alive in there!

Praise the Lord! says Matt and starts burrowing into the snow like a dog. *Praise the fuckin Lord!*

The camera team's got the lens on the hand and it's pulsing in and out like a heartbeat. Carlton TV's putting it out to all their stations.

It's Big Eddie's hand that, says Matt, *I'd know it anywhere.*

Well some amazing goings on here up on this Salzburg mountainside this morning. Eight hours buried in an avalanche and it seems there's somebody still alive. As to his condition we can't say at the moment but there's a paramedic team standing by . . . The reporter's genuinely amazed at the whole thing. But he's stopped cos there's another shout in German.

Com at zee here. Yalla yalla.

A Policeman's found another body. Well – it would be a body if it was dead. There's a flurry of digging.

By this time Eddie's face has been uncovered. And a smile! First thing he sees is Matt and Jimbo smiling down at him.

He's managed a smile the big man . . . he's managed a fuckin smile, says Matt to the rest of the team. *It's a miracle.*

137

And the whole thing's going out live to every news station that wants it right round the globe. And an Internet Optical Digi-link. It's all overlaid with the reporter being more amazed than he was five minutes ago.

Bailey Bloggs's watching the news. A football team trapped in the snow. It brings back the memories right enough. And he feels for them. He hopes they're alright. There comes a point when he's about to switch it off. A point where he can't take any more. And just as he's about to shout *off* Jimbo shouts about somecunt being alive in there and Bailey can't switch it off. He slumps back in his chair with a tear in his eye. Not tears of despair. Or tears of memory. Tears of relief. Tears of hope. Not dolphins. Not yet. But shoals of fish roaming a reef. Flicking this way and that. And beyond them in the sparkling water's something good. You just know there's something good. Hope that at least one of these young guys have got out with their life. He turns and blows his wife a kiss and makes a signal to her that means pray for them. He joins his palms together. His wife smiles back from the silver-plated photo frame. She's twenty odds. Looks exact same as she did the day before she died.

Mary Maglone watches in Coatbridge. Her heart goes out to the wifes and relatives. You'd think she'd be biting her lip. With this being her favourite team and the boys being mostly local. But she's not. She looks happy. At ease. She turns and smiles like she's smiling at somebody. But all there is is an empty chair.

Up the mountain the rescuers dig and dig. Eddie Duncan's brung out conscious but he slips into a coma soon as they try to heat him up. Like the cold was keeping him awake. He's flew away in a helicopter. There's another one standing by to land just as Eddie's helicopter leaves.

One by one the seven other players are brought out conscious. First they think it's bad practice to heat them up too quick. They expect them to slip into a coma like Eddie but none of them do. In fact they're quite chirpy.

Barney's that well he gets a fag off Matt and lights up. His clothes are like toast with the frost. You could bend them out of shape and they'd stay there. In fact the back of his jacket's all bent up. The newsmen are astounded. But they don't know how astounded they are. It'll all be apparent when they get away from the place and wonder how eight men trapped under ten feet of snow survived eight hours. They should have suffocated in minutes. Alright one or two of them might have got into a pocket of air. They might even have had the savvy to get their elbows out in front of them and leave a gap in front of their face and breathe easy on that air. But that would have lasted an hour at the most. And that's assuming you could breathe with all that weight of snow round about your rib cage. No sir – there's no fathoming this one out. But right now. Right in the moments that follow one another where there's no past and no present – only the moment you're in. Right there on the mountain it all seems plausible. Engrossed in their work they've no time to think.

Barney doesn't even want to go away in the air ambulance.

A change of clothes'll do me fine, he says, *and maybe a wee half?*

But they take no notice of what he says it's up up and away and the next copter's landing. Every player dug out is feeling OK. In fact some of them's commenting on feeling great.

Like I've been snorting coke, says Jonesy Mark. *Maybe the snow's really all coke?*

And all this's going out live. But the people watching think the poor boy's delirious. He's that bad he thinks he feels good.

The last helicopter takes off and the flurry of snow lands. The sun's coming up on the hills. It's a red line like a wane's drew with a magic marker on the edges of the snowy mountains. The birds come down out the upside-down snow trees and settle into position. There's nothing different about this patch of snow. Even the footprints of the hundred-odd people have been wiped out by the snow blast of the last helicopter. For all any lone man passing might know there's never been a footfall in this area for over a hundred years.

Intensive care. Salzburg City Hospital. Eight beds have been prepared. Drips ECGs – all the usual works you get in crash rooms. Specialist hypothermia doctors are there. A team of nurses called in from their days off. The corridors have been cleared. Outside a congregation of media wait. The first ambulance arrives. Out rolls Eddie on a stretcher. Coma. Flash flash. Microphones sticking everywhere. Bright young things with long hair nice tops and tatty jeans tell the world in all the languages who it is. How he is. And how likely he is to die. But what they can't understand, they say, is the reported wellbeing of the other seven of this football team that are due to arrive any time now. Any time now at all. And they point the cameras up the long road. Except for the sly Internet guys who are sneaking about trying to site minicams on anything that's going into the hospital.

Eddie's took straight up to intensive care and wired up like an experiment. He's trussed in tin foil and thermometers are placed at all the extremities of his body. He's in a room of his own. His fingers are black with cold.

Outside the ambulances arrive with the other players. The media take on the solemn look needed for such an occasion. They've seen their colleagues report on the state of the other seven but they don't believe it. They've seen it. They've heard it. But they don't believe it. They've got to see it in real flesh. Real time. Touch it. Smell it. Interview it.

The ambulances come to a halt. There's no rush. The drivers look happy. And their assistants. They're laughing. One door opens and there's four Rovers players playing cards. The only thing that looks wrong with them's the crazy silver paper wrapped round them. They're having a smoke and waving out to the winking eyes of the cameras. The peering eyes of the world are upon them and all. Barney flashes his arse. And he gets well away with that cos the media and the public put it down to hypothermia. Not to the half bottle he's managed to acquire on the way over. It's an hour's journey from the air base.

Excuse me excuse me – can you tell us something about your night under the snow?

It was freezin hen, says Jonesy Mark. *Fuckin freezin.*

All the others laugh and they're shepherded inside like a pop group. Not like seven guys who should have died but didn't.

It's Brian Rogers' house. His Da's trying to find out who drank the Ginger Beer. The belt hisses through the trouser loops. He wraps one end round his fist and leaves the brass buckle shining like fear.

Right this is your last fuckin chance. If whoever it was owns up that's the end of the matter. He's staring right in Patrick's eyes.

Silence.

Right, the Da goes, and he's just about to tell them to get their pants down when Jean bursts in.

It was me Da.

Everybody's astounded.

I done it.

They look round at her. But only with their eyes. Their heads don't move.

I drunk your rotten Ginger.

The Da grins and looks along the line.

See, he goes, *that's all I was wanting – I only wanted to know who it* was...

And he grabs Jean and throws her to the ground.

Right – every one of youse cunts – up the stairs – scoot!!!

He swishes the belt at them as they scatter out the room. The Daleks have got Doctor Who cornered miles from his Tardis.

From up in their rooms they can hear him laying the brass buckle into Jean. The thud/slap. But she doesn't yell. She doesn't scream out.

Scream ya bastard, he's shouting,

scream.

But she won't scream. And it goes on

And on.

And he's still doing her in. Now and then he picks her up and throws her about the room. Brian can't see it but they've all had it that many times they can put a strike to a noise.

Salzburg. Three days after the rescue everybody's out the hospital. But big Eddie's still in a coma.

The rest of the players finish their holiday. But they take it in turns to spend four hours at Eddie's bed. Talking to him. All about the Rovers. Or the pub. Rena's even flew out and she's there most of the time. She's staying in the same hotel as the players. All their wifes have flew out and all. Airdrie Travel's seen to that. The publicity's been amazing for business.

But time passes and Eddie doesn't stir. It's looking grim for the big man. The machines say he's all but dead. Matt's thinking the doctors are going to suggest switching the life-support off. And he's got a feeling. Fuck knows where he's getting it from but he's got this feeling that Rena would say aye right away without thinking. He's like that Matt. He can tell a lot about what kind of person you are. And Rena's no good.

The rest of the players have a slow two weeks. Moving about the city with their wifes. Eating out. Talking about the future. But if the truth be told the seven are being dishonest. They really feel for big Eddie – don't get me wrong. They feel great inside. There's an energy in them that's making them want to burst out laughing all the time. And when they do. Especially when Pegg Davidson does it in Intensive Care on a visit – the nurses and doctors and the wifes put it down to shock. Post-traumatic. But the other six players know what it is. It's the same as them. They can't wait to get back on the pitch. For the first time since they were boys they can't wait to play the game. They feel fit. They're fat but they feel fit. Their wifes notice they're different too but they say nothing in case they upset them. They've been through enough already poor souls.

They stay in the city. Far away from the mountains. Well away from the snow.

It's only Jimbo and Ingrid that wander in the snow. Jimbo's been having nightmares so Ingrid thinks it'll be good for him to go back to where the trauma started and see how peaceful it is. She knows the peace of the hills's a therapeutic thing. She knows the power of the hills well. So they get a picnic together. Some warm coffee in a flask. Some different cheeses. One of them big loafs you get in Europe that you tear lumps off. They get well togged up and go out for the long walk.

When they come to the place it's peaceful right enough. White. And the sky's blue. And the birds are whistling in the trees. There's nothing wrong here. Nothing wrong at all. They lean against a tree and fall asleep for an hour. The clean air draws up their nostrils and clears away the stress. And they sleep deep. Like in fairy tales. And the birds watch them before they fly back down onto the snow picking the bits of bread round about them and even being bold enough to pick bits off of their jackets and out the bag. Jimbo and Ingrid don't stir. And it's a good job they don't cos they'd see something they'd never believe.

Duncan Edwards. Or the ethereal ice-blue version of him rises out the snow. And he shouts on his mates.

Tommy!

The birds move away.

Roger!

The birds fly to the trees. But then a force starts pulling on him. He's bent out of shape. He looks as surprised as you or me'd be if it happened to us. You always think ghosts are in control but it doesn't look like it here. No sir. Big Duncan's trying to resist. And he's a strong big cunt. So his feet are rooted to the spot. His head's straining back. But his middle's stretched away ten – twenty feet and moving all the time. Eventually he can't resist.

Whooooooooooooooooooooooooooooosh.

He's whipped away at the speed of light. And he leaves a vortex and the air moves into it and a wind comes rushing through the pine trees. Jimbo and Ingrid come slowly awake to the smell of fresh air and pine resin. They're totally refreshed. They look at the spot and there's nothing moving. Still and tranquil. That's what it is. Peace itself.

Duncan Edwards' spirit zooms through the hospital ward.
It's like *Star Wars*. A ball of blue light goes up one corridor
turning right without swerving – turning left in an instant. It
passes doctors and nurses going about their business. Some
of them are amazed but most don't see it it's that fast. Or
they put it down to tiredness. Or a trick of the light. Or
refraction. Or diffraction. Or reflection. Or something to do
with the rods in your eyes. Or something to do with the
cones. Or a slight misfire of neurones across the synaptic
passes. There's a million ways to explain away a passing ball
of light. The last in the list being a passing ball of light.

But it's much harder to explain away Eddie Duncan
jerking suddenly awake and full of beans. But that's what he
does in full view of the doctors and nurses that have
gathered round him to discuss how to bring up the subject of
switching off the life support machine. Duncan Edwards'
spirit thrums into him and BING he's up there.

I'm Hank Marvin! he says. The gathering's amazed.

I'm starving! They still don't seem to understand. He starts
doing eating motions.

Essen, he says, *essen*.

The doctors laugh in amazement.

When they bring Rena in they're more puzzled at her
reaction. She thinks she's in to make the decision on the life
support. All that's been going through her mind's Flannagin
and putting the insurance money into Flannagin's scheme.
When Eddie's sitting up smiling she boaks her guts up on
the floor and faints. The nurses put it down to a release of
stress.

When they're back home the players carry on with their lives as normal. Or they try to. But there's a couple of reasons why they can't. They feel funny. More energetic. More optimistic. Like they're just off a positive thinking course. In training they're coming away with some new moves. Moves that cause them to stop and look at each other in amazement.

But off the pitch – going about their everyday things it's their wifes that notice the difference. Cole Edwards – lazy cunt. There's a story about him. This night his wife comes in from MILLENNIUM MART USA first thing she hears is screaming.

Anna Anna! For fucksakes hurry,

he's screaming. She drops the fifty-odd carrier bags she's carrying and runs into the living room. There's Cole lying beside the fire squirmin.

What is it – what is it!? she's going.

He twists his head round to her. His face's all contorted with pain.

Turn the fire down I'm burning, he goes.

That's how lazy he is. Well the first thing that looks out of place for him's the Sunday. It's eight in the morning and the wife smells cooking. She gets up and sneaks out to the bedroom door cos there's only her and him in the house. She creaks the door open and she can hear somebody moving about down the stairs. Clashing and clanging of pans and stuff. She turns to whisper to Cole that there's a maniac in the house. But he's not there. No Cole. Gone.

Anna leans out the door. *Cole,* she goes, *is that you?*

Aye, he shouts up, *away you back in your bed – I'll be up in a minute.*

What are you doing down there it's only eight o clock?

Away back to your bed and you'll find out.

So she goes back to bed puzzled as to what he's up to. But she's not that bothered and falls asleep. Next thing she hears,

Anna, Anna!

She opens her eyes and there's the fat cunt with a big tray with the works on it. Teapot. The wee thing for holding toast. Sugar. Milk. A big plate with ham, eggs, tomatoes, tattie scones, fried mushrooms and two jumbo sausages.

What are you after? she goes pulling the duvet up to her chin.

Nothing, he says not even catching her drift, *I'm away out a jog. D'you want anything when I'm out – the papers or something?*

No. Thanks. No. I'll . . . I'll – eh – eat my breakfast.

Ta ta then, he goes and kisses her.

And that's the way it is with the eight players that were in the avalanche. Wee differences. Stuff that outsiders wouldn't notice. The one biggest thing is they've all been spotted by fans jogging up the lochs. Team jog. And sweating like pigs. There's been talk that there's a push on for fitness cos these lazy bastards wouldn't run for a bus usually. So there's a wee bit of expectation in the lead up to the first game since they came back. It's the first round of a Scottish Cup game against Forfar.

Saturday. The Scottish Cup game against Forfar. There's a thousand Forfar fans made the trip cos they've signed some African players and they're expecting a good run in the Cup. Rovers have got their usual hundred and odd supporters. And a few more that's been persuaded by the faithful that there's something in the air.

In the Rovers dressing room some of the boys drink beer and smoke. There's one sub – Johnny Dillon – never had a game for two years. He's eating a pizza. Matt looks at him.

Brung it home last night!

Matt stares.

What d'you want me to do – let it go to waste?

Matt shakes his head.

Could be worse – could be a kebab!

He bites a chunk out the pizza crashes open a can of super lager to wash it down. His adams apple's going up and down like a bouncing ball behind a curtain. He takes a good long last slug and without looking passes it to Barney. Barney waves it away. He's deep in thought. There's a few nods and winks. First time Barney's refused a drink. First time ever. Johnny Dillon shrugs and pours it in Benny's bowl. Big Eddie's watching Barney.

Are you alright Barney? goes Eddie.

Aye I'm alright – how?

Eddie says nothing.

Are you alright? Barney says to Eddie.

Aye. Feeling quite good in fact, goes Eddie.

You sure you should be playing?

Barney shouts to Matt through the throng of players getting their kit on and off.

Hey Matt you shouldn't be playing him so soon after the the . . .

Eddie butts in. *Coma? Don't bother about that for fucksakes. I feel like I could run a million miles.*

Matt shrugs at Barney. He drops back to reading the

horoscope in the *Millennium Sun*. The dog's lapping up the lager.

George the goalie's sleeping off a hangover under a bench. Through his snoring you can hear the Forfar fans singing outside.

Better wake that big cunt up, says Pegg Davis. He gives the goalie a kick. George's lips smack together a few times like they're trying to take a draw of an imaginary fag.

Grunt, says George the goalie.

His wife's flung him out again, goes Taylor Thomas. Taylor Thomas is the centre forward and well past his sell by date.

George comes round right after his lips. He slides out from under the bench. Johnny Dillon nods at the can of lager. George picks it up and guzzles the lot. Crushes the can and flings it in the bathtub. Benny dives in after it. Splash. Two other dogs dive in too – splash splash. He fumbles about in his jacket and lights a fag.

Time's it? he goes.

Time you were in your gear, says Matt and whips out Padre Pio. *And get them greyhounds out that bath. We've got to use the fuckin thing*.

Matt blesses himself and kneels down beside the statue.

Awaken us Padre Pio to Glory
Dispel the darkness of defeat
Destroy the heaviness of foot . . .

Some of the players join in for a laugh.

If you're going to make a mockery out of it just shut up and get outside, says Matt.

But when he glares he sees that even if some of them's ripping the pish out him – two or three have got serious looks on them. Eddie – fuck – Barney too – and some other cunt – Brent Geogh. It's like they're really into it. He smiles,

takes a deep breath, and goes into the praying with a bit
more gusto.

> *Cure the lank of limb and fat of gut*
> *Give us gentleness of touch*
> *Encourage a sense of adventure*
> *Bring us an awareness of space*
> *Awaken our jinkiness*
>   *and Padre Pio make us slinky*
> *Glory be to you for ever more*
>   *and the greatest gift of all holy benefactor*
> *Padre Pio Give us a goal.*

When he's finished the whole place's quiet. Even the
greyhounds in the bath are staring up. Their heads are wet
and their paws are over the edge. Like beings just arrived
from another planet bewildered at the goings on.

Young Eddie Duncan's sitting greeting by the side of the road. As the old woman walks away she rubs his head. And that wee touch on the head's what does it. It goes flooding out and the images come flooding in.

It wasn't the wee boy that got hit with the train. Not the wee boy that was singing 'Karma Chameleon'. It was Pat Brogan. Pat and Eddie were playing chicken. That's when you stand on the track and watch the train coming. You and at least one other person. Better with four or five. The one that stays on the track the longest's the winner. Pat Brogan was the champion. Was great at everything Pat. Football. Captain of the school team. Played for Scotland in the under-sixteen internationals. Already had an S form for Celtic. Going to be the greatest footballer that ever came out of Scotland. The big guys used to kick his head in after playing against him – he took the cunt right out them. Made them look like diddies. There was nobody like Pat Brogan. The ball was glued to his shoe.

Pat and Eddie's been sniffing glue all morning down the tunnels.

C'mon – chicken, says Pat. Eddie offers him more glue but the rush of popping braincells is not good enough. Pat wants the adrenaline of steel against steel and tons of certain death coming at him. That's a rush. That's one big fucking rush.

So they're out on the mainline. Pat's standing like a soldier about to get a medal. He's breathing in diesel and the metallic whiff of railway. He's daring the distant trundling to be a train. He lights a half fag. But Eddie's feart. He's looking at Pat and then at the wee speck coming round the bend.

Here, Pat says and hands him a fag. *Two draws and gimmi it back*.

Eddie takes three quick dizzy draws and gives it back. He's staring at the arrogance in Pat's eyes.

Pat, says Eddie, *Pat!?*

But Pat's not looking at Eddie. He's looking straight at the distant train. Like it's alive.

C'mon to fuck train. C'mon just try it. Just you fuckin try it, he's going. He takes the last draw of the fag and flicks it. It hisses out in a puddle of oil. He gets another one out the top pocket of his Wrangler jacket. A three quarter dout. He sticks it in his mouth. He hands another worse fag to Eddie.

Light, says Pat without flinching. The train's two hundred yards away now. They can feel it in the soles of their boots. The wooden sleepers are vibrating. Eddie fumbles and lights Pat's fag. He lights his own but he's not really smoking it. Pat takes a long cowboy draw. The train's a hundred yards. Eddie tries to talk but his jaws creak like they're made out of wood. You can tell he's wanting off the line.

Pat!!? he goes.

Shut the fuck up, says Pat into his fag, *here's the train.*

But he doesn't say *here's the train* like Eddie's not seen it He knows he's seen it. He says *here's the train* cos he wants him to get ready. This is chicken for real.

Albion Rovers. Cup game against Forfar. Outside Forfar limber up on the tacky park. They're avoiding the particularly mucky bits. They look great in clean new strips and lean bodies. Fit and ready for action. Hup – star jumps and soaring in the air headering balls. Some of the Rovers fans feel like walking out right away. Before a ball's kicked.

The Rovers straggle out. It looks like closing time in that pub in *Star Wars* – all kinds of things. The game gets underway. Rovers fans brace themselves for the onslaught. Last time it was Forfar six – Rovers nil. But it's unusual today. Rovers are in an early attacking spell. It'll last a couple of minutes and then they'll be knackered probably. That's what the fans think. Some of them's hoping Rovers don't score early cos then Forfar'll come back with a vengeance and hammer them.

Rovers play OK five minutes.

OK ten.

Fifteen minutes into the game George the Goalie comes lumbering onto the pitch. No one notices. Not the Ref. None of the players. Or even the crowd. And the reason they don't notice is – all the play's up at Forfar's goal. George hides a can of super lager behind the post, lets a ripper of a fart out and takes up position.

And the Forfar end is packed. The Forfar supporters can't believe their eyes. Even their rosettes and hats and shiny kids are stunned. Every Forfar player's in the penalty box and there's shots and headers going in from all angles. Rapid. Even the Ref looks surprised.

At the Rovers end the hundred and odd jump up and down singing the Padre Pio song.

♪♪ *Padre Pio give us a goal give us a goal give us a goal*

Padre Pio give us a goal give us a goal give us a goal

Padre Pio give us a goal give us a goal give us a goal

Padre Pio give us a goal give us a goal give us a goal.

They can't believe it. Once a season a pish team might have a display like this. But with The Rovers it's once in a generation. Most of them's only heard about good games from their Da or Maw. The legendary Cup Final against Kilmarnock in 1936.

The only one that's not dancing a jig's Mary Maglone. She looks really interested in the goings-on. She watches one player – makes some mental notes and then watches another. There's no goals yet but there's sure to be. Soon. The only thing that's stopping Rovers belting a few in's the belief in Forfar that they are by far the superior team. And they are. Or they were. But there's something not right here. Something not right at all. The Rovers are playing with an overwhelming fluidity.

It's a free kick. Taylor Thomas's to take it. But Brent Geogh steps up.

Let me. I feel it's mine, he goes.

You're a fucking donkey! Taylor goes. *You never hit a ball straight in your life,* and goes to take it.

Brent steps in front of him. *I'm not,* he says.

Taylor looks at him. The crowd's shuffling about jostling for position. Wondering what the talk's about. Rovers have never discussed tactics before.

I'm not going to hit it straight.

Taylor puzzles with his eyebrows.

Banana, says Brent. *Banana.* And he curves his hand round in the air.

Taylor nods sarcastic and moves aside. The Ref gives it an are you ready now look and blows his whistle. There's a wall in Forfar's penalty box. Ten in it!

Brent scuds the ball. Banana? It looks like it's heading out for a throw in. But the curve on it swings it back in from the last twenty feet and in behind the goalie who's still smiling from thinking it's a miskick. Taylor's trying to get his sarcastic grin off his face. Brent starts running about in circles. Rovers go wild. They run the length of the pitch to the fans and take their plaudits. Forfar's manager's on the pitch giving his players a right verbal boot up the arse. He's throwing his arms about like he doesn't want them.

In the huddle at the other end the Rovers players are ecstatic.

I feel – I feel – electric, says Brent.

Me too – like charged up – energised! goes big Eddie.

Barney Wheelan shakes his head, *I've not felt like this since my first drink,* he says.

There's big white smiles all round and skin stretched over the surface of happy faces. And behind the players the Rovers fans are going wild. A sea of smiles. Unexpected joy and sudden vitality. Like sea anemones in a whirlpool.

Except one man up the back. Flannagin.

Flannagin's thunderstruck. He looks worried. Above him a monolithic concrete structure. But the cranes have stopped. There's nobody working or moving about even. There's these white and yellow building site hats dotted about like daisies and daffodils in a scrap yard. Every joiner, steel fixer and concrete labourer's leaning over the scaffolding transfixed at the Rovers display. The play resumes. Forfar get to the Rovers goal. But they lose the ball there. To Big Eddie of all people.

Big Eddie runs the length of the pitch. Round three defenders. The goalie comes out. Eddie's still coming. The goalie's a giant multi-coloured frog spreading his legs and arms wider and wider. But it doesn't put Eddie off. No sir. Big Eddie flicks the ball up over his head – runs in – gets under it before it starts falling and – wham – heads it into the net. The crowd are crazed.

Barney Wheelan'll not forget this one. Forfar are on the break. It's two nil to the Rovers. Rovers are running back. Barney takes the ball from the feet of the Forfar player. He strides up the pitch. But there's no Rovers players there. Just him and three Forfar defenders and the goalie. He rolls the ball five feet forward and to his right. He's thirty yards out. He takes one stride and whammmmm over the defenders and into the net.

It's a landslide from then on in. Rovers goal after Rovers goal. The only Rovers players that don't score's Jimbo and George the Goalie. Even Johnny Dillon got one. At the end of the game the hundred and odd Rovers fans are packed down the front. The whole building site is silent. All the scaffold's took up with thick forearms. Rovers fans are going wild. All the Forfar fans have left. Long ago. And the players wish they could have went with them.

Away from everybody Mary Maglone sits smoking. She's got that look on her face you'd have if you seen something unbelievable. Well – everybody's got a look on their face that you'd have if you seen something unbelievable. But she's seen something else. Not just the display from her team. Something much bigger. Like you'd just been visited by every one of your dead relatives. You'd just found out there's life after death. She's awe-struck.

It's the final whistle and the place erupts. Except Flannagin. He implodes. There's a quiet explosion in his head that only he can hear. Like an elastic band snapping. He's up the back on his own. Above him in the labyrinth of steel-titanium towers and concrete beams the workers sing the Padre Pio song. Benny the greyhound struts up to Flannagin and snarls. It looks like Flannagin's ignoring him. Benny looks at the briefcase. His back leg's lifting a bit off the ground and twitching. But the briefcase is covered in polythene. Flannagin grins and clicks the dog over. He's got a bit of fried liver in his hand. Benny growls. Benny sniffs.

Benny growls. Flannagin click clicks. It's a stand off.

Here doggy doggy, Flannagin's going, *come to daddy*.

Benny's jaws are rivulets of saliva. He gets closer. Too close. HISS! Flannagin stubs his cigar out on Benny's head. You can't hear the yelps above the crowd. All you can see is Benny running about with his eyes shut bumping into screaming fans. Crashing into the uprights on the barriers. Flannagin's laughing. Laughing till he remembers the final score.

Albion Rovers twenty-one – Forfar nil. And there's somebody else who won't be laughing either.

It's Glasgow. Pollockshields. A big house on the corner.
Sandstone. Bay windows manicured gardens the whole
fuckin bit. Nice wee trees. A million at least it's worth.
There's a plush office in there with Aromatherapy and Air
Conditioning. Flannagin's stopped pacing cos the Boss has
sprung out of his chair.

The Boss wrecks the building model. Smashes it to
artificial little pieces. One of the trees spins through the air
and lands in one of the henchmen's whisky like a cocktail
umbrella.

Twenty nothing, he shouts, *you're telling me it was twenty
nothing?*

There's an electric pause. All the eyes are on Flannagin.
He's reluctant to speak. He's just been plugged into the
floodlights and the life's draining out him. That's what he
feels like.

Twenty-one nothing . . . Boss, Flannagin goes and drops his
head like it was his fault. *It was twenty-one nothing.*

Twenty-one, says the Boss, *ti-wenty-one. Hmm. Is that what it
was?*

There's a biblical pause.

Twenty-one, the Boss says again and lifts the replica of the
Rovers ground and hurls it across the room. Even the model
is looking in dire need of repair. It smashes into red and
tangerine matchstick piles in the corner. He calls Flannagin
over.

What do you see here Flannagin?

Flannagin looks at the wrecked model.

Where?

The Boss points at the space where Rovers' ground used
to be.

There. Right there! And he's thumping his bending finger
into the table top.

Flannagin looks round the room for an answer but no pair
of eyes'll meet his.

There? Flannagin goes pointing at the space.

Yes – there!

There's nothing there Boss. He feels like the King's Gold Clothes. Like he's in for a roasting. But Boss calms down a bit.

Exactly, he says sitting down, *exactly. That's what I want to see there – nothing. Nothing at all so we can get on with this operation.*

He lights a cigar and considers the case closed. But Flannagin can't leave with all this bad feeling in the air so he starts blabbering on about Lang.

I'm on my way – nothing'll stops us now. Lang, you know – in the council – he's the man. I'll pressure him into the CPO. That way it doesn't matter what Rovers get up to. They could win the cup for all it matters if they've no ground.

But he's getting led to the door at the time and out into the corridor. Whumph – the door shuts and he's looking left and right up long corridors wondering what way to go. He can hear murmuring in the room. Paranoia sets in big time. And he wonders how he ever got to this stage in his life.

It's the steelwork. A young Flannagin grapples a wire twisting-hook from the wall and swings it without looking. Next thing there's silence. Flannagin's got his eyes shut waiting for the sledgehammer blows to come in but there's none. The whole work breathes in. Flannagin opens his eyes. There's the Bam standing with this hook through his cheek. He's running about taking the weight of it with his hands in case it rips right through. A couple of the men try to hold the Bam and guide him to first aid. But he shakes them off and walks away. There's blood running down the steel hook. It looks black against the metal.

Flannagin's up in front of the bosses. There's two of them sitting. In walks Flannagin with his overalls trailing down behind his heels and his chin sinking into his chest. His curly hair's an explosion and his face is red from two kinds of fear. The bosses. The Bam. One's as scary as the other. The high head bummer starts talking.

Right young Flannagin . . . I believe you were involved in... but he can't get the sentence out. He bursts out laughing. So he tries again.

I believe down on the shop floor today you . . .

But his shoulders are going up and down. So's the other boss. And so's two other independent witnesses. They can't stop laughing. Flannagin gets interested in a knot in the table while they calm themselves. There's no way he's going to laugh. No way he's going to smile even.

They go to talk:

Well . . . t . . . t . . . today . . .

But it's no use – they burst into hysterics again. Flannagin doesn't know what's happening. He's looking at his overalls to see if his zip's down or something.

Eventually the one that started talking waves Flannagin away with his elbow up in the air and hand flipping through the room like a table tennis bat. Backhand.

Flannagin goes back down through the foundry and

they're all asking him what happened. All he can do is shrug his shoulders.

The next day the Bam comes in with ten stitches in his cheek. And all day he says nothing. Flannagin's working alongside him in silence. He looks up and there's a big hole in the side of his little metal church. The money's escaped. But he says nothing. Does nothing. That's the way it is for days. Weeks even. But time passes and the tension lessens.

Time passes and they start talking.

Time passes and they start laughing.

Time passes and Flannagin and the Bam get on great guns.

Time passes and Flannagin and the Bam are drinking together. And there comes a time when Flannagin knows he's the Bam's pal cos the Bam tells him the answer to the riddle of the two doors.

You want to know the answer?

Aye.

You really want to know?

Of course I want to fuckin know.

Watch your language son.

Sorry Bam. Right tell me.

The Bam takes a long slug of his pint and lights a fag.

You go up to any one of them and you say – If I asked that other guy what the door into Heaven is what would he tell me?

Flannagin looks puzzled.

Well if you asked the Devil he'd tell you the other guy'd point to the door into Hell. Cos God would point to Heaven but the Devil'd tell lies and say he pointed to Hell.

Flannagin's still puzzled.

And if you asked God the same question he'd point to the door into Hell. Cos the Devil'd tell lies to God too and say the door into Hell's the one into Heaven. So God'd point at the door into Hell and all.

Flannagin's getting it.

So both – no matter what one you asked – would point to the *door into Hell. So you ask **If I asked that other guy what the door into Heaven is what would he tell me?** And whatever door they point to – no matter who it is – don't take it. Take the other one.*

So with that Flannagin becomes one of a gang of two. And all he wants to do is work all week with the Bam and drink all weekend. There's nothing on his horizon except the weeks folding into months into years. He's happy with his life. But that's about to change. For good.

The Bam's above the ladle this night. He's leaning right out over it watching the pour go down into the roll. Glowing white like heaven. Or red like hell as it cools. Whatever way you want to see it. It's the wee ladle. Just about the size of your living room. They use it to top the hundred tons of white-hot steel. The Bam hears a click. He feels his body move forwards. Half an inch. No more. He looks down to see what the click is. Nothing else. He thinks nothing about it. Then the railing he's leaning against gives way. He's moving down through the blast of hot air coming up from the pour.

A scream goes out.

A klunk as his upper body hits the edge of the crucible.

A splash as his lower half sinks in.

Pause. The electromagnetic thrum of fear travels the whole work in a second. Everybody turns even though some can't possibly see it for the walls. And by this time Flannagin's running at the pour.

Bam – Bam – for fuck sake,

he's screaming.

Other men look about frantic, realise and run at the crucible. Somebody's shouting to the crane operators.

Shut it down . . . shut the fuckin thing down.

Men hammer on stop buttons. Machines start shutting down.

Flannagin's reached the crucible. The Bam's up to his waist in white hot metal, hanging on to the rim trying to pull himself up. And he's smiling. For fucksakes. Smiling. His hands and face are blistering.

Bam – oh for fucksakes Bam, Flannagin's going.

But he knows the Bam's as good as dead. Half of him is missing already beneath the surface. By this time men have gathered round. They've got their hats off like men at a graveside. And they're looking at Flannagin. Flannagin bends down and kisses the Bam's forehead.

God bless you Bam, he says.

The Bam closes his eyes. Flannagin's face is blistering with the heat. He stands up and shoves the Bam under with his boot.

God forgive me, he says.

All the other men look on. It's never mentioned again. Never. Flannagin walks out the work. He's working for no boss ever again. He's going to make his own money.

Bailey Bloggs's watching the telly. It's the bit at the end of *Universe At Eleven*.

And finally... there's all these shots of the Rovers celebrations after the game and some of the goals on an amateur disc.

. . . the worst team in Britain confounded their critics today with an incredible display of football. Following a recent scare where eight of the team were feared lost in an avalanche Albion Rovers beat their opponents by twenty-one goals to nil. And their Manager puts it down to divine intervention. Ian Ferguson reports live . . .

And there's Matt with all the team going wild behind him and the town turned out. The place is wild. There's this Reporter sticking a microphone up in his face. Matt's blabbering on,

. . . since I was a wee boy my Maw said all about God and praying. In this day and age nobody believes – but the power of prayer's a big thing.

Ian Ferguson grins at the camera.

You can laugh if you like sonny jim, goes Matt, *but Padre Pio – he's the main man. It's him that got us out of the mess we're in and gave us the goals . . . I've been praying constant to him all my life.*

He's interrupted by the Reporter, *So you're suggesting Padre Pio intervened and helped your team?*

The crowd behind's singing the Padre Pio song.

♪♪ *Padre Pio give us a goal give us a goal give us a goal*

Padre Pio give us a goal give us a goal give us a goal

Padre Pio give us a goal give us a goal give us a goal

Padre Pio give us a goal give us a goal give us a goal

. . . och laddie I'm not suggesting it – I'm saying it. That's exactly what I'm saying. Matt holds the statue up to the camera for the benefit of thirty million people.

See if you need help, anything at all, he goes, *pray to this man, he'll help you . . .*

But the Reporter's shoving his way in front of Matt trying to finish the report off. Matt's shoving the statue round in front of the Reporter's face. You can hear his muffled voice going, *And don't forget anything you need Padre Pio's your man . . .*

There's fuzzy lines on the screen and we're back in the *Universe At Eleven* room. The anchor team's laughing their heads off.

Well that's Ian Ferguson Universe at Eleven *at Albion Rovers. Goodnight.*

And in Cardiff Bailey Bloggs's watching with interest cos here's the team that was trapped in the snow weeks ago and now they're up to all sorts on the pitch. He wishes them well and laughs at the crazy manager. He switches it off and heads to bed. But there's something in his mind and he can't sleep. It's nagging away. He blinks. He closes his eyes hard. Eight stars appear in the squeezed-in darkness. He opens his eyes. The after-image of eight stars shoots across the wall and out the window. If he wasn't so tired he'd have thought it was real. He puts it down to the old trouble. It is the old trouble – but in a completely new way. A way that's going to change his life forever.

And in Coatbridge Mary Maglone's watching. She's thrilled her team's made it to *Universe at Eleven*. She laughs at Matt's evangelism. His wee holy statue and all that. She's just the glow of a white smile moving across the living room. And a glassy sheen in her eyes. The surface of them's been painted by tears of joy. And eight lotus flowers shimmer on the miniature seas. She switches it off. As she switches it off she senses someone somewhere else switching the same thing off. Someone with the same warm glow she's got. And she smiles again. She goes into the stars and moons room and sets up the ouija board.

You'd think you'd never see the likes of it again. But it's repeated. Week in week out. Rovers demolish bigger and bigger teams in the Cup. They're top of the League with unbelievable scores every game. The Cup scores are incredible.

ALBION ROVERS 20 – DUNFERMLINE 5
ALBION ROVERS 11 – DUNDEE 7
ALBION ROVERS 12 – ABERDEEN 1
ALBION ROVERS 7 – RANGERS 1

The crowd's building and building every game. By the Rangers game there's thousands packed into the rickety stadium. But the management are not daft. They've hired huge video screens and outside the ground a few thousand watch the game. You're supposed to pay two quid each. Some watch for nothing but most of them's that impressed they pay at the end.

On the building site it used to be hard to get the men to work on a Saturday. Even if you got a hundred to say aye only twenty'd turn up after a Friday night on the drink. But now there's fights every Friday to get the Saturday shift. Men are even turning up without pay so as they can see the game. There's men with their wifes and wanes with site helmets on. And yellow or orange waterproof jackets on. It looks like a field of orange and lemon trees from a distance. There's even Grannies dressed up with nail-bags and hammers. Wrinkled like crazy old fishing witches.

At the Aberdeen Cup game Flannagin comes onto the site. He's with the Site Agent and the Architect. They're walking along talking about the progress. Flannagin's sweeping his arm over the sitescape and the Site Agent's answering. But he notices how quiet it is. There's machines running alright. The big saw's buzzing round. The generators buzz away. But the wires lead to power tools orphaned on fields of concrete. It's like the workers went home in a huff.

How's there nothing happening? Flannagin goes.

The Architect and the Agent look at each other and say nothing.

Where's all the men?

The Architect looks at the ground. The Agent starts switching generators off.

It's only three o clock? Flannagin goes.

Next thing there's this big roar. Flannagin knows it's the Rovers scoring again. Another fuckin goal. But what he can't figure out is why the scaffolding's shaking. It's bouncing up and down. He's not that daft. He figures out that the Rovers fans in the ground are so energetic that it's transmitting its energy onto the scaffold. The roar is at the resonant frequency of the scaffolding. A couple of extra tubes here and there'll bang it up a few hertz and that'll put a stop to that.

But when he turns the corner blanked out by a huge concrete retaining wall he sees what it is.

One end of the site's thronged with building workers and their wifes and wanes. And they're all wearing Rovers scarfs.

Flannagin marches at them. The Architect and the Agent stay where they are. In the distance they see Flannagin pulling the scarfs off people and threatening them with the sack. One or two straggle back to work. Or that's what it looks like they're doing. But they walk the whole perimeter of the site with a plank on their shoulder and come back into the crowd at the other end. But most of the people tell him to fuck off.

One gorilla with his wife and six wanes is grabbed by Flannagin.

Are you familiar with who I am? says Flannagin. But the gorilla puts his hand round Flannagin's neck. The fingertips touch at the back.

Are you familiar with the phrase Get to fuck before I rip your fuckin head off?

GULP! goes Flannagin and gets to fuck.

Flannagin's on the phone. He's mad-dog crazy. Every time he presses redial it's the same message.

Bee-bob-bee-bob-bee-bob-bee-bob-bee-bob-bob.

Hello. You've reached the office of Mr Lang. Your call cannot be taken at the moment. So please leave a message after the tone. If you require another extension please dial that . . . now. If you require to be returned to the switchboard please press star . . . now. If you have an Opti-Link blink . . . now.

Fuck, says Flannagin and slams it down. *Fuck!*

And all day long it's the same thing. He drinks. Smokes. Redials.

Bee-bob-bee-bob-bee-bob-bee-bob-bee-bob-bob.

Hello. You've reached the office of Mr Lang. Your call cannot be taken at the moment. So please leave a messa . . .

Slams it down.

And every now and then his own phone goes. But he lets it ring. And the machine comes on.

Hello. Your call cannot be taken at the moment so please leave a message after the tone.

Bleeep.

Flannagin. Flannagin if you're listening pick up the phone . . . Flannagin – he's not answering sir –

And there must be a wave of the hand in the big house in Pollockshields – cos the Boss's secretary hangs up. Quietly. And the silence is filled with adrenaline rushing into Flannagin's veins. And Flannagin makes for the phone right away and redials.

Bee-bob-bee-bob-bee-bob-bee-bob-bee-bob-bob.

Hello. You've reached the office of Mr Lang. Your call cannot be taken at the mo . . .

ARGHGHGHGHGHGHGHGH GHGHGHGHGH!!!!

He flings the phone to fuck and withers into the chair. He sits with his chin on his chest for a long time. The square of light from the window moves up and across his body as the sun goes down. Eventually Flannagin looks out over the town. It's dark. He can't do a thing tonight. Not a fuckin thing. He pours a big whisky.

Brian's Da's still doing Jean in. Now and then he picks her up and throws her about the room. Brian can't see it but they've all had it that many times they can put a strike to a noise.

Scream, he's shouting and it sounds like the boot going in.

And in.

And in.

Cry – cry! Brian's going. He knows that whimpering is the only way he'll let you go. And he's crying. And his Da's still doing Jean in. But Jean won't cry.

He looks about and Patrick's away.

Where's Pat Johnny?

He's away for the Polis, Johnny goes and Brian can't tell if Johnny's scared cos of the Da or cos Pat's away for the police. It's all too confusing for a seven-year-old boy. Too much.

All Brian can do is sit on the bed and rock back and forwards. He doesn't know his Da's kicked Jean to a pulp. Kicked her so that her mind's in a place she'll never come back from. All he can do is rock on the bed and wait on the police coming.

Rock on the bed.
Rock on the bed.
Rock on the bed.
Rock on the bed.
Rock on the bed.

Morning. Flannagin's been up all night worried sick. Been sick in fact. The green boak. Then the yellow stuff that tastes like rotten lemon skins. His breath's hot as he squeaks along the corridor. He dunts past a joiner on the way. Turns a corner and bursts into Lang's office. The door skelps off the bookcases. Bump. The glass cracks.

Right Lang what the fuck . . .

But he stops talking cos the chair swivels round.

Yes, can I help you? says a complete stranger. Dark well-combed hair and interlocking fingers.

There's a noise at the door.

Here sir? says a joiner.

Yes. Same place.

The joiner starts unscrewing Lang's nameplate. The other one he's got to put up says Wilson on it. Wilson and a load of letters after it.

I'm Mr Wilson, he says to Flannagin. *Is there a problem?* he goes, looking at the cracked glass. Flannagin looks at Wilson. Looks at the glass. Looks at Wilson. The Joiner's listening as he takes a screw out.

No – wrong room, says Flannagin and blunders off.

It's dark. The site looks like a half-finished city on a forbidden planet. Or a half-destroyed city on a forbidden planet. It's all black geometric shapes. Beams of orange street lamps criss-crossing and falling on expanses of white concrete. Strange shapes of stone. Steel shining silver in the moonlight. In light cloud it looks like water. Now and then a nail or a drip of water falls and echoes round the place. You're always scareder in places where there's certain to be nobody. It's mad really. But that's how it is. And that's how it is for Lang as he waits for Flannagin. He's even got his fag cupped in his hands in case anybody sees it. A repeating arc of red light – a blaze of publicity on its soapbox of darkness.

Thump thump go the scaffolding batons that he's on. He can feel the steps. The end of the retaining wall's the meeting place. The wall's five hundred mil. In case it's not Flannagin, Lang slips in through the reinforcing steel bars. He stands in there and his body shape's broken by the dark brown criss-cross shapes. There's no way anybody's going to see him in there. No way at all. Even if you shone a light you'd not see him.

Flannagin comes up. Lang decides to watch him for a while. Flannagin looks left and right. He hears something away at the other end. He listens. He shivers. He looks vulnerable. Lang's never seen him like that before. Scared. He's shaking. Or is that the vibration from the sodium lights? And even though Lang's not one for a joke he decides on one tonight. Under pressure you can never tell what people are going to do. Flannagin pulls out a cigar. He's slapping about his pockets for his lighter when a match scratches and lights in the mesh of steel. He's just getting the adrenaline rush for that when the hand comes out towards the cigar with the match burning like a comet. Flannagin drops the cigar and runs. The scaffolding batons are bouncing about.

Fucksakes Flannagin it's me. Lang.

Flannagin gets his act together and walks back up.

What the fuck are you trying to do – give me a heart attack? he whispers as loud as he can.

Lang squeezes back out the steel and the two of them go for a walk into the vault like interior.

So what's the story then? says Flannagin.

What's the story? Lang says as if Flannagin's daft. *D'you not know what's happened?*

Flannagin shakes his head, widens his eyes and shoves out his bottom lip.

I've been burning folders and papers all week. Flannagin doesn't understand.

There's a corruption investigation. They've been into our systems for weeks. Every computer file's been downloaded to the CID.

What about the deal?

Lang can't believe his ears.

The CPO, says Flannagin. *What's happening there?*

CPO? CPO!? There's no fuckin CPO. I'm heading for two years. Look – I've still got all the money. I'll get that to you this week. But right now I've got to watch who I'm talking to.

There's a clang of metal in the distance. Lang and Flannigan jump. Lang shakes his head.

Christ I'm risking it just coming here man! he goes.

Flannagin grabs Lang by the lapels. He's speaking through his teeth.

How the fuck d'you expect me to get things sorted out? Eh?

Lang stares him out and he drops him.

Look, says Lang, *you'll have to find out what drugs the Rovers are on. Get that fixed and they'll revert to the heifers they really are. Then there's no problem.*

Drugs? goes Flannagin.

Well you don't believe all that shite about miracles do you? Nothing.

Well do you?

All there is is dripping water and some rats or something scurrying about. And a flash of blue-white light moving past on the tier of scaffold below. They put it down to the reflection of car headlights.

The Rovers make it to the Scottish Cup Final. Celtic it is. At Hampden. And the build-up is tremendous. They've become world curios the Wee Rovers. There's two angles the press are taking:

1. What's the reason for the sudden upsurge in their talents?
2. Is it possible there really has been some kind of divine intervention?

And another thing's happened. The Padre Pio statue outside the ground's grew into a shrine. There's all sorts of holy medals and candles burning constant. There's even a Fan Club vigil. There's somebody there all the time. Night and day. Some people's even claimed cures from touching the statue. Or walking past just. All sorts of holy rollers have started to gather outside the club. Nut jobs and UFO hunters. Sandal eaters and tree huggers. Priests and nuns. Producers and publishers looking for that next great idea.

The week of the Cup Final Rovers fans turn up with a lorry. They load the shrine onto a low-loader trailer. So that they can take it into Glasgow for the game. Fans pass each object careful along a line. It could be bone china. At a distance Flannagin watches. An old woman creeps up on him.

It's the work of God.

Shit missus you should ring a bell when you're walking about.

God works in mysterious ways you know, says the old woman and walks away.

And Flannagin thinks. He looks at the last of the divine objects being loaded on and set up as they were on the ground. He watches the old woman fade into the distance.

Fuck it, he says and strides off.

St Augustine's Chapel's well over a hundred years old. It's in bad repair. Hardly anybody uses it since the new priest took over in September ninety-nine. When you walk in there's the smell of musty books. And snuffing candles. Some of the floorboards have sprung up and never been fixed. It looks like the deck of a dilapidated ship.

A few old women are dotted about. Nobody else. Probably the only reason they've not hightailed it up to St Pat's for their holy stuff is it's too far to walk. Even if St Pat's ran by three of them African priests they've been importing – it's still too far away. Father Bolyle's got a captive audience of knock-kneed coffin dodgers. And that's strange in itself. And even stranger in Coatbridge considering events of the past few months. The media attention's had the effect of holies flocking in from all round the country and some parts of Saltcoats. Even as far as Japan they've come for some cure. You can't get in any of the newly sprung up bed and breakfasts.

But the first thing to happen is the local Catholics start going back to mass. Dribs and drabs at first but then the chapels are packed. Even the young folk are going. And not just the Tims. No sir. All the Protestant churches are mobbed. The Baptists. The Wee Free. The Mormons have reported an upsurge in interest in the Church of the Latter Day Saints. The only church that's not benefited is the Jehovahs. And St Augustine's.

He must be pretty bad that Priest if there's no cunt in his chapel in this climate, Matt said when Eddie was on about it this day.

And he's right he must be pretty bad. And he is. It's not just his unmoving glass eye or his big lanky walk. Or the way his cassock hangs off him like a bad curtain. Or his dyed-black hair.

What kind of priest's got the vanity to dye his hair? Matt says. *Why should a celibate dye his hair at the age of sixty?*

Who knows. And he's more to be found out on the golf

course with the local Virtual Dealers than hearing confession. This day when he was late for his golf he leans out the confessional and shouts, *Mortal sins only*. The queue of old women evaporated. The best they could do was having bad thoughts about the milkman or that wee cunt on *Titanic Three – A Ship In Space*.

But it's still not all them things that keeps most people away from his church. It's a feeling. There's a gloom hangs from the altar. And there's this undercurrent that he emanates. When you're next to him you feel like you're being emptied of your energy. Your soul maybe. Emptied of your soul. Looks more of an advocate for the Devil than any man of God. The old women are too doted to see through the guy. Not unless they secretly want to join his coven and run about in the scud with him patting them on the wrinkled arses. Who knows? Stranger things have happened.

So Father Boyle's sitting having a fag on the front pew. Looking over him's the Virgin Mary with the Baby Jesus in her arms. Boyle's flicking his fag ash into the cupped hands of the Holy Child. The pale blue Virgin's looking down not too pleased. She's got her head tilted to the side in disgust. But he flicks away. The hands of Jesus are full of douts anyway. And he's got a bottle of altar wine but he's swigging it out the chalice. He hears the door and crushes the fag into the hands. You can almost hear Jesus going *awch!*

And even before he turns round Boyle's carrying the chalice in two hands above his chest to the altar and chanting one of them crazy Monk chants. ♪♪ *Sal-vey Regina*, or something.

Gimmi a swig of that – I need it! shouts Flannagin as the door bangs shut on the outside world. A wee woman opens it right away. She's got her rosary beads dangling from her clasped hands. Flannagin shoves her back out.

Sorry hen we're shut, he goes, *away home and light a candle.* Boyle smiles and there's some of his teeth missing. He's that ugly his rotten teeth almost enhance his looks. The rest of his teeth have fled his face. Flannagin walks the squeaky length of floor and plonks his arse on the altar. Boyle goes over to the tabernacle and gets another chalice. He sits beside Flannagin and fills the two of them with wine.

Fag? he goes and flicks one at Flannagin. He's got no matches so he jumps up and lights it off the sanctuary light. It goes out.

Fuckin thing – it's always going out that so it is, he goes.

It's OK I've got a lighter, says Flannagin.

Boyle sits down.

So what brings you here this time? More forged marriage documents?

No.

Baptism?

They were good by the way – thanks.

I'm doing a good wedding certificate the now. I've got a wee thing going with the registrar.

They sit in silence for a while. Flannagin smoking and drinking and looking about the decayed splendour of the chapel. Boyle flicking the pages of the bible.

There's some right good crack in this you know.

Flannagin's lost in thought.

The Old Testament! What a fuckin book.

There's more silence. Flannagin breaks it.

D'you believe in divine intervention?

Fuck off, says Boyle, *Divine intervention – are you mad?*

Flannagin turns his palms out like he might be. He might just be mad right enough.

Mad as a fuckin brush, he says, *is it possible but?*

What? goes Boyle.

That God or Paddy fuckin Pedro can make people better.

Aw – right it's them fuckin players up there you're on about. The Rovers.

Aye.

Then Boyle looks puzzled.

What're you interested in them for? He gets it. *Aw you've got money in the development. I see. That super train thing.*

Well is it?

Is it what?

Is it possible that can happen. Possession or something?

I can't believe you're asking me all this shite. Of course it's not.

They drink a bit and have another fag. The sun's came round on the stained-glass windows. There's a particular bit that's blue. Well blue-white really – the sun's making it blue-white. Flannagin's drawn to it. But no more than you or me'd be drawn to a puddle of light on the surface of a river. It's something to look at before Flannagin speaks again.

Well how's it happening?

It can't be possession. Even if you did believe in it.

How?

Cos Padre Pio couldn't possess them all at the same time, Boyle goes.

But I've been looking. There's only eight of them got any good. The other two and the goalie's shite.

He couldn't possess eight either. They'll be full of them stereos.

Flannagin looks at him.

Steroids you mean.

Whatever. Look – there's always a rational explanation for everything. Go home. Think about it. And phone me when I'm not in.

Flannagin gets up to walk away.

And another thing, says Boyle.

Flannagin looks.

Even if he could possess them all at the same time – Padre Pio – he was shite at football so it'd make no difference.

Boyle laughs at his own joke. Flannagin moves up the aisle like a man refused a loan.

Praise the Lord, shouts Boyle and laughs and whoops, *Praise the Lord.*

Aye, goes Flannagin, *right yar*. Boyle's cackles are tombed in as Flannagin closes the door and walks on into the day. The old woman he shoved out the door's only at the end of the street she walks that slow. He passes her.

Hey we're open again hen.

She stops. She shuffles. She turns and heads scliff by scliff back the way.

It's Glasgow. Pollockshields. A big – big house. Sandstone. Bay windows manicured gardens. A million at least it's worth. There's a plush office in there and that's where Flannagin is.

Outside the room you can hear the Boss going berserk. And you know who's getting it. Flannagin. And he's reminding Flannagin of something he needs no reminding of. The fact that he's borrowed a lot of money from some acquaintances of the Boss. Does he know what could happen if these guys don't get their money back?

Flannagin swears he's got an answer. He's got a way to stop Rovers even playing in the final with Celtic.

That's good. That's good, says the Boss, *good for me and more to the point Flannagin – good for you.*

When he comes out the room he's white as a shirt. He doesn't know what to do. Then bing – his face changes and he's off down the corridor with a purpose.

Back on the railway line a young Edward Duncan's standing with Pat. In the distance is the big yellow front of a train. They draw the smell of oil and diesel up their nose. And fear. The smell of fear.

Shut the fuck up, says Pat into his fag, *here's the train.*

He wants Eddie to get ready. This is chicken for real.

Eddie looks. And the same time he looks the train driver looks and there's two boys on the line. And as Eddie's head swings for Pat the driver sounds the mighty horn.

MANAHAA

MANAHAA

Eddie reacts. He jumps and rolls down the bank through the long summer grass. But not before seeing Pat outstare the driver.

The driver sees Eddie tumble down the slope. He waits for Pat to move. But he's a lamppost Pat. The only thing moving is the swing of his arm up to the fag and the line of smoke coming out. His feet are sunk into the ballast. The horn screams again. Pat's a rock. The driver realises he's up against something here. He jams the brakes on and these sparks come out the wheels like instant comets. Bits of red hot are landing on the back of Eddie's neck where he's tugging at the grass and pressing his face in. Burning into his skin. He can smell the burning flesh.

The last thing the driver sees is Pat disappearing below his vision cos the train's so high up. He's not sure if he got out the road but he hopes he did. He's sure he did. There's a

lot of chicken on this track and some of the madder cunts
stay till the driver can't see nothing and then jump. Fuck
sake he's got a son looks the same age the driver. Hope to
fuck he's alright. That's probably what this wee cunt done.
Waited till the last second and sprung to the side. Aye that's
it. That'll be what's happened here. I mean you'd feel it.
Something anyway. Wouldn't you? A wee bump even?

The train comes to a stop away up at Kirk Street. The
driver's out and running down the track. But it's a long
distance half a mile over lumpy ground and ballast that
gives way under your feet. Like running on sand and the
tracks are shining waves on the shores of steelwork. That's
the crazy stuff that's going through the driver's head as he
puffs his way back.

My son's just the same age. My son's just the same age, he's
going over and over blocking out the emotions.

It's training at Rovers three days before the final. There's traffic cones and the team's dribbling through them. Nothing too strenuous. It's going well. Everybody's feeling great. There's hundreds of supporters lying about in the sunshine watching the training. One leg bent so their knees are like a range of pink mountains on the green plains of hope. There's TV cameras from the most obscure countries. All the usual football nations and Sierra Leone. Honduras. And a few others. Every chance they get they interview a player. They're fed up with Matt's story about divine intervention.

Outside there's all sorts round the shrine. Some's praying. There's a hamburger stall. **Eat at Holy Joe's** it says. A black car draws up and six men get out with suits. There's two with cases. If it wasn't a football ground you'd think they were door-to-door salesmen. Time share – or something worse – if there is such a thing. Flannagin's there at the shrine trying to see if there's anything magical about the statue. It's all been loaded onto the low-loader and waits transportation to the final. One of the men has a wee word with him before they all troop into the ground.

In the ground the training goes on. Reporters grab a player if they can. Nobody notices the suits.

Excuse me, one of them shouts, *excuse me.*

No one turns. One of the suits strides onto the pitch and lifts a cone. The players dribble to a halt. The snoozing supporters sit up. Matt tilts his hat back.

What the fuck's going on here? he says to himself. *Who are these cunts?*

When they've got everybody's attention they state their business. As they do up at the back of the terrace Flannagin watches.

Excuse me. Thank you for your attention. We're SAFTYS – Scottish Association For Testing Your Sportspeople.

The whole place is silent.

Drugs. We're here to test for the misuse of banned substances.
The players look at each other amazed.

Could we have the following people in the dressing room please,
Brian Rogers. Taylor Thomas. Pegg Davidson. Barnie Wheelan.
Cole Edwards. Jonesy Mark. Brent Geogh. Edward Duncan.

The players troop off grinning and shrugging their shoulders. The crowd waits.

And waits.

And waits.

The shadow of the Leisure Complex and Tube Terminal moves across the ground.

Flannagin sits smug on the steps of the terrace.

It's an hour and a half before the players emerge again. It's been like a father waiting for a birth.

Eddie Duncan and Barney Wheelan raise their arms. The crowd cheer. Next it's Brian Rogers and Taylor Thomas. Then Pegg Davidson, Cole Edwards, Jonesy Mark and Brent Geogh. All clear. All drowning in the cheers of the crowd.

The crowd bursts into the Padre Pio give us a goal routine.

♪♪ *Padre Pio give us a goal give us a goal give us a goal*

Padre Pio give us a goal give us a goal give us a goal

Padre Pio give us a goal give us a goal give us a goal

Padre Pio give us a goal give us a goal give us a goal.

The SAFTYS go over to Matt and give him the test certificates for all the players.

Sorry, goes the guy, *but we've got to act on information received at a high level.*

At the back of the stadium Flannagin's sneaking off. Five feet behind him – matching his movements step for step – Benny growls and moves. Growls and moves.

It's the Scottish Cup Final. Albion Rovers against Celtic. Celtic have won the European cup twice since Kenny Dalgliesh took over. That's them equal with Manchester United's record. It's such an event people all round the world are watching.

And in Cardiff. There's a telly. It's just a guy watching football. That's what it looks like. But when you see the look on his face the situation changes. It's Bailey Bloggs. He fingers a lucky medal. Rovers are whizzing about with skill and elegance. Mr Chinn the commentator's rambling on.

And I honestly haven't seen football like this since . . . since . . . since . . . oh and there's another shot on goaaaaaaaaall. Ooh well that just went past the post there. I've not seen football as fluent as this since . . . since the Busby Babes . . . there I've said it. It's too late now to take it back . . . Over to John . . . oh my word what a pass. These guys are telepathic. John . . .

And it brings it all back again. The flight. The fear holding itself inside. The quick-eyed staring about. The questions within questions that eyes can ask – disembodied from your voice. And the guilt. The guilt. Right there in his chest. It's been brung under control through the years. Like when you want to divert a river. The slow but sure building of a dam. And that gives you a new valley to walk in. A new place where new grass and trees grow. First it's mud. A wasteland. Then the tiny tips of green show through. Then the double-leafed sprouts of trees and bushes and flowers. Then birds and rabbits. Before you know it there's a whole valley and forest with maybe a wee stream running through it. But a good stream. A clear stream. A stream with stones on the bottom you can see. And you can walk there. There's the place you can walk right enough. Trailing your hand off the leaves. Sitting down maybe with your socks off and plunging the feet in the water. Cold. Great.

But it's all back now and he's immersed in the black waters behind the high wall of the dam. Engulfed. That he lived and they died – that's what it is. He tries the usual tactics. Think of something else. He switches the telly off and sits down with his paper. But he can't read it. Flick flick from page to page he's going. Trying to find something to focus on. But nothing. He tries meditating. The breathing – just the breathing. On the air coming in at the nostrils – that's where to concentrate. Concentrate. Cold in. Warm out. Cold in. Warm out.

But it's no use. He switches the telly back on. The Rovers are running rings round Celtic still. But against the run of the play Celtic score. Bailey's disappointed. For a man that's trying to block things out his mind he's helluva concerned that the Rovers are one down. One down in the Cup Final. The Cup Final that if they win'll put them into Europe. Into the European cup. They've done away with the Cup Winners and the UEFA cap. It's the European Cup for all the big teams. And what a tournament it is. Bailey Bloggs's glued to the screen. Glued. He's found something to focus on now. And he does. With every fibre.

Celtic lead one nil. The Celtic fans are singing.

♪♪ *By lonely prison walls*

I heard a young girl ca-a-a-a-llin

Michael they have taken you away . . .

Flannagin joins in. But he's watching the way Rovers are playing. Recording them through a button camera. And the information's being fed back to a massive database. Millions of moments gleaned from all the amateur discs of them playing and the CCTV that's in the building site. And the conclusion that's coming back is these men in the Rovers strips can't possibly be the same men whose jerky movements the computer knows off by heart.

The Rovers are stunned. Celtic have been lifted and they're playing their flamboyant brand of football in top gear. It looks like the end of the Rovers Roller Coaster. Outside the ground the mobile altar – the Padre Pio shrine – is covered with Rovers scarfs and jerseys. But there's something else. Cos of the Catholic thing with Celtic it's covered with Celtic stuff too. There's three Police guarding it cos before the game Rovers fans tried to stop Celtic fans sticking their stuff on the shrine. A scuffle broke out and the Police moved in.

Back in the ground Rovers get a penalty. And who knows why. Maybe it's sentiment. Maybe it's faith. Or something deeper. The players decide Jimbo's to take it. It's wild. Ingrid's on the pitch kissing him before he takes it.

The Celtic fans are singing,

♪♪ *Who's the slutbag?*

Who's the slutbag?

Who's the slutbag on the pitch?

Who's the slu-ut ba-ag on the pitch?

The Ref hunts her off and Jimbo sets up the ball. He turns into the silence of the Rovers' end. They've all got their teeth clenched and the words are pressing through. *C'mon Jimbo. C'mon.*

Jimbo runs up and scuds the ball. It sails right up over the bar. The goalie doesn't even move. He hunkers down laughing. All you can see is his hair falling down over his eyes and his shoulders going up and down. The Celtic fans go wild with laughter. It's derision for Jimbo.

♪♪ You're a wanker

You're a wanker

You're a wanker Jimbo Brown

You're a wa-an-ke-er Jimbo Brown

But not for long. Rovers come charging at Celtic. They plant three in the net in quick succession.

Roggggggggerrrrrrrs!!!!!!!! Chin says.

Wheeeeeeeelannnnn!!!!!! Five minutes

later.

Dunnnnnncannnnnnnnnn!!!!
It's all over for Celtic now.

And it is. Cos it's the final whistle. The Celtic players
are dejected. And they've got to stay on the pitch and
collect runner-up medals. Runners-up? If you'd bet on
the Rovers being the runners-up at the start of the season
you'd have got a million to one at least. It's silence as
Celtic collect their medals. All their fans have left and the
Rovers fans are waiting in delirious silence for their
players to file up.

And when they do there's something every fan notices
about them. The Rovers walk they had at the start of the
season. The rounded backs and the dangling arms. The
skinny gorilla look – it's gone. A new walk's been installed
and it's straight-backed and strong-armed. And their heads
are up as they take their medals.

Eddie Duncan lifts the cup to the roars of the fans. He's
crying.

♪♪ *Padre Pio give us a goal give us a goal give us a goal*

Padre Pio give us a goal give us a goal give us a goal

Padre Pio give us a goal give us a goal give us a goal

Padre Pio give us a goal give us a
goal give us a goal . . .

And if the crowd could hear what Eddie's saying they'd
think he was mad.

It's for you Pat. I done it for you.

And Pat The leg lying on the railway track's the picture in Eddie's head. The picture he'll never get rid of.

On the telly Rovers players are passing the cup from one to another as they run round Hamden. The fans are on the pitch running with them. Mary Maglone's right in the throng. There's nothing but party atmosphere. The camera man goes right in on the joy on Mary's face.

Bailey Bloggs is watching it out the side of his eye as he looks through the phone book. He looks at Mary. He stops as the camera moves over her face and onto the crowd again. He dials a number.

Hello – Cardiff travel agents? How much for a ticket to Glasgow?

Matt the Survivor's getting interviewed now and Bailey Bloggs sits down to watch.

The interviewer's asking him what it'll be like playing in Europe next year.

It won't be that bad, he goes, *most of the guys have been to Spain and stuff on their holidays. Tenerife. That's hot. Pheww!*

Matt wipes his forehead to show how hot it is in Tenerife. The interviewer's got no comeback to that so he mingles into the players looking for more sense.

Bailey switches off, and looks out his old training gear and boots.

Coatbridge. The streets are lined with team colours. From Bargeddie to Jackson Street. The town's seen nothing like it. The bus comes off the M8 with a trail of tangerine and red-winged cars behind it. It's like every car in the vicinity's suddenly vomited out its entrails and the entrails are tangerine and red. Rovers are on the move. And they reach the Coatbridge hotel and the bus is down to two miles an hour at the most. Nudging through the bedlam. From the sky it's a red and tangerine river and there's something moving in the middle of it. But that's red and tangerine too so that it looks like the river is trying to swim up the middle of itself.

All the pub doors are flung open. The drink's free. Nobody cares. In the distance the railway bridges are painted red and tangerine. On one it says,

ALBION ROVERS
INTERNATIONALE

♪♪ *Hello Europe here we come,* the fans are singing.

Even a train that's been stopped by the swarms on the line's been part-painted. It'll look right weird when it gets to Inverness. Right weird.

The train calling at platform four is . . . tangerine?

It's three hours later they get to the Fountain. It's so crowded the bus stops. And it's dark now. Next thing all the lights go out. The lights in the streets and the lights in the shops. It's pure dark till the eyes adjust. Then everything is silhouetted against the lighter darkness of the air. But the crowd know about the lights going out. This is planned by the local council. While the Rovers eyes are adjusting there's this swoosh. A light quiet swoosh but a wide one. One that runs through the crowd all the way up to Airdrie and back to Bargeddie.

And when the eyes are adjusted there's thousands of wee candles burning away. And when they look closer there's thousands of wee Padre Pio statues. The crowd starts singing low.

♪♪ *Padre Pio give us a goal give us a goal give us a goal*

Padre Pio give us a goal give us a goal give us a goal

Padre Pio give us a goal give us a goal give us a goal

Padre Pio give us a goal give us a goal give us a goal.

And if they looked up in the sky they'd see something strange. But they don't look up. They don't look up at the blue lights that do a dance and swirl in and out one another and shoot back into each Rovers player unnoticed while the party swings on.

Brian's in the bedroom with Johnny. His da's still doing Jean in down the stairs. All Brian can do is sit on the bed and rock back and forwards. He doesn't know that his da's kicked Jean to a pulp. Kicked her so that her mind's in a place she'll never come back from. All he can do is rock on the bed and wait on the police coming.

And when the police come that's the end of them as a family. They're stuck in a home. Then they're fostered out. Then they're adopted. It's a middle aged couple that adopt Brian. No kids. Right set in their ways. But he settles in. They're not that well off. He's retired early from the Virtual yards in Glasgow. Engineer. They build Virtual Ships and a hologram of the stages of the work is projected into dry docks in China and South America. The workers there copy the actions of their Glasgow *doppelgänger.* Only for a twentieth of the wages.

They don't give Brian much in the way of money. But they give him a life and that's fair enough. They live in New Shettleston and three or four days a week Brian's in Glasgow with his new Maw. At the weekend his new da goes and all.

Glasgow. A big – big house on the corner. Sandstone. Bay windows manicured gardens the whole fuckin bit. A million at least it's worth. There's a car outside and in the passenger seat Rena sits doing her lips in the wee vanity mirror. Inside there's a plush office and that's where Flannagin is. He's walking about the room cos he can't sit down. If you thought he was nervous the last time you should take a look at him now.

The model has been rebuilt since the Boss smashed it last time. And the wee people walking about in the model look weary with walking. If you saw them through a magnifying glass now they'd all be loosening the necks of their blouses and shirts. There'd be creases appearing in their short efficient skirts and blue business suits. Sweat marks under their arms. Even the woman with the go-chair has lost her pink happy face. Next thing she'll be slapping into the wane cos it's crying with its face screwed up. Looks like it's shat its nappy ages ago but there's nobody changed it.

The happy-looking students in full colour are stoned out their heads. And there's another couple of figures appeared. One's a glue sniffer begging microscopic coins on the steps. And he's selling his own poetry.

He's pestering everybody going by. There's an invisible swerve line going round about him. Swerve this way it says.

But the other figure is more frightening. He looks like Flannagin. Well – he's shaped like Flannagin but he's down and out. He's hiding in the shadows with a minuscule bottle of Buckie Turbo.

It still looks like we're entering a new era. The human race strides forward. But it's leaving a lot of cunts behind. And it's not sure any more what that new era's going to be. Not too sure at all. It's striding forwards in the dark. Losing hope. Lacking faith.

The Boss's staring at Flannagin. There's no words said.

He's just staring. He's got that look. He's trying to make up his mind what to do with Flannagin.

He says one thing. One sentence. No energy in it. No cadence or venom. It could be a computer voice. A machine that's disconnected from the world it's speaking about.

I want Rovers wiped off the face of the earth, is all he says and signals for Flannagin to leave.

And Flannagin leaves.

A train draws into platform one Glasgow Central Station. Bailey Bloggs gets off. To see him you'd think he's just another Glaswegian arrived home from London. Another ordinary guy finished a few weeks' work demolishing the Millennium Dome. And now he can't wait to see his wife and wanes. Maybe get down the boozers – have a bit of crack with his mates.

He's looking up at the board. Down again at a bit of paper. Coatbridge Central he's looking for. And there it is. Platform eight.

It's a Saturday. Pre-game. In walks Bailey Bloggs to the dressing room with Matt. Matt's got the Padre Pio under his arm.

Hey lads guess who this is? Matt goes.

Brian Rodgers and Taylor Thomas look blank. Pegg Davidson, Barnie Wheelan and Cole Edwards shake their heads. Jonesy Mark, Brent Geogh and Edward Duncan are not that interested. Most of them's been on a bender since the cup final. The Goalie's under the bench as usual. Johnny Dillon's finishing a can of Super Lager. Jimbo's probably outside with Ingrid.

C'mon have a good look, goes Matt framing Bailey's face with his arms.

There's no need for all this, says Bailey tugging at Matt's elbow.

Don't tell me you don't know who this is?

Is it your Maw? says Brent Geogh.

It can't be his Maw – she's got a beard, goes Cole Edwards. And that gets a good laugh. It starts them all off.

Mickey Mouse?

Shergar?

Monica Lewinsky?

Donna Summer?

Saddam Hussein?

Lord Lucan?

Mo Johnston?

Suzy Quattro?

Slobodon Milosovic?

Don't tell me – they've found Bill Clinton after all these years!

It's Bailey Bloggs for fucksakes! Matt says it with a da-da tone in his voice and waits for the recognition.

Bailey Bloggs the baker from Airdrie? says Pegg Davidson. *What's good about that? Is he doing the pies from now on?*

The pies? The fuckin pies!? Matt goes. *No he's not doing the fuckin pies. It's Bailey Bloggs the fringe Manchester United player. Ya bunch of toe rags.*

They're all staring.

The Busby Babe! Matt goes.

Big Eddie chokes on his Lucozade.

Once they know who it is it's all apologies and my Da says yous were the best team that ever lived and all this stuff. They can't do enough for him.

So what brings you up here Cream? says Barney.

There's a bit of a silence.

D'you call me Cream there? says Bailey.

No . . . don't think so – did I?

You called me Cream.

I never, says Barney.

Nobody's called me that for years.

Probably your imagination old yin. Bailey – Cream and all that. But what you doing up here anyway?

I came to see you lads play.

The players fall about laughing but Bailey Bloggs's still looking at Barney. Matt slaps his arm round Bailey's shoulder. *C'mon,* he goes, *the game's about to start.*

They all trip out onto the park. When the game starts there's Bailey next to Matt on the bench pointing and discussing tactics.

If they win this game they've won the League. But Bailey's not watching the game. He doesn't even know the score. He's watching the individual players. He's quickly ascertained that George the goalie and Johnny Dillon's shite. Jimbo's not bad but he can't kick a ball. It's the eight other players he's watching one at a time. And he remembers the moves. The wee back heels. The flicks. The turns. Even some of the set pieces they were taught at Old

Trafford all them years ago. It's them alright. Sure as shite sticks to the arse of a donkey. No doubt about it. The Busby Babes. Reincarnated. Rovers annihilate East Fife.

Bailey Bloggs smiles.

Young Eddie Duncan's hiding in the summer grass. The train comes to a stop away up at Kirk Street. The driver's out and running down the track.

My son's just the same age. My son's just the same age, he's going over and over blocking out the emotions.

The screaming and the grinding metal's still ringing in Eddie's ears. Residue. But the silence's enough for him to lift his head. He sticks his head up like a rabbit. Away in the distance there's crunching feet. That'll be the driver. Eddie's not daft. He knows how long it'll take him to get here. As he moves his own breath's loud like deep-sea divers. But there's this other sound piercing it. It's like crying.

Oh for fuck sake – Pat! he goes and starts scrambling up the bank. But it's like running in sand when he gets to the wee round railway stones. And when he sees the track he hears it's not crying. It's laughing. It's Pat and he's laughing. Eddie lets out a sigh. He's looking about.

C'mon Pat stop fuckin about! He shouts. He's expecting Pat to spring up out the nearest bush and light up a couple of douts. But there's nothing. Just the laughing and the crunching feet of the driver getting closer.

C'mon to fuck Pat there's the driver coming!! But Pat keeps on laughing.

Pat for fucksakes he's got a big stick!!! C'mon.

I can't, says Pat and bursts out laughing again.

Eddie's walking towards him. He notices the blood but he's kidding on to himself that it's not Pat's. Probably a rabbit. Not Pat's blood. No sir. A fox maybe. Or a dog or something from the last train. Not Pat's. Can't be Pat. The bold Pat'll have got off the track. He's lightning. Fast as fuck Pat. But the blood's still advertising itself in Eddie's eyes.

Here I'm here, it's saying. And he's getting closer to Pat. He can see him the other side of the line. His blue Wrangler jacket's sticking up and reflecting on the mirror surface of the track.

Pat! Eddie shouts.

But Pat can't stop laughing. He puts his hand on the track and heaves his head up so it's just his chin resting on the mirror.

It's hot this, he says and bursts out laughing again.

Eddie smiles. The tears are streaming down Pat's cheeks. But it's tears with sharks in them. Eddie's just about to say, *Fuck sakes Pat I thought that blood there was you* . . .

Hey youse cunts! shouts the driver.

He's nearly there but he's stopped with his hands on his knees coughing again. Trying to get his breath back.

C'mon Pat, says Eddie, *we'll need to run like fuck!*

But Pat's laugh's so loud and strange it's starting to frighten Eddie. Next thing Eddie trips over a mangled lump of dead dog. Red and pink. Stringy bits. And white fat. And stuff oozing out it.

But what the fuck's a dog doing with trousers on? he's just thinking. *And a Doc Marten?*

When Pat shouts out, *I can't fuckin run I've not got any fuckin legs.*

It's Pat's leg that's lying there like a lump of butcher meat wrapped in canvas. A Sunday roast. Eddie runs. He only gets a wee bit away and he boaks his lot up and faints. Next thing he knows he's in school. Doesn't have a clue how he got there. Pure blackout.

You'd think Eddie'd be up the hospital visiting Pat with sweeties and stuff. But he doesn't go. It's one of them times when you just want to forget. Pat never said nothing about Eddie being on the railway to the Police.

There was another laddie here, the driver's saying to the

Police but Pat denies it. And it's six months later he gets out the hospital and they've saved one of his legs but the other one's metal.

It's the dressing room after the game. It's only big Eddie that's left. He's been lying in the bath relaxing. Rena's away to the WWW Bingo in Glasgow with her Maw. So she says. He hears the door going.

Who's that?

Nothing.

Who's that? He gets up out the bath and starts drying himself. Get the soap out of his eyes.

He turns full frontal to a bench where Bailey Bloggs's sitting staring at him. Eddie covers himself up right quick. Holding the towel over his balls.

What the fuck is this?

Bailey continues to stare.

What's your game sir – are you a poof or something?

Bailey shakes his head.

I wish it was as simple as that, he goes.

What? What do you wish was as simple as that? Eddie checks his body out for anything strange that might be growing out of it.

What the fuck is your game mister? Eddie goes struggling into his boxers.

Something I can't believe so I can't expect you to believe it son.

Eddie strides towards the door but Bailey gets up and blocks his way. Eddie lifts a fist to punch him.

I'm telling you sir I'll hit you a helluva dunt if you don't get out my road! Eddie goes.

But their eyes meet. Eyes. Eyes. Eyes. He can't do it Eddie. He can't punch the old cunt. So he leans towards the door over Bailey's shoulder.

Matt! Matt! Is there anybody out there?

Nothing. His voice flies out the door and flattens over the silent grass on the pitch.

Look, says Bailey, *sit down. I'll say what I've got to say and I'll be off. OK.*

Eddie stares.

OK?

Eddie sits down.

OK – it better be something good.

Bailey walks about telling his reincarnation theory.

Eddie gets ready with his mouth hanging open for the whole story. The plane crash. How he can't cope with the guilt. The psychologist – that was a mistake – Eddie smiled at that bit.

I've got a right weirdo on my hands here, he's thinking, *a right fuckin weirdo.*

And Bailey feels the thought but he keeps going anyway. If he could just get the whole story out maybe at the end Eddie'll believe him. Or maybe at the end Bailey'll believe himself. Who knows? There's nothing sure any more. Nothing certain. It's a whole other ball game.

He tells Eddie how he seen them on the telly in the accident. How he's seen them playing. Their miraculous rise to fame. How they're possessed by the ghosts of the Busby Babes. When he's finished he looks to Eddie for a reaction.

Eddie puts his jacket on. *That's the biggest load of shite I've ever heard old yin. A right load of codswollop. You should be in Hartwood Mine.*

Hartwood Mine?

Aye – Hartwood Mine – it's a fuckin loony bin. Under the ground. The night shift dig out tons of rock and take it to the surface. The day shift takes it back down again.

Bailey's not dejected but. You'd think he would be but he's not. He's not that daft he'd expect such a story to be accepted. That's why he's brung the bag of memorabilia.

I've got this, Bailey says and starts taking handfuls of stuff out the bag.

Big Eddie laughs as polite as he can and leaves Bailey standing in the dressing room. Looking into a photo like a teenager with a dear-john. There's a silence except for footsteps on the red ash. Bailey hears the footsteps receding. The steps stop. They get louder again. Eddie comes back in.

C'mon ya old cunt – we're all going down the pub. We've won the league for fucksakes!

In the pub. It's momentous. Mostly Rovers players and their wifes. Red mini skirts black tops. Hairdos from *Titanic – A Space Oddyssey*. They're talking loud. You can't hear anything in particular except the electric buzz of triumph. The clink of glasses. It's an old-fashioned pub – it doesn't sell drugs.

Over near the bar there's four men at a table. It's Bailey Bloggs, Edward Duncan, Brian Rogers and Barney Wheelan. There's nothing inherently peculiar about the situation. It's just four men sat at a table looking at a bunch of photos. They could be any photos. But if you look at all the other groups in the place you'll see something. They've all got their party faces on. They're high but not pished out their heads yet. Their faces are red and pink – eyes bright. But these four have got their quiet serious faces on. And that's how they look out of place.

Matt walks past them with a young bird on each arm. And he's amazed. But he doesn't say nothing cos they're so engrossed in the photos. It's not the fact they're so sombre or that they're looking at photos he's amazed at. No sir. Not Matt. He'd not notice anything as subtle as that. What he's amazed at is the fact that they've been in the pub two hours and Barney Wheelan's not pished out his head yet. He's usually dancing along the bar nude by now. Or fighting with the bouncers and getting lifted. But there he is sitting discussing photos with Bailey Bloggs. Old football photos.

Photos like:

MATT BUSBY WITH THE TEAM IN JERSEY.

Like:

MATT BUSBY AND JIMMY MURPHY TOGETHER AT THE 1958 FA CUP FINAL AGAINST BOLTON WANDERERS.

Like:

BOBBY CHARLTON, DAVID PEGG AND TOMMY TAYLOR HAVING A LAUGH.

Like:

PHOTOS OF THE PLAYERS IN HOSPITAL AFTER THE CRASH.

But the ones that make the biggest impression. That stun them in their subconscious. They know something's happening but they don't know what. The photos that stun them the most are the ones of Duncan Edwards, Roger Byrne and Bill Wheelan. Especially the ones when they're all together. The three of them.

Bailey Bloggs leans back once he's got them enthralled.

You know something, he says, *I've got this weird thing to tell you three.*

They look up from the photos.

I'm going to say something you might think's crazy here.

Big Eddie sighs and looks away.

No no hear me out. Hear me out, goes Bailey.

The other two are interested.

What's he on about? What's up with you? goes Barney to Eddie.

Nothing. Nothing. Listen to this. Eddie goes smiling and shaking his head. The other two look at Bailey who's leaning back now. Leaning back quite sure they'll want to hear his story.

Well, Bailey goes rubbing his hands together, *no point in beating about the bush so here goes – it looks to me that somehow your team's picked up the spirits of the Busby Babes.*

The three look at each other. Brian goes to stand up.

Eddie pipes in again. *Don't get up and walk away. It's the same stuff he came away with today to me in the dressing room so it is. Mad.*

C'mon! says Brian. But Bailey's got his deadly serious face on.

The eight that died, Bailey says, *eight of your team's been possessed or something – I don't know.*

How d'you make that out old yin? says Barney.

Bailey points into his own eyes.

With these! I've watched. You play just like them. In fact sometimes I forget I'm watching Rovers.

You're crazy.

Might be – but there's nobody better equipped to tell than me.

This is . . . I'm out of here. Brian goes to stand up but Eddie shoves him back down.

No wait. Give the man his say.

I can list who's possessed by who even! goes Bailey laying eight photos out on the table.

Aw c'mon now you're really going over the score.

No – I can. The way you play's like your signature. How d'you think I cottoned on in the first place?

The three look more interested. They are in fact. They think it's just the weird story they're wanting to hear but they don't know about the other forces at work deep within them. Forces looking to connect. Looking to communicate.

Right who's in me then? says Barney swinging his head and grinning at the other two. *I hope I'm somebody good.*

Bill Whelan. Inside right. And he's Irish.

Barney looks a bit stunned. He slugs his pint.

And you, he goes to Brian, *you're Roger Byrne. Left back.*

And I'm Duncan Edwards? says big Eddie.

Bailey nods his head. The three of them's quiet for a bit. Then.

Fuck off! says Barney, *anybody want another drink?*

Barney stands to go to the bar. *Whooo hoo,* and all this Brian and Eddie's going.

Get me a spirit. Get it – spirit! says Brian.

Hey Casper what you wanting to drink? Barney says to Bailey. Bailey kids on he's joining in the fun but he's tore apart inside.

A pint of lager, he says, *get me a pint of lager.*

But his face changes. Cos from behind they look like three guys from the late fifties standing at a bar. Brian's even got a DA haircut. And the three's wearing drainpipe trousers. They look like Teddy Boys. Bailey is mesmerised. He smiles.

No change that, he says. *Get me a malt whisky. A double. I'm celebrating.*

So it's late on and they're all well on. They're going on about the thing again. Taking the piss sometimes and sometimes being interested. Specially in the descriptions of the plane crash. So he gets their respect. He gets that at least. It's coming up to closing time. Bailey goes for it one more time.

OK prove me wrong, he goes. *Come with me to a medium. You three. Us all together.*

A medium for fucksakes, goes Eddie, *I'm an extra large at least!*

And they all laugh. But they agree to meet the next day at one at the Fountain and go to Alice's in Kirk Street. She's a medium supposed to be.

They walk out into the street singing the Padre Pio song. Bailey joins in and their four faces are like grotesque but happy beach balls floating down the main street. Singing.

♪♪ *Padre Pio give us a goal*
give us a goal
give us a goal
Padre Pio give us a goal
The Albion Rovers faithful . . .

And where the fuck have you been? Rena says to Eddie when he stoats in drunk. How could he know she's just left Flannagin and got in herself.

What the fuck d'you think you're doing landing in at this time of night. Eh?

Eddie laughs and falls into the bedroom.

C'mon Rena darling. I want you. C'mon.

Want me – you'll not be getting a mile near me the state you're in.

Eddie flops onto the bed. Rena sits on the edge taking her make-up off. Eddie's staring at the ceiling with this mad grin on his face.

Rena – guess who I am.

Shut up Eddie.

No guess who I am Rena. Who am I?

You're you. She leans forward and checks for wrinkles in the mirror.

No I'm not. C'mon guess who I am.

The fuckin Queen Mother!

No. I'm really Duncan Edwards.

That's good.

Duncan Edwards! he says and flings his palms out like a black and white minstrel.

Is that supposed to impress me?

Duncan Edwards!?

Who the fuck's he when he's at home?

Only the greatest player that ever lived.

Well how can you be him you big lump a lard? She scans his body like it's vile.

That's how we've been playing so well. We're possessed.

She takes a keener interest.

Aye! How've you been playing so well? Is it drugs right enough? C'mon you can tell me. It'll not go further than these lips.

He stares at her big red pouting lips and laughs.

Drugs? He falls back on the bed laughing. *Drugs? No it's spirits.*

Eddie, what the fuck are you on about.

The whole team – no . . . no . . . eight of us's been possessed by the ghosts of the Busby Babes!

Rena stares at him. She screws her eyebrows up.

Remember the avalanche?

Avalanche – aye, she goes dead slow.

That's it. That's where we got possessed. That's how we're so good now. Beat any cunt.

Rena's right interested now. She moves over and sits astride Eddie. He can see the white flesh at the top of her stocking. He yanks the trousers down.

C'mon baby. Give it to your big Busby Babe.

She leans forward and gives him the sexiest kiss ever. When she leans back up her blonde hair trails over his face and chest like silk over rocks. But she shoves him back every time he tries to touch her.

Tell me again.

C'mon Rena – I've not had my hole for ages.

Tell me that story first.

Then am I getting it?

Aye.

My hole?

After the story.

Say it then.

You're getting it after the story.

No Rena – say it right!

Rena sighs, *After the story you're getting your hole.*

Eddie tells her the lot. And after it, while she's shagging him she rolls the whole unbelievable tale over and over in her head. Wondering if it's possible. Or is it drugs right enough and that's how Eddie's havering? The side effects with the drugs.

It's Mackenzie's. There's the usual jakies about the bar. This guy's about fifty looks seventy. He's skinny and he's pished his jeans and there's a brown stain at his arse. Some fat slag's taunting him.

Hey Joe I think you've had a wee bit of a follow-through at the bog there.

But he's not listening. He hears everything but he's not listening.

Behind him's all the other drunks and wasters. And the tables are full with women and men that don't like daylight. Away in the corner Flannagin's looking at the man at the bar with the wet patch and brown stain. And there's something going through his mind. He's thinking about a glue sniffer begging microscopic coins on steps. And the miniature future Flannagin. Hiding in the tiny shadows with a minuscule bottle of Buckie Turbo. He doesn't want to be that future. He doesn't want to be the man at the bar. Or worse. Something worse.

The door opens. The bad air tries to escape. Suddenly you can breathe. And a fusion of light. The door shuts and in the new darkness's Rena. And she's smiling. Not her usual automatic hello Flannagin smile. She's got her happy smile on. Genuine happy. She gets the usual from the bar and skips over.

I've got something to tell you Charlie, she goes. And lights up a fag.

D'you believe in ghosts? she says.

Kirk Street. Alice the medium's house. The four sit on the couch and two chairs. Alice walks about up and down the living room. You can see mostly the whites of her eyes just. And she's got the frizzy hairstyle you need to be a medium. She's talking to somebody.

Yes. They're here. I know. It's so hard.

Then she's bent over in anguish for a few seconds. Like she's got a bad attack of the runs. Then she corkscrews up. And she's back to smiles and conversations.

Yes I know. It's fine. She's moved into the light now.

They've been there fifteen minutes and she's ignoring them. Barney leans across to Eddie.

Ten quid each for this shit! he says. But right away Alice points at him.

Do not scorn the power of the spirits, she goes with her eyes bulging out like ping pong balls on sticks.

Barney's a wane at school. He lowers his head and looks up at her through his eyebrows. Brian's shoulders are going up and down.

Alice swings round to Bailey. *What do you want to know? Something heavy is weighing on your mind.*

Me? Bailey says.

You my child. Your aura is darkness itself. Ask. Ask . . .

And at that she folds into the painful diarrhoea grimace waiting to be asked so she can transfer messages.

I want you to tell me is there anything strange about these three men here?

Alice blinks one eye open. It looks amazingly calm in the pain she's in. It fixes on them one at a time then shuts.

They're sportsmen, she says, *it's coming through what did you say Ebeneezer yes yes great uncle Jeremiah moved into the light . . . Footballers that's what they are.*

She blinks the eye open again to see what the reaction is.

Every cunt knows we're footballers, Eddie whispers to Brian.

Alice goes for something else. She whips round pointing

at them all with a sweeping finger. *Beware the lure of fame. The drink. The drugs. The women. Beware. The corruption of the dark one. Beelzebub!*

Bells and fuckin bubbles, Barney whispers. Brian's shoulders start going more.

Bells and fuckin bubbles, Barney says again.

Brian's shoulders are infecting Barney's cos it's them two that's on the couch together. Bailey interrupts.

Yes – but Alice –

Psychic Alice, she goes.

Psychic Alice – is there anything you can detect about these three that makes them – well – different?

She lifts big Eddie's hand. She's rubbing it. A bit too much really. Eddie's stressed right out.

Europe, she goes, *I can see a trip to Europe. A trophy.*

That's enough. Barney and Brian burst out laughing. They're falling all over each other.

Ya old tart, Barney goes, *it's worth a tenner right enough – you're a turn – a right comedy turn.*

If you were walking up Kirk Street that day you'd hear some cups and plates smashing.

Get out. Get out you good for nothing bastards. I knew I could smell the drink when you came in.

If you were walking past outside you'd hear Alice shouting that. And then the front door flies open and out run four men. An old guy at the front vaulting the fence with difficulty and three other younger guys that can't run for laughing and can't clamber over it. And there's empty bottles flying at them from the rectangle of darkness in the doorway.

And I hope you roast in your own pish in hell when you die. And I'll be making sure you get a right hot welcome when you get there. I've got plenty friends on the other side that'll see to the likes of you. Plenty. Whaaaaa, she goes wiggling her fingers at them.

Whaaaaa!

SLAM

The door goes and the four men make off down the street laughing. Howling. Except the old guy.

Never mind Bailey. Medium my arse. She was an extra large at least, says Barney.

That's my joke! says Eddie.

And off they go slapping Bailey on the back and ripping the pish out him all over again.

They go for a few beers. Bailey's doubting the whole thing now. The boys put it down to the guilt he's had all these years since the crash. But they like him. He's not a bad old cunt. So they invite him up to stay in Coatbridge for a while. Brian Rogers' wife's Da's not long died. He can move in there for a while. As long as he likes fifties music.

I'm starting to quite like it myself right enough, Brian goes, surprised that he does.

♪♪ *Well a well a hulla-a-hoo . . .*

It's two weeks later and Bailey's settled right into Brian Rogers' house. He's being treated like a king. The wife thinks he's great. Goes to the training with Brian.

This day at breakfast he knows there's something in the air. There's an extra silence. First he thinks they want him out. Fed up. And he can understand that. But it's not got that choking feeling with it. That crushed in can't breathe feeling you get when there's too many people in the one space. No. It's got that secret Christmas present feeling to it.

Bailey, what you doing tonight? Donna asks. Like she doesn't know. Like he's not being doing the same thing every night since he got there. But he does the polite thing anyway.

Nothing. Nothing at all Donna, he goes.

It's just that we're inviting a friend round for dinner tonight.

No problem, I'll go to the pub or something.

No no – I don't mean that. I want you to be here.

Oh!?

It's a woman Bailey, says Brian with a wink.

Mary Maglone. We're inviting her round. Thought a foursome'd be good.

Bailey looks shy. *OK*, he says. *Do I need to . . .?* he points at his clothes.

No no, Brian and Donna say at the same time. *Nothing special – casual.*

So he meets her. It's the four of them at the table and candles. It goes well the meal. So well that Bailey plucks up the courage to ask Mary out.

St Augustine's chapel. It's dark and the rain's sheeting down. Flannagin stands outside. He bangs the door.

Nothing.

He bangs the door again.

Nothing.

A taxi goes by. The tail lights flick across Flannagin's eyes. For a second he looks like a black figure with red fiery eyes. Like the Devil. Inside the taxi's warm and cosy. There's a soft light. Two figures inside. And their hearts are going faster than normal. And they're trying hard to keep their smiles down. It's Mary Maglone and Bailey Bloggs. They don't see Flannagin. Flannagin doesn't see them. And what if they did see each other? It'd not make any difference they'd just be two people in a taxi and a guy sheltering in the arches of a chapel out the rain.

Except there's a lurch in Bailey's stomach as he passes. And there's a darkness passes through Mary. She senses Bailey's feeling and holds his hand. He gives her a squeeze and she smiles. The tangerine streetlights pass over the surface of their eyes. And they're like little galaxies passing. One heaven after the other going past. And Bailey can see them pass in Mary's eyes. And she sees them glitter in his.

Brian lives in New Shettleston now. This Saturday he's ten and he's in the town with his new Maw Janice and his new Da Alistair.

The telly's there in Sauchiehall Street. Filming the shoppers. It's nearly Christmas. The lights are up in George Square and that's where they're going next. But first Maw Janice needs to buy the cakes. And a few pies for Daddy Alistair.

They're moving about shopping. Brian's looking in the shop window.

Gregg's

Old Time Cookies Buns And
Rock Cakes – Bridies Bread and Pies

Pies and cakes Janice's in for. Brian's standing outside watching the reflection of the world in the window. Like another parallel world exists right beside us all but we can't see it. He's in the pane of glass running away into the streets. Following a bus into the distance. The people in the shop are blurs and strange energies moving in the place where the bus is heading. But never quite reaching.

Next thing the place erupts. Janice is frantic. She's got a brown coat down to between her knees and her ankles. Brown boots with fur inside them. And a hairnet. And there's this brown leather shopping bag dragging her down so she walks *tilt* tilt *tilt* tilt like a brown penguin. She's seen something out the window and she's ran out the shop. Brian runs after her but he can't catch up. He can just keep the distance between them the same.

Janice's eyes are this way and that way. And they're blue her eyes. Really blue. Fear – that's what they're saying to one person before butterflying off to another.

And the crowd that's parting to let her through can see their own fear imprinted in her eyes. They move and they part and they glance back when she glances away. And they see the wee boy following her.

That's a sin – that's her wee boy, is all Brian can hear as he tears along the street. Maw Janice is stopped up the street a bit. And she's talking to the telly. That's a laugh Brian's thinking. My Maw Janice is not famous.

Brian's starting to hear what she's saying cos this reporter's got a microphone shoved in her face. She passes the camera and it swings. It swings and keeps its monstrous silver eye on her. It doesn't blink or look away. It follows Janice and the reporter jostling through the outskirts of the crowd.

The crowd is quite a cosmic thing. It's like a star's exploded and flung all its debris out. Sauchiehall Street's the cosmos. There's a smattering of people on the edges but as they go in they get tighter until they're congregated on the rim of what must be a black hole. Gravity. Brian's pressing his way through.

Maw Janice – Maw Janice – what's up? he's shouting.

So they're out for a meal. Bailey and Mary Maglone. The talk's the usual about pasts. Then it gets round to husbands and wifes. How hers died and so did Bailey's. And they're across from each other knowing that what they're really doing is asking each other out on a more permanent basis. But it's never them words. Just – *Would you marry again?*

Who knows – if the right person came along I'd maybe.

An impressive silence and then Bailey goes, *Are you wanting coffee . . . Mary?*

Yes please . . . Bailey.

And when they've finished the coffee Mary offers to take Bailey up Loch Lomond the next day to see what the country's like. What it's really like. Not all this urban decay and construction. And they'll go by road. Not the underground Tunnel Direct from Glasgow that surfaces in the middle of the loch – waits for half an hour and zooms back into the city. Tourists take their photos and move on. And he agrees. The road sounds good. He agrees totally. His heart is lighter than it's been for years.

On the way home in the taxi it's a drenched Flannagin they see crouched on the steps of the chapel. The light in his eyes has went out. All he sees as they pass is the puddle in front of him light up and go dark again. So dark you'd never bet on its depth.

Next day they're on the hillsides Mary and Bailey. They find snow in this shaded valley and make a snowman. Bailey makes the body – Mary makes the head. Bailey sticks a smile on its face with stones. Mary – the Rovers fan – wraps her red and tangerine scarf round its neck. And they're up there against the white. Laughing. Holding each other up. Happy clouds of fog coming out their mouths.

Then they're still. A giant bird glides past overhead. When they tilt their heads back down their faces are level. Eye to eye – an inch between their noses. What's to do then but kiss. Their first kiss. And that's what they do. The soft impact of lips. The morning sun's shining on their shoulders. The wind's breathing out flowers and pine trees.

And they wander about the hills all day. Mary's got a right good picnic in her rucksack. So it's night and dark by the time they're coming down out the hills.

At the edge of the loch Bailey stares at her face forming in the glistening light of stars. And the black loch surface is smattered with stars too. And eight of the stars are ice-blue. A Walt Disney film. Bambi could jump out the trees any minute and it won't surprise them. Or Snow White. Or the Dwarfs. Rumplefuckinstiltskin even. They wouldn't bat an eyelid. Far as Bailey's concerned anything's possible now. Anything.

Bailey's looking at the stars thinking the maddest stuff. Stuff he's never thought before. Or if he has he's forgot he's thought it. Poets stuff.

See the stars Mary?

Aye? she goes and her voice's tight cos her neck's stretched up.

See if we put all the poets that ever lived onto the job of naming them all. You know with perfectly precise names?

Aye? she goes listening hard.

If we done that we'd still not know what they were all about.

Right at that moment he realises he's falling in love. If he's not already fell. Frightening. They sigh into the big empty spaces between the stars.

They look into the edge of the loch. It's dead calm. And so are they. Tree tops reflect on it like roots grabbing at the water, sky, water, sky. They lean into its topsy-turvey world and one thing seems to be another.

She's squeezing his hand. And he's thinking he could happily drown there with her. The two of them entwined. Sinking forever. Unnoticed as funeral tears. The wind skates the surface. The eight ice-blue stars are the only ones visible till the loch settles again. But Mary and Bailey are too engrossed in each other to notice.

Mary she kisses him again. Sticky mouths, fingers in black hair and mingling breaths. She laughs.

This is brilliant, she goes.

Bailey's coming over all poetic again. There's this stream. You can see the stones clear on the bottom. And last year lies on the bottom and all. Leaves, dead insects and stuff. Forgot. He points it out to her.

No matter what happens, he goes, *no matter what happens. I'll never forget you.*

She kisses him again with one heel lifted off the ground. Way the other side of the loch cars wind by.

The rush of river far away and the wind fracturing on trees. And the clouds going dark light dark light dark light in time with their emotions. He turns and kisses her light on the cheek. Fuck me – you can say that much not saying nothing. The whole place is an orchestra. Birds singing. Rabbits thudding out the rhythm. The song is composing itself.

The sky is black as fuck. They're kissing. Mary sees this shooting star through her eyelids. She opens her eyes,

whizzzzzzzzzzzzzzzzzzzz

. . . it goes, lighting the tops of the pines. And it's not white the way you'd expect a shooting star. It's blue. An ice-blue. They're pressed against this wire fence and Bailey's facing the wrong way.

Did you see that? Mary goes.

Bailey spins round looking about into the different darkness.

A shooting star right across the sky – whizzz – you should have seen it you could have made a wish so you could.

Bailey looks kind of sad. Cos by now they both knew the wish.

Mary goes, *Do you believe in God Bailey?*

He nods his head. Mary turns him by the shoulders.

God, we never seen that shooting star you sent us there could you send us an . . .

Whooshhhhhhhhhhhhhhh

Right across the sky. Darkness lights up like daylight. This gigantic shooting star right to left across the hills. And it's ice-blue. Definitely ice-blue.

Oh my God. Oh my God. Oh my God, Bailey's going, and running up the path and running back down and looking at Mary in wonder. And looking at Mary in fear.

What the fuck is this Mary?

It's nothing. I knew the other one was coming.

You knew?

Aye. I'm a medium.

I've met one of them before, says Bailey.

Aye Alice? She's an alky just. I'm the real thing.

Bailey says nothing.

Is the shooting star not enough? Mary goes.

Bailey stares at her. *I think I'm falling in love with you,* he says.

That's good cos I know I am. With you, says Mary.

So they head off the hills holding hands. Miles away – in the sky – the ice-blue shooting star fragments and breaks away into eight smaller stars. Some wane, looking out the window gets the celestial event of their life-time.

But, by the loch, Bailey's thinking whether or not to tell Mary the story about the Busby Babes. Eventually he plucks up the courage.

Mary can I tell you the reason why I came up here?

I know, she goes. *I know exactly why you came up here.*

Bailey thinks she's thinking about something else.

No, not the mountain – the reason I came to Scotland. To the Rovers.

I know – that's what I'm on about Bailey. I know. She kisses him and skips on ahead like a wee lassie. She shouts back. *Come on. We'll go back to my place. There's something I need to show you.*

First thing Bailey notices about Mary's house is all the books in the living room. Well not all the books. A certain pile of books. And a certain book on top of that pile.

The Busby Babes.

And discs. A pile of discs about the Busby Babes. But Mary acts like they're not there. She swans past them and into this room with stars and moons painted on the door. Bailey follows her in. He's fascinated by his falling in love with her and fascinated more by her interest in the Busby Babes.

In her back room there's all sorts of crystal balls and ouija boards.

Here, she goes and pats a sofa beside her. There's a massive crystal ball the size of a football on the table. First time Bailey looks at it it's made out of glass. Next time he glances it looks a bit opaque. Next time it's a football that's sitting there. He blinks and it's back to the clarity of glass bending the room out of shape on its surface. And there in the middle's him and Mary. Bailey goes to speak. Mary places her finger on his lips to shoosh him.

I'm going to contact the Busby Babes.

Bailey's nervous. He stands up knocking a few things over. *Is it OK . . . d . . . d . . . do I have to leave . . . can . . .*

Sit down Bailey, she laughs at him.

Watch this, she goes.

Hey Duncan Edwards are you anywheres about?

Her voice is plain and clear. Like she's shouting into MILLENNIUM MART USA or something. Or a crowded pub. There's nothing ethereal or metaphysical about it. Bailey thinks he gets the joke and laughs. His face is just realising she's taking the pish out him – starting to wonder how she done the trick with the shooting star when there's this voice.

Aye lass I'm here. How's things with yourself then?

Fine fine Duncan.

Did you get him?
Aye I did that.
You took your time!
You can't hurry love!
Oh no she's going to burst into song next, Duncan goes.
He's right here now anyway.
I . . . I . . . I . . . Is that you Duncan? Bailey says.
But there's nothing.

Mary leans across. *See that's why I'm a medium and you're a footballer. He can't hear you. You've not got the voice. The frequency. It's in here,* she points to the middle of her forehead, *not in here,* she points to her throat. *If you hold my hand they can hear you.*

He wants to know if that's you Duncan?
It sure is. Tell him to look into the glass.
Look into the glass, Mary goes.

Bailey stares into the crystal ball. Mary slaps him.
Daft get. You don't believe in that shite do you? Crystal balls? He means the mirror.

Mary nods at a full-length mirror.

Bailey near shites himself. Cos there's the eight Busby Babes stood there in their old Man U strips.

HI BAILEY! they all shout together and double

up creasing themselves laughing at him.

For fucksakes!!! Bailey's making for the door.

Jesus Bailey . . .
Watch your language Roger, Mary says to Roger Byrne.
Bailey. Where are you going man? We're not that ugly.
Bailey turns and scans his old team mates.

Roger Byrne 28. Tommy Taylor 25. David Pegg 22. Bill Whelan 22. Eddie Coleman 21. Mark Jones 24. Geoff Bent 25. Duncan Edwards 22.

Des Dillon

Bailey sits back down again. He's hyperventilating. Mary pats his knee.

Hey Bailey is that your new bird? Mark Jones says. *She's a bit of alright.*

Mary's coy. *Hey stop that talk you lot.*

C'mon Mary, for your age you're a good-looking woman, says Geoff Bent, *we've been saying that since we met you. Nat right lads.*

Mmm mm aye yeah! the lads are going.

Bailey can't believe it.

This is fuckin crazy.

Innit, says a voice from mirror world. *Innit just. How d'you think we feel? One minute we're rumbling down the runway in that crate and next thing we're eternal!*

But how – why – wh . . . oh fuck it.

We've been trapped in that snow up there for years Bailey. There's a fault line in space-time there.

Space what? says Bailey.

Magnetic, says somebody else, *Re re re . . .*

Resonant Magnetics . . . it's not been discovered yet – but that's what the future is Bailey – Resonant Magnetics believe me. Get your money into that soon as you hear about it.

Bailey looks at Mary.

Resonant Magnetics. It's when their spirits passed over the gravity fault it sucked them in. The avalanche was caused by the same fault only much lower in Resonautics.

Resonautics. What the fuck is this a science class?

In the mirror the figures are now the ethereal blue of spiritdom. Incandescent white one minute – a shimmering blue the next.

I'm puzzled, says Bailey. *How come Duncan's there with them when he died two weeks after it?*

Resonant Connection, big Duncan says as he headers a ball and it explodes away with the tail of a shooting star on it. *How was your walk up the hill?* he goes.

Good, Bailey goes, *good.*

See any good stars? Eddie Coleman says and they all have a right good laugh at Bailey.

Ya bunch of cunts. You mean to say I've been ripped apart with guilt all these years and all you can do is play tricks on me and laugh at me.

Bailey – the last thing we wanted was you going through all that pain.

Yeah yeah, says Bailey.

We couldn't wait we had to go. It was pulling us. And then wham we're on the ground playing football with a star and then wumph we're buried.

Ten feet of snow, David Pegg butts in, *and next thing we know we're resurrected inside these cuddies. Carthorses. It's like playing with three players sent off.*

Or putting a Rolls Royce engine in a Lada, says Mark Jones.

Want a wee cup of tea? Mary goes.

We'd love a wee cup of tea Mary!

they all shout at once.

They always do that. That's what they miss the most. The tea.

Get the players to drink plenty tea Bailey we can taste it.

Tears are streaming down Bailey's face.

Jesus I've missed you fuckers. D'you know that?

Language, says Mary.

We've missed you Bailey.

Bailey bubbles away for a bit.

Bailey. Stop bubbling Bailey. We need your help.

You need my help?

Yeah. We should have been in Heaven fifty year ago. Well most of us.

They all laugh and argue about who's going to Heaven and who's not.

Serious Bailey. We should have been there only for that Resonant Gravity crap.

How can you not go now?

It's hard to explain.

Try it.

Well now that we're anchored by the RG there's another anchor on us.

Bailey's puzzled.

Because the lower scale of the RG is earthbound we're tied to the earth by things that are human. Earthly things.

Like what?

Like football.

Football!?

Yeah. Nat right Mary.

Listen to them Bailey. They're talking sense.

Sense? Right. Sure enough that's what all this must be – sense, Bailey says.

Roger goes on.

Because we were on our way to win the European Cup we're tied to the earth till we do it.

Or till the end of time, says Tommy Taylor.

Shut up Tommy – you're a right doomer, goes Eddie Coleman.

Or the end of time right enough – if we don't win a trophy, says Bill Wheelan.

In comes David Pegg. *We'll be sucked back under the snow up that hill again and it's fuckin boring with this lot.*

We've done all the jokes a million times already, says Geoff Bent.

So you win the European Cup and you're off to Heaven?

Simple as that.

Fuck sake this is like something out a comic. Roy of the fuckin Rovers. . .

Bailey – it'd make a great film, says Roger. *You could write it as a book and sell the rights.*

Stay away from them producer bastards, says Eddie Coleman.

Is this really happening?

You've got to help us Bailey! says Duncan Edwards.
OK what the fuck. What d'you want me to do? Tell the players?

NO! they all shout at once.

Roger pipes in, *There's only three you can tell.*

I hope it's not Roger, Wheelan and Duncan cos they think I'm off my fuckin rocker as it is.

There's silence.

There's more silence.

Aw fuck I might have guessed. It's them three.

Good man Bailey.

Bailey gets up to go but Roger Byrne remembers something.

Bailey – another thing.

Bailey drops his head expecting something weird.

It's nothing mad, goes Roger. *It's ordinary in fact.*

On you go then.

See that boy Jimbo?

Aye. The young lad that can't . . .

Kick a ball – aye him. Well we want you to start training him. You could fair kick a ball in your time Bailey. Spend all your spare time doing it.

Training one player?

It's important Bailey. You'll find out later.

Bailey looks at Mary. She reassures him.

OK. OK. I'll do it.

Good man Bailey. Good man.

Next day there's Bailey running down the wing and passing the ball to Jimbo. Wham – Jimbo strikes it. And whizz out it goes sailing past the empty net like a strange round fish that's saying – *Oh ho here's the old fishing nets out again. I'll just whizzzzz off this way.*

But Bailey doesn't get mad. He thinks of the Babes in the mirror and them saying it's important. Jimbo's dejected. He's trying his best to please Bailey.

They swap round and it's Jimbo whizzing down the wing. And he can move that boy. In and out the traffic cones and flicking the ball up. There's been nobody like him since Jimmy Johnston. But when he goes to pass it to Bailey it's miles away. Bailey's got to go and collect it every time.

Sorry Bailey. Sorry about that Bailey. Are you sure I'm not taking up your time Bailey? is all you can hear coming from Jimbo.

Ingrid arrives with cookies buns and rock cakes and they break.

Pat loses one leg and the other gets sewed back on. Not been right in the head since. Goes to a special school. He's got a metal leg and he can swing it about better than Bruce Lee. Pat the Leg they call him now. Not to his face but. He'd batter your cunt in for that. But that's what he sprays on the walls.

PAT THE
LEG
SHAWZ

But he's not even in the Shawz – they won't go near him cos he's too crazy.

So it's a year later. A year after the accident. Eddie and Bonzo's up on the British roof getting lead. It's shut down. There's all these roofs that are like saw teeth black against the sky. In the troughs is where the lead is. You rip it out and drag it over the peaks to the edge of the building and drop it. You drag it in long strips cos it's easier. Sometimes if the moon shines on it it looks like a stream on a dark hillside. And with the stars out and some Buckie and a joint it can be Heaven up there on the roof. And when they've got their quota down sometimes Eddie and Bonzo sit and look out at the stars. And they wonder is there two guys

on some other planet stripping lead and watching for
the Police.

One night they're walking off the roof casual. Like
walking along a country lane. Bonzo slips through. It's his
legs hanging into nothing that's frightening. The vast
darkness of an empty steelworks. His legs going like duck's
under water. Trying to get a purchase on nothing at all.
Nothing between him and the concrete floor. Only the echoes
of his screams if he falls. The rotted corrugated steel's up to
his chest. He looks like a man fishing in chest-high waders.
Only the river bed's suddenly disappeared and he's
connected to the world just by the surface tension of the
water. Eddie gets Bonzo to grab onto his ankles. Eddie holds
onto this pipe. Bonzo claws himself out. For weeks there's
this big scab running right round Bonzo's middle. Like two
different guys joined together.

Welded like a Q-plate car, says Bonzo.

But this is a different night. They're well wary to only
walk on the bits where the sheets are bolted onto the steel.

They've dragged the lead over the sawtooth ridges and
folded it best they can and shoved it off. There's the grunt as
they push the bundle. The silence as it moves through the air.
And the thud as it packs into itself on the ground. They
climb down the black ladders.

They're dragging it under this tree when a figure appears.
It's four in the morning but there's somecunt out walking
their dog. Eddie and Bonzo's still. But the figure keeps
walking over. And it's a funny walk. Not the kind you get
when it's an old guy that can't sleep. There's a slight limp.
But there's menace too. They know who it is before he gets to
them. Pat the Leg. And he's got his mad dog Krooger with
him.

Hellllo Eddie, he goes.

He's poking the lead with his tin leg.

What you up to? He's talking slow with staring eyes sweeping over the place all the time. Back and forwards. Up and down.

Just getting some lead Pat, Eddie goes. And they're the first words Eddie's spoke to Pat since the railway.

Lead? he goes. *Lead? What lead?*

His eyes are off again. Up on the roof this time.

Eddie nods at the roof and goes to say, *Off the roof Pat . . .*

But Pat bursts right in, *That's all mine . . . all mine,* he says like a madman sweeping his arm over the whole work. And Krooger barks to back him up.

But Pat we're . . . Bonzo goes.

Shut up, says Pat.

He says up like two words. Bonzo nods at the pile of lead under the tree.

We've already got a load down.

It's all mine! says Pat again and whips out a sawed off slug gun.

Pat points the slug gun at Bonzo's head and shoots him. Eddie looks at Bonzo – looks at Pat. Pat's reloading.

Arghghg! Bonzo's saying. *What the fuck did you do that for?*

It's what he says next that frightens Eddie.

You ruined my football career Eddie.

Eddie can't think of anything to say. Pat pulls out this big bowie knife.

Eddie and Bonzo run like fuck to laughing barking and trains going past at different distances.

Ruined my life Eddie, Pat the Leg's shouting, *my football.*

Albion Rovers. New season training starts. The League starts in a week. Bailey's there every day. His input's that good he practically takes over from Matt. Matt spends most of his time out the front painting the flaky red paint back onto the statue in the shrine or chatting with the priests nuns and wheelchairs that turn up looking for their own personal miracles.

After training Jimbo stays behind for extra how to kick a ball lessons. But there's only a wee bit of improvement.

Matt sits watching when he's not at the shrine. Alternating between feeding the greyhounds and praying to the saint in the bag. One thing he does notice is that the clock on the outside brick wall of the changing rooms's stopped. Seven o' clock it says.

Even the ground's been cleaned up a bit. Bits of paint here and there with the money that's coming in. There's even a new terrace being concreted in. And rising above it to the east is the huge growing edifice of the Leisure and Retail park. A great shadow over the club. And underground is the geological anomaly that the Boss will stop at nothing to own.

At night Bailey's in Mary's talking to his old pals. They're having a right laugh now. It's like they never died. Like he never carried that immense burden of guilt.

Like it's a bunch of guys meeting up for their regular night out.

Albion Rovers Football Ground. They've been promoted. Somebody's painted

ALBION ROVERS INTERNATIONALE

along the wall. The place is crowded for the unfurling of the league flag. It's the Padre Pio song drowning out all the other noises. Rovers run out to the rapture of the crowd. The world media's there wondering if the phenomenon'll keep up this season.

It does. Rovers beat Airdrie six–nil. Coasting.

In the dressing room at the end of the game Bailey's giving some advice to Jimbo. Edward Duncan, Brian Rogers and Barney Wheelan are sitting near them. The gear they're putting on's much more fifties than before. Brian slides up to Bailey. He talks low to him. He thinks the others can't hear cos of the noise the crowd's making outside.

Bailey, mind what you were saying in the pub?

Aye? says Bailey.

All that stuff about . . . about . . .

He leans forwards and whispers in Bailey's ear.

About the Busby Babes!

Bailey smiles and nods for Brian to look behind him. There's the two big faces of Eddie and Barney. And they're listening. Cos the seed's been planted and it's been growing. And some things have been happening to them. Things that's making them think.

Bailey takes one look at their childish faces.

C'mon, he says, *let me show you something. I think you'll like it.*

Mary Maglone's. Mary is more in awe of having three Rovers players in her house at the same time than having footballer ghosts talking to her. She keeps them in the front room at first. Mary and Bailey slip into the stars and moons room to set things up.

Eddie picks up a few of the books.

Busby Babes, Busby Babes, Busby Babes – it's all Busby Babes. So's these discs, says Barney.

The three of them sit nervous and quiet for a while. Fiddling. Like schoolboys waiting to see the headmaster and they don't know if it's good or bad.

Maybe they're just a pair of Busby Babe nutters – like Elvis freaks! Brian says.

Star Trek, goes Barney, *beam me up Scotty!*

But Mary comes back in. The hairs on her arm stand up. She knows what they're thinking. But you wouldn't need to be psychic to know that. The room's dense with stress.

Look maybe we shouldn't be here, Barney shouts through to Bailey.

I'll be in in a minute, Bailey shouts back, *hold on.*

Would you like a wee cup of tea? Mary asks.

Next thing all these voices shout from the next room,

We'd love a wee cup of tea Mary!

The three of them jump.

What the fuck's that? goes Brian.

Bailey comes out of the room and closes the door soft.

Who's in there Bailey? Barney asks.

Nobody. Nothing. You'll find out in a minute.

Aww – I get it you're ripping the pish out us, goes Eddie. *What d'you take in your tea?*

So they're in the stars and moons room sipping out the wee china cups and looking round at the paraphernalia of the occult. Brian's bent over with his face pressed right into the crystal ball.

Whoohahahah, goes Barney and crushes Brian's balls – *hear about the gypsy with the crystal balls?*

Brian hasn't.

He could see himself coming!

Eddie's floating his hands over the ouija board.

Bussssbayayaya Ba-a-a-a-abes are youse there. Give us a signal, he's going.

♪♪*Knock three times on the ceiling if you wa-ant me,* Brian sings, *twice on the pipe – if the answer is no-o-o . . .*

Bailey's sitting like a teacher watching kids.

Finished? He's got folded arms. *Quite finished now?*

The three sit back and try to get their fingers in through the impossible holes in the china teacup handles. They're a bit embarrassed. They never meant to offend but Mary's got tight lips and her face's like hard plastic.

Sorry Mary, Brian goes, *sorry hen.*

Barney's fed up. Any faith he had in Bailey's story's gone now.

OK – sorry Mary let's do your stuff and we can get out here, he goes.

Mary looks at them one at a time to see if they're ready.

Got all the carry on out your heads now? she goes.

They nod like three monkeys.

OK.

She puts her hand in the middle of the table. Bailey lays his hand on top of hers and gives them the eyebrows to do the same. One at a time, slowly, they lay their hands on top.

Busby Babes come in please – over, Mary says.

The three laugh. *Tee hee hee.*

There's an eerie silence. The kind of silence you feel like something's just been took away but you can't tell what.

Mary tries for contact again.

Busby Babes come in please.

Eddie looks deep into the crystal ball.

Not in there you big lump, Bailey whispers.

Shh, Mary says, *they're coming.*

There's a rushing sound like water falling over a cliff but not reaching the ground.

Come in, says Mary.

Hello Mary, says this voice.

Aye right – good stuff, Barney says looking about for the trick.

ARGHGH!!!!

he says and makes for the door. Eddie makes for the door after him. He doesn't know what it is but he's running anyway. His fear's overwhelmed him. There's a terror moving up the back of his neck. Brian's still looking about for what it is when he sees in the mirror. There with their faces pressed up against the glass, not saying nothing, are the Busby Babes.

ARGHGH!!!!

Brian says and makes for the door. When he gets the door open the living room's empty. He makes across the floor. But he feels like he's in one of them dreams where something's pushing against him all the time. There's a heat rising up his back and through his neck. A dark fire's engulfing him. He makes it to the other door. The cold breath of outside is rushing up the lobby as he leaves the living room. Cos the front door's wide to the wall. Out he goes onto the street. There in the distance are the two tiny dots of Barney and Eddie still running.

It's half an hour before Bailey finds them in the pub and persuades them to come back. It's only a joke. The Babes having their wee bit of fun at their expense. So they go back. After three quick doubles each.

When they get in Mary's in good form. She's chatting away with the Babes. Soon as the Babes see the three nervous figures peering round the doorway they laugh.

Come away in lads. Don't bother with us. Just our little joke! It's Roger Byrne.

So in they go. Mary indicates to put their hands back. They've got their hands on the pile alright but they're leaning towards the door that much you'd think there's a hurricane blowing through there.

Is there anything you'd like to communicate to these three boys? Mary asks the Busby Babes.

By the time they fill the three in about how they need to win the European Cup everybody's relaxed. The conversation's mainly between Roger Byrne and Brian Rogers. Bill Whelan and Barney Wheelan. Duncan Edwards and Edward Duncan.

So you can taste tea and stuff when you're inside us?
Yea. Drink too.

There's a laugh. It's weird that ghosts should like a wee drink. While they're laughing Brian gets an idea into his head. He shouts in through the laughing and rocking about.

Hey wait a minute, he says, *wait a minute – what about when we're in bed with the wife? Are you guys . . . well . . . there?*

There's a pause. A long pause. The kind of pause you just know somebody's waiting on somebody else to answer. Ghosts are the same as us when it comes to that. Exact same.

Well? goes Brian.

No – no never – not us – nope. Would we do a thing like that? No us. No sir. We're ghosts for fucksakes. We're on our way to Heaven. To cover their tracks the Babes all start singing:

♪♪ *We're on our way to Heaven we shall*
   not be moved
On our way to Heaven we shall not be moved
By the groaks the sproaks or the zeelbebubs
We shall not be moved . . .

What's that? Eddie says.
What?
The spoats and the beeblejoos or whatever it is.
Oh you don't want to know, Mary says.

Maw Janice is bumping her way through the crowd. Brian's following.

Maw Janice – Maw Janice – what's up? he's shouting.

She was only out to buy some pies with her man. And her wee boy. He decided to look in A.T. Mays while she was in the shop. She's still moving through the crowd. Towards the clear circle in the centre. Brian's right behind her now. It's when she reaches the critical lip and bursts through into the vortex Brian hears what she's saying.

Is ma man hurtit?

Silence.

A cough and the shuffle of feet.

A gust of wind.

A distant siren.

Is ma man hurtit?

But there's nobody answers. There's just the reporter and his microphone hissing like a snake between the words. And the people in the crowd can't answer her eyes. She's grabbing them by the shoulders and shaking them.

Is ma man hurtit for Godsakes?

But they still won't answer. Next thing she slumps down to her man crumpled on the slabs. Stabbed by a junkie for a fiver. She's saying his name,

Alistair! Alistair!

But it's not to him she's saying it. She's on her knees like she's praying. The rain's dripping onto her palms and she's saying his name to the crowd. Like they can bring him back. Brian's got his arms round her. It's hard to tell if she notices or not.

There's blood on her hands now. Blood and water. She stretches them up to the sky and wails. The circle she's kneeling in could be a spotlight on any stage. Or a rock in deep space.

Barney Wheelan goes home. Carol's surprised by five things:

1 The fact he's home so early.

2 The fact he's sober.

But her surprises ain't over this night.

3 *C'mon get the wanes ready hen we're going out to the pictures*, he goes.

She's shocked and so are the wanes.

4 Barney gives her a peck on the cheek before they go out into the boggin close.

5 *We'll need to get some cash together and get out of this midden*, he says.

Brian Rogers goes home and sits on the new pink couch. He gets up and looks through the CDs. His wife gets a couple of surprises too:

1 She comes in from her dancing classes and finds him listening to Buddy Holly. 'Peggy Sue'.

2 He starts dancing with her.

I thought you hated fifties stuff, she goes. Brian flings her on the couch.

It's got a good rhythm, he says. *Let's take it for a groove babe.*

Rena's surprised too. Cos Eddie usually comes in late when he's with Barney:

1 The door goes while Flannagin's pounding it into her. Flannagin fucks off out a window. Eddie comes in the room as Rena's shutting the window

2 Eddie kisses her, *I love you*, he says,

3 Eddie goes to the window. *Is that Flannagin running down our street?* he goes, not making any connection.

4 The story he comes away with about Mary Maglone and the Busby Babes.

But she's interested in this story. Oh she's interested alright. Very interested. Rena plies him with more drink and can't wait to get round and tell Flannagin. Big Eddie's definitely getting his hole tonight. Any way he wants it.

And it's not just them three that changes. The voltage goes up in the whole team. Everybody's glowing like Americans. Meanwhile the Padre Pio shrine is attracting more nuns priests and wheelchairs. From all over the world. The tunnel for the Zoomph MAPTT – Magnetic Air Pressure Tube Train has come to a halt half a mile underground and a mile from the ground. The Leisure Complex is towering higher and higher. And yes it is casting a shadow. And yes you can see the shadow on the ground. But the wild thing is the ground seems to be shining like a pin. Bright like springtime.

OK there's been some money spent on it. But even at that it should still be dilapidated. And it is. But instead of architectural despair it's took on this new look. Rustic. That's maybe it. Rustic. Lived in but welcoming.

The season's moving on. Before every match Bailey and the Three discuss tactics in Mary Maglone's with the Babes. They're the managers of the team now. If the truth be known.

Rovers have drew Real Madrid in their first European Cup game. The Three and Bailey are in Mary Maglone's discussing how to play. The Busby Babes flew over and watched Real playing. It's no bother for a ghost. Whoosh and you're there. So they chat away about what players to watch and who to keep the ball away from and the usual football stuff. Bailey's taking notes and doing wee drawings. It's all going great. Great except for one thing –

Unbeknownst to them Flannagin's planted something in the room. It's a device that detects any change in the electromagnetic flux about the ring-main circuit. The very plugs in the walls. They sit at fifty hertz all the time. But sound waves cause them to distort slightly. Enough to digitise and decode and separate the distortion into words. Flannagin's also got the end of a fibre optic shoved through a crack in the window frame. It's all being fed back to an Optic 5000 – the fastest finger-ring computer on the market. Flannagin's left it in a flowerpot.

It's three weeks after the lead on the roof incident with Bonzo. Young Eddie's sitting in his garden minding his own business. Watching the clouds go past overhead. Shutting his eyes and listening to a tin can rolling along the ground. The shadows of birds moving over his eyes. That's when Bonzo comes up with the news.

Pat the Leg shot himself through the head with a shotgun he found in a farmhouse he broke into.

Eddie goes to the funeral. There's a wreath the shape of a football on top of the coffin. Green white and gold it is. Celtic. And Eddie feels guilty. He ruined Pat's career. His life. It's his fault. He's to blame for Pat doing himself in.

At the altar Eddie prays for Pat. He glances up at the flowerball again and it comes to him. He decides he'll devote his life to football. And that's some decision for a carthorse like him. And with all the will and determination in the world he'll be lucky to get far.

Glasgow. A big – big house on the corner. Sandstone. Bay windows manicured gardens the whole fuckin bit. There's a car outside. Rena sits doing her lips in the wee vanity mirror. Inside there's a plush office and that's where Flannagin is. And there's a group of them sitting round watching this disc. It's a disc of some ordinary people sitting talking. But now and then there's these ghosts dressed in ancient football strips. Every time a ghost floats past the screen the Boss snatches a glance at Flannagin. Flannagin smiles. But he's not sure what he means by his own smile cos he's not sure what the Boss means by his glance.

The disc comes to its hissing end. All the men in the room look at the Boss for their clue as to how to feel about this thing. But he's silent. He's staring at Flannagin. Pressuring him into doing something with silence. And he does. He can't take the silence pressing against his forehead.

There it is folks, Flannagin says clapping his hands together. *There it is – that's what's happening. Aye. That's it right enough.*

What? says the Boss.

The folks give it a what is he on about look?

Well – it's obvious – Albion Rovers have been took over by the ghosts of The Busby Babes! Possessed!

*

Outside the big – big house on the corner. There's a car. And in the passenger seat Rena sits filing her nails. She hears a noise and she looks up. Flannagin's being booted out by two heavies. He keeps trying to get back in.

One word – that's all I need. One word.

But the heavies keep buffeting him about and down the path.

Tell him I'll phone, he shouts before he jumps into the car. Rena flashes her startled new eyes at him. Her lashes are like two spiders sliced in half and stuck above and below her eye.

Well? she goes.

Well? This is it. It's my last chance, he goes.

Last chance or what? I hope we're not going to lose our money?

Lose our money? I wish that's all it was.

What d'you mean?

Flannagin draws a finger across his throat with his left hand and turns the key with his right. The car bumps forward and dunts into a black Merc. Flannagin stares at Rena.

I stuck it in gear in case it rolled when I was doing my eyes, Rena says and leaves her mouth hanging open.

Flannagin manages to get the car going and out onto the street before the two heavies come down the path to inspect the damage.

St Augustine's chapel is well over a hundred years old. It's in bad repair. When Flannagin walks in there's the smell of musty books. Only a few old women are dotted about. Father Boyle's down the front drinking.

Flannagin walks down. He sits beside Boyle and lights up a fag. He goes to talk but Boyle says, *shoosht*. He's got his eyes shut and he's concentrating on something. Flannagin thinks he's maybe got the wrong man here cos he looks like he's took up praying. It's ages and nothing's said. Flannagin finishes his fag. The wee cupped hands of Jesus are full so he's got to stub it out on the floor.

Boyle eventually comes round.

Hello Flannagin, what can I do you for? Something holy perhaps?

What were you doing – praying?

Praying? Me for fucksakes? I gave that up at priest school.

He pulls two small earphones out his ears. Flannagin looks down and there's the personal stereo on his waist. Amstrad – best you can buy now.

No – I was listening to the races. I've got a double up at Goodwood. Fifty to one. So what's it about this time? Boyle laughs, *Divine intervention again?*

No – exorcism.

Fuck off!

I'm serious.

No you're not.

I've never been more serious in my life. He takes the video disc out his inside pocket.

See this, he goes. *When you see this you'll change your mind.*

OK then c'mon. I've not had a good laugh since old Mrs McGinty caught her tits in the wringer and wanted the last rites.

So they go into the inner sanctuary of Boyle's little kingdom. In the library there's the leather-bound books where the smell comes from that permeates the chapel.

They're covered in cobwebs and mildew. Three giant spiders scurry for corners when Boyle comes in. They remind Flannagin of Rena's eyes. A fourth spider that's not so sharp is squashed under the MILLENNIUM SUN that Boyle's picked up and smashed it with one fell swoop. Graceful as a dancer. Compassionate as religion.

Where's the video? Flannagin wants to know.

Boyle winks and pulls a bookcase away. There's a door behind it. In they go.

This is our wee secret, he says.

Sure. No bother, goes Flannagin looking about the place. Its black leather furniture. A three-seater a two-seater and a single seater. Boyle swoops and lifts a set of handcuffs off the single. He tucks them down the side. But when he turns Flannagin's got a whip.

Whiplash whiplash, he's saying and whacking it into the couch.

Gimmi that!

Boyle tidies up his love toys and straightens out the nude books.

Where's the video?

Boyle points to a slot in the wall. Like a letter box. He takes the disc off Flannagin and shoves it in. The whole wall lights up like a cinema. The film starts playing.

Jesus fuck, Boyle says at the end, *Jesus H Christ – is all that real?*

Aye it is real. How d'you think they've got this far?

But Boyle's not listening he's rewinding the disc and listening to everything they say. But it's all about football and tactics.

Did they say anything about God?

Flannagin looks at him like he's mad. *What?*

God – Jesus and that. Did they mention him or anything?

No – all they can talk about's football!

Boyle looks a bit scared. He's running about hiding all the implements of depravity.

Don't tell me your bottle's crashed?

Well you can't expect to show a man that life after death exists and for him to act normal.

What the fuck is up with you?

What if there is a God?

A God? A fuckin God?

Oh fuck, goes Boyle.

I thought you believed in all that stuff anyway – that's your job.

I never really believed it up to now.

So does that mean you're not going to do it?

Boyle looks round the room and then at the freeze-framed disc. There's a thump and a wad of notes lands beside him. Boyle picks it up. But you can tell he's still not sure.

You can have a share in the profit from the Complex – if you're successful.

Boyle lights up.

OK. I'll do it.

Boyle starts up the disc with the sound down. He watches for an hour.

Boyle and Flannagin's on the couch. The disc is freeze framed. Boyle's got an ancient tome opened on his lap.

There's only one problem.

Eh?

I've got to have a physical object connected with each individual dead player.

It registers in Flannagin's mind.

Well let's get to work then.

Flannagin shakes Boyle's hand hard. But not hard enough to cause the slight tremor that rushes across the wooden planks under the plush carpet. An ice-blue light flashes through a crack in the floor and is gone.

What the fuck was that?

Padre Pio probably, says Boyle.

They laugh. But it's a stunted uneasy laugh.

In the stars and moon room Mary Maglone picks up an iniquitous ripple in the force. She calls up the Busby Babes and warns them.

There's something directed against your spirits. An entity connected to the Sproat.

You'd think in the year 2004 there'd be no more mucky pitched corrugated steel football parks. But there is. Nine miles east of Glasgow. All pies and greyhounds. Red and tangerine. Just been painted. Four winos shelter beneath bent-over corrugated steel.

But today you can't see the tackiness for two reasons. One – there's a certain glow about the place that makes it rustic. Two – the place's saturated with the world's media. Here's the story of the century as far as football goes. Wee Rovers meet the mighty Real Madrid. Never has something so insignificant made it into the world's headlines since Clinton's Dick. And Clinton's disappearance. There's only the hushed buzz about the place. The Rovers players are already in the dressing room tense as fuck. Photographers are checking their cameras. Aperture. Film. Flash. Setting the distance. Some's taking photos of the nuns and wheelchairs round the shrine. Maybe get a feature in the Sundays with that. But most of them's focused on the roundabout at McDonald's Multi-storey World Burger. Where you can get burgers the flavour of any cuisine in the world. Curry flavour. Sweet and sour. Fahita. Black pudding. Porridge. Frogs' legs.

And the Telly's there. BBC. NSTV (New Scotland Television). WEB CAMERA – allsorts. And Matt's there in the middle stroking his wee statue. He's like a man in the firing squad. Only he's not going to be shot to fall in a crumple where he is. When the time's right he's going to get sucked through the lenses onto the photoreactive electronics inside. From there he's going to be broken up and synthesised into zillions of wee pulses and digitally fizzed round the globe. To be reconstituted through decoders onto millions of screens.

But the time's not right yet. The time's right when the Real Madrid bus arrives so they can get Matt in all his madness with the Spanish players trooping out the bus as a backdrop.

Real Madrid are staying at the Salmond Leap hotel.

The time's coming. Round Burger Bend the double-decker comes. In the colours of Real Madrid. The crowd bustles forwards. Rovers fans with pens and paper. Photographers start whirring and clicking like robots. Flashes are bouncing off everywhere so that the whole area's like a battlefield without the explosions.

The bus draws up. There's a silence. Its long rows of black windows tell them nothing. The crowd surges quietly backwards leaving a good two metres between them and the bus. It's like a UFO's landed and they don't know what to expect.

The only living things that have breached this quarantine cordon's the greyhounds. Benny's right up there and pishes on the corner of the bus. The hissing brakes are disgusted. It's like Benny's a fan welcoming the visitors. The other greyhounds are waiting eager at the door.

Hisss it opens. There's gasps and the first dark-skinned Spaniard steps down. He stands in the free zone. Looking about. He can't believe the place. A shed in the middle of a building site. That's probably what he's saying back to his mates on the bus. But it sounds like *No Nintendo No Nintendo*. Like he's got no Nintendo game. The others come off with their hair slicked back. Wee fat Spanish men are opening the locked side doors of the bus and carting the training equipment in. Hundreds of bags and bottles. Lotions and potions.

The first four or five players are greeted by the good old greyhounds. Snorting their balls and shoving their noses up the crack of their arses. The macho Spanish men don't know what to do. They smile at the cameras, trying to shove the dogs away. Placing the heel of their palms on the foreheads of the dogs and pushing. At the same time they're trying to keep a happy rows and rows of nice teeth smile for the cameras. The flash-flash is going on everywhere so that the morning papers show five guys bent over and they've either got a dog growing out where their balls should be or it looks like they've farted and a greyhound-shaped cloud's coming out their arse.

Soon as Real Madrid start making their way through the paper-waving and pen-pointing crowd the telly starts interviewing Matt. It's got the background it wants. And even though Rovers have proved how good they can be you can tell by the tone of their voices – the condescending twitch in their words – that they expect Rovers to get a right tanking here. To get thundered. For their luck to run out.

So how do you expect the game to turn out Matt?

I reckon we can hold them out and maybe snatch a goal or two, he says.

You can see the twitch of a smile on the media. Their voices go up ten points in the condescending scale.

And what's Padre Pio got to say about it Matt? Any messages from beyond?

Oh – he'll be with us all the way. Every minute of the game. Every kick of the ball.

D'you think he's actually on the pitch with the guys Matt?

Aye of course he is. Every ball that's kicked he's got a hand in it.

A hand?

Sorry – a foot. Every ball that's kicked he's got a foot in it.

This fat bastard shoves a microphone in Matt's face and points the camera at the shrine.

And how d'you explain Matt that Padre Pio's in there helping your players meanwhile he's out here helping the – pause for comic effect – *lame and the afflicted.*

Bi-location.

Eh? says Fatty.

Bi-location son. D'you not do any research at all? That's what he's famous for Padre Pio. Being in two places at the one time. Matt takes a long deep breath through his nose. *Smell the flowers?*

The what? goes Fatty losing his cool.

The flowers son – tut tut – your researcher's really let you down there. Every time he's about there's a smell of flowers.

No no I never . . . what about the second leg Matt. D'you think Rovers can travel?

Well – we've been to Forfar.

Real Madrid reach the dressing room. Creak. The wooden door's just made out of floorboards with a z-shaped bit on the back to hold it all together. The windows are either cracked broke or boarded up with cardboard. The money Rovers have made has gone into the red hole of debt. But they're almost in the black now. There's a right rotten smell in the place. The smell that you get out the back of hotel kitchens. And maybe something dead. There's black water in the bath with a pink scum round the edges. And there's a plumber there. He's got a plunger on the end of a floor brush.

Don't worry – I'll have this spick and span for full time.

The Real Madrid players look at him.

What ees thees speek and span?

The Real manager takes one look at the place and takes a flaky. He storms out shouting all this stuff in foreign.

So the game's delayed. Cos it looks like the Real players have left. But the Ref's still on the pitch so Mary and Bailey know the game's going on. But where's the opposition? Rovers are running up and down the pitch. Practising.

It's just European tactics to put us off! Matt's shouting. *Don't worry keep the head and we'll be OK.*

Next thing this big rumbling happens. The main gates open. It doesn't matter cos the ground's full – and most of the crowd that would have snuck in are up on the scaffolding or packed about the Complex somewhere. Better view. And what they can see but the supporters in the ground can't is the Real Madrid bus coming in.

Bailey nudges Mary. In it comes and parks behind the goal. The Real players troop out dressed to kill in their shining gear and boots. They line up. The Rovers supporters that were behind the goal are on top of the bus now or stuffed round the edge of it. Watching. Kick off – a roar goes up. Except in a far corner of the ground. Flannagin and Boyle's watching with screwed up eyes.

And they're even more dejected at half time cos the expected doing for Rovers hasn't come. The Real Madrid players troop onto the bus and the Rovers retreat to their dressing room. It's been a hard game so far. Rovers are defending. But a couple of times they've broke out and played well. Couple of chances and their confidence has been growing towards the end of the match. Maybe they're not so high and mighty as they seem these Real Madrid. And the supporters are of the same minds.

♪♪ *I think your name is Kid on Madrid*
Kid on Madrid
Kid on Madrid
I think your name is Kid on Madrid
You come from Bar-ce-lo-na.

And the second half's different. Rovers come out and attack on all cylinders. Ten minutes of pure pressure. And Eddie and Barney score one each. Then it's back to the wall defending as Real throw everything at them.

♪♪ *Padre Pio give us a goal give us a goal give us a goal*

Padre Pio give us a goal give us a goal give us a goal

Padre Pio give us a goal give us a goal give us a goal

Padre Pio give us a goal give us a goal give us a goal.

Ten minutes to go and Jonesy Mark runs straight through the centre. He holds it up cos there's nobody there. It's been solid defence. But Brian Rogers's steaming up from the back. He's seen the run Jonesy made. He's like a train. Twenty-five yards Jonesy just lays it onto him ninety degrees and wham it's in the back of the net.

That's it. Real give up. Rovers win three–nil. The town erupts. Party time. Second leg in two weeks. The press go mad. They can't get enough. Some of them's even interviewing the greyhounds. The only two people not cheering are Flannagin and Boyle. Boyle picks up his bag. He feels something wet on his hand. He sniffs the air with his hatchet nose.

Yeeargh, he goes and drops the bag. Benny's walking away and flicking his leg.

It's Sauchiehall Street. There's blood on Janice's hands now. Blood and water. She stretches them up to the sky and wails. The circle she's kneeling in could be a spotlight on any stage. Or a rock in deep space.

It's the hospital. The place is mobbed. Brian's in the waiting room. There's a few people there. Mostly he's looking out the big window at the snow falling and the rows of lights on the wards.

News at Ten comes on. The door opens and some important people come in like horses out the frost. Snowflakes are falling in droves past the window and the fire's on. Two bars. Cosy. It's all shaking jackets and kissing cheeks. The snow is starting to lie. Maw Janice's still in the intensive care with Daddy Alistair.

The Scottish news comes on. Brian's amazed to see his Maw on the telly. And him and all. There he is running down the street. But he can't take the look on his face. He forgot what fear was for a while. He turns away to the window again.

The reporter tells the whole story and after Janice goes, *Is ma man hurtit?* there's this silence. Brian looks round expecting sympathy.

Is ma man hurtit! goes this blonde through her nose. *Well! Talk about giving Glasgow a bad name? Really. Is maa maan huuuurtit!*

There's another pause. The snow is still whispering its edges off the glass. Then the blonde's red lips part – and part – and part – and explode in super-nova laughter.

When it's died down this young guy says to her, *Field of willows that's what it means.*

Eh? says red lips.

Field of willows – Sauchiehall Street – that's what it means. Gaelic.

Iiiiiiis iiiiiiit? she goes in these long vowels that only snobs and teenage schoolgirls use.

That's when the door opens and a doctor looks about. He stops on Brian.

Brian son – could you come out here.

Brian leaves the snow and goes. The room is left in silent curiosity. All they can hear outside is the low voice of the Doctor. The c-c-c-crying starting in Brian and a wee woman wailing in the distance.

All through the next few days Brian thinks of his old Da and his new Da. And both of them gone out his life forever. And this hole in his belly. And that's when he decides he's never going to hurt anybody in his life. He's going to make sure he doesn't destroy nobody. And he's never going to get hurtit either. Never. He's going to be good.

It's one of them wee schemes that's sprung up the last fifteen years on land that used to be factories or railway land. Tan-coloured bricks and wee white windows with hundreds of wee squares in them. In one house the curtains are Hollywood pink. An American car sat in the driveway this morning. But Donna's away to work in it. Brian Rogers is away to the extra training laid on by Bailey Bloggs for the European game coming up. Return leg. Real Madrid.

Flannagin slips up the driveway. He's got a tammy on and his collar's turned up but there's no mistaking who it is. From the front a passing cat whips its head round and sticks its ears up at the sound of breaking glass. It slides up to the wall and slinks along to investigate.

Inside Flannagin shuffles along the hall. One kind of wallpaper on the bottom. Rag rolling on the top and a dado rail. Coving and a few B&Q paintings.

He comes into the living room. Elvis statues. Buddy Holly posters. Rockabilly paraphernalia. He heads off up the stairs. Into Bailey's room. It's neat and tidy. He's got plenty time. He looks under the bed. Nothing. In the drawers – usual pants and socks. But in the cupboard is where he finds the old brown leather case. Under a pile of shoes and neatly folded jumpers. He dunks it onto the bed.

Click   Click

He opens it and there's what he wants inside. He rummages through it. Photos. Badges. Letters. Postcards. Medals. All the things belonging to the eight Babes. He grins and empties the stuff into the training bag he's got with him. He clicks the case shut and puts it back in the cupboard and places the shoes and stuff back on top of it. He makes off down the stairs.

He shuts the door and he's off.

St Augustine's chapel's in bad repair. Hardly anybody uses it since Boyle took over in September 99. Nine nine nine that is. 999. When Flannagin walks in there's the smell of musty books. A few old women are dotted about. They've not high-tailed it up to St Pat's. The walk seems further every day. Even if the shrine up at the Rovers's a world icon now. There's talk of a soap opera based round it.

Boyle's lying smoking on the front bench. There's two empty wine bottles beside him. There's three books on exorcism and two video discs. One's the disc Flannagin made of the Babes in Mary Maglone's. The other one's *The Exorcist*.

Got it! says Flannagin.

Boyle swings his legs down.

The stuff! goes Flannagin, emptying it all out on the altar in front of the candles. There's light flicking off the medals and the photos. And Boyle's smile.

Is that what you need?

Boyle gets up.

Is there something for them all in there? he goes.

Flannagin looks at him. *I'm not sure. C'mon we'll look.*

So they set about trawling through the stuff. On the altar beside the chalice they set up neat wee piles. And slowly they build up an inventory of one two three four five six seven eight players. When they've got it all Boyle turns to the wooden head of Christ hanging down.

Thank you Lord. Thank you so so much.

He turns to Flannagin and says, *How much did you say I'd get – percentage?*

Never mind that the now. Can you do the job?

C'mon! Boyle says and they go down to the bench where he was reading the books and stuff earlier on.

There's a wee notepad.

I've been working it out. It's not a simple as it seems.

Don't try and fuck me about Boyle!

No – no – it's all here if you want to check. All the stuff. This is an old Catholic book. I got it in Chesters. It tells you the whole thing from a Catholic point of view. I've even got the Proddy book to make sure. You can't be too careful!

Right right – I don't want to read that shite. All I want to know is when and how!

Boyle looks at his notebook again.

Well, he goes, like he's calling out the procedure for building a house or baking a cake, *the whole procedure – exorcism – eight men – time for preparation. Prayers – devotions – communion with the Prince of Darkness . . .*

When – when for fucksakes? goes Flannagin.

Boyle shows him the date underlined in red at the bottom of the page. Flannagin opens his filofax. Flick flick flicking the pages in the candle-lit darkness of the chapel.

Jees! He holds his filofax up for Boyle to see. Boyle looks at him. Flannagin closes his filofax.

That's OK. That's fine. At least we can make sure they don't win the European Cup! Boyle says.

You sure Boyle?

More than sure – I've got faith.

Flannagin looks half convinced.

They might trip up of their own accord by then anyway, Boyle says.

Flannagin looks at his diary. Looks at the book. Considers.

OK. OK. Let's go with that. I can't wait to see them turn back into the ball-booting carthorses they really are. Cunts.

Boyle sees Flannagin to the door of the chapel. When they open it the same wee woman as the last time sees Flannagin and turns round and shuffles away muttering to herself.

I have to get to work, Boyle says. He sticks a closed for repairs sign on the front door of the chapel, gathers all the Babes' stuff and makes off into the inner sanctuary.

The date for the exorcism's the same date as the European Cup Final.

It's one of them wee schemes that's sprung up the last fifteen years. Tan-coloured bricks and wee white windows. In one house the curtains are Hollywood pink. An American car draws into the driveway. Donna's picked Brian up on the way home from work.

A cat slips up the driveway. It's yamming trying to talk to them.

Here kitty kitty, Donna's going. *I think it wants something to eat,* she goes.

But it's saying, *Hey missus your house's been screwed. A big fat cunt with a tammy broke in and took all these photos and stuff.*

But all Donna hears is the meeaww. She turns the corner. Puts the key in the lock and she's got the door half open when she notices the broke glass.

Brian – Brian – this glass's broke! she says.

He bolts into the house picking up an Irn Bru bottle on the way into the living room. He moves about the house springing into each room with the bottle raised like American films. After shoving the door open with the sole of his foot. Only they do it with guns. When he's searched the whole house and up the loft he goes back down. He's feeling sick cos of the adrenaline.

Make us a cup of tea Donna – there's nothing missing that I can see.

She comes in and gets the kettle on. Outside on the window ledge the cat's going meeaww again. *He's got a bunch of stuff from that room up the stairs,* it's going.

But they're not listening. They're wondering why anybody would break in and not take nothing.

Bailey comes in and they spend the rest of the night looking for stuff that might be stole. Every time Donna remembers another bit of jewellery they all run up the stairs and whip open its hiding place. There it'd be shining away like a good laugh. Eventually they come to the conclusion that whoever it was seen the car coming up the street and bolted. After all it's a right sight that big pink car. You'd see it for miles. Everybody knows who owns it. So they decide to get an alarm fitted and Donna feels much better with the thought that nobody's been in the house. No violation.

Bailey looks through his meagre belongings before he hits the sack for the night. There's hard training every day for the return leg with Real Madrid.

Pants socks. Watch. Jackets. Shoes in cupboard. Folded jumpers. Brown leather case. Nothing touched at all. Must have been startled right enough.

We're in a plane going to Madrid. The players are singing. But there's none of them drunk. They can't believe their luck. Some of them's never been to Spain.

Brian's sat beside Barney. There's nothing much to talk about so it's quiet. The constant drone of the engine's knocked most of them out.

Oh I forgot to tell you Barney – we got our house screwed the other day! Brian goes out the blue.

Fuck sake what did they take?

Nothing!

Nothing?

Not a thing. We think we disturbed them when they were just going in.

There's silence for a while again. Brian can't see it but Barney lets this big grin slide across his face. He waits for a while.

Brian, he says.

What? goes Brian without looking round.

Are you sure nothing was touched?

Nothing!

Not a thing?

There's silence again but Barney's grin won't leave.

Did I ever tell you about the time we got our apartment screwed in Spain – me and her?

No.

Well the door'd been kicked in. We came in after a night out. Five in the morning. Pished. The door'd been splintered. I goes mental. Wanting to kill every cunt. Know the way you are when you're drunk. Take on the world.

Brian nods.

Well we get the Rep – a wee scouse bird – and she gets the Polis. Spanish Polis. The Polis come up and we're going through what's been stole. Guess what?

What?

Nothing – not a jot. Just like you. And know what the funny thing was?

What?

There's this camera. A Pentax sat right there on the bed. I mean how the burglar never seen it I don't know.

Nothing stole?

No. We counted it as a stroke of luck.

Brian sits back. Barney's grinning away. He waits five minutes. And that's a long time for a pause in a conversation.

Brian, he goes.

Eh?

See two weeks after we got back from Spain that time?

Aye!?

We got the photos developed. I takes them home and there's me and her sat flicking through them. Sliding them off the pile one at a time. Beach. Sea. Donkeys. Spanish dancer with castanets. Me spilling wine down both my cheeks at the same time drinking out one of them mad things you get over there. And then – you're not going to believe this. There's two photos of our apartment. And there's this wee Spanish cunt on top of the bed bent over. And he's nude. He looks more like a Mexican really. The kind you get in them old Clint Eastwood films. A gringo. Fat and spotty. His arse that is. And he's twisted round to the camera with a teethy grin. Big wide eyes like he's laughing at a good joke. But he's got something sticking out his arse. It looks like a short blue stick and a short pink stick.

Brian's mouth's hanging open.

Me and her's giving it the what the fuck's this look? But it's when we slide onto the next photo we see it. It's a close up. The wee gringo bastard's got our toothbrushes up his arse.

No way! says Brian.

I'm telling you – stuck right up his arse, Barney goes and screws his face up like he can smell shite.

Brian reaches for the sick bag and boaks. But you can hardly hear him for Barney laughing.

It's one minute into the game and Rovers get a penalty. Here's a chance to go one–nil ahead and Real'd have to score five goals to go through.

Bailey waves Jimbo up to take it. Crack – it hits the bar. Jimbo collapses on the ground as the Real Goalie boots it up the pitch. Bailey and Ingrid console Jimbo. He must be getting better – nearly scored in a top-class game.

Rovers hold Real back. At the end of the day it's a two–nil victory for Madrid. Rovers go through. There's no noise cos hardly any Rovers fans have been able to afford the journey.

It's one of them wee schemes that's sprung up the last fifteen years. Tan-coloured bricks and wee white windows. In one house the curtains are Hollywood pink. An American car sat in the driveway this morning. But Donna's away to work. Brian Rogers's away to Spain.

Flannagin slips up the driveway. He's got a tammy on and his collar turned up. The cat whips its head round and sticks its ears up waiting for the sound of breaking glass. But there's none. It slides up to the wall and slinks along to investigate. Flannagin's at the door. He's got a chisel out. He removes the astricles from the wee pane and slips the glass out. Hand through and turns the key. He's in.

First thing he does is replace the glass. Pins the astricles back with a wee toffee hammer he's brung and locks the door. The cat's up on the ledge peering in.

Off up to Bailey's room he goes and he opens the cupboard careful. There's the suitcase under the shoes and the neatly folded jumpers. He draws the case out and dumps it on the bed.

Click   Click

He replaces the stuff. At a glance – or even a long look – it seems the case has never been touched. But there's things missing. Eight things to be exact. One belonging to each of the following:

Roger Byrne. Tommy Taylor. David Pegg. Bill Whelan. Eddie Coleman. Mark Jones. Geoff Bent. Duncan Edwards.

Flannagin places the case back in the cupboard. He puts everything back just as it was. And he's off back to see Boyle who's getting the exorcism together. He's got the eight things he needs and the process is going well.

It's only hours after Flannagin's left the house that Donna's back. And she's relaxing in a hot bath with Chuck Berry singing. She's expecting Brian any minute. But what she doesn't expect is the way he arrives. He comes rushing up the stairs, into the bog. He kisses her in passing.

Toothbrushes, he says.

Eh? she goes sitting up and turning round so that sheets and blankets of water's falling off her edges.

These, he goes picking them all out the jar like dead flowers. He runs back out the bog, down and out the back door and chucks them in the wheely bin.

Eyuck! Donna says after when he tells her Barney's story.

Rovers are top of the League. They're winning by amazing scorelines. Nothing can stop them. Bailey Bloggs's still working on Jimbo and he's getting better. Slowly better.

And on the European trail the games get harder and harder. Until it seems like luck when they win the semi-final. Against Benfica. One-nil and that's a penalty. But through it all the Goalie and the other player Johnny Dillon have started training better. Eating better. And they're getting a kick at the ball. Now and then. Getting better all the time.

So they get to the final. And Irony of Ironies who's in the final with them but the mighty Manchester United. It's a week away. Wembley it's to be. Every spare room in Coatbridge is rented out to the world media. Every kick and swerve of the Rovers players recorded and packed off. Their clothes. Music – the whole bit. The town's red and tangerine. There's not a Celtic supporter left in the place. It's Rovers all the way.

Wembley. The noise can be heard for fifteen miles. One end's all red and the other's tangerine. Rovers have attracted support from all over the world. Outside the mobile Padre Pio shrine's getting prayed at that much you'd think it'd fall to bits with the strain.

It's a happy day. The microcameras in Manchester United's boots are flashing all the best POV's round the globe. It's one each and it's extra time. The game's been well matched. But if the truth be told the Man U side's had more of the ball. Big Eddie scored for Rovers just before the end after Man U were up one–nil since the end of the first half. The supporters are in good spirits. Except one. Mary Maglone's scanning the park. There's a black presence but she can't locate it. It's a sea of shouting screaming people.

Except two. They've paid for a box Boyle and Flannagin. And that's where they are. And they're pushing it a bit tight. But he's got everything together. Another couple of minutes that's all. Just a couple of minutes and the Exorcism'll be there.

So it's extra time and it's one each. They've done away with that golden goal shite so it's half an hour of football left. The players shake hands before they restart the game to the applause of both sets of fans. But high up in a box above the crowd Boyle's coming away with all this mad stuff:

And when he had called unto **him** *twelve* **disciples** *he gave them* **power** *against unclean* **spirits**.

to cast them **out** –

and I **command** you to

leave the

bodies of these young men

now!

Roger Byrne. NOW
Tommy Taylor. NOW
David Pegg. NOW
Bill Whelan. NOW
Eddie Coleman. NOW
Mark Jones. NOW
Geoff Bent. NOW
Duncan Edwards. NOW

Suddenly big Eddie trips over the ball and lands on his face. The eight spirits pop out the bodies and continue to play whizzing through bodies. It takes them a while to realise they're out the bodies.

They're playing a totally different game. And now the deflated Rovers are pinned to their own goalmouth. Like they've all caught a heavy flu at once. It's that obvious Alex Ferguson turns to Matt and shrugs his shoulders. But Bailey Bloggs knows what's happened cos three minutes ago Mary shrieked and fainted. The ripple in the force went right through her like a thousand volts.

The spirits realise what's happened. The Babes gather in despair. In a huddle in the centre of the field. Every now and then a Man U player runs through them. And they feel it the Man U players. They shiver and they start taking the ball round the centre circle. Cos there's something not quite right in there. Not quite right at all. In fact there's frost starting to form on the grass. And ice.

The Ref goes over to feel it. He stops play for a minute. Nicky Butt's standing with folded arms and a foot on the ball. That gives Bailey a chance to go over and set the players up for tight defence. He pulls the Three aside and tells them what's happened. But they already know. They felt it.

Like getting a Christmas tree dragged out my arse, Barney says.

Always the poet, goes Bailey, *but these guys need this win to get to Heaven. All we've got to lose is the game.*

The Babes realise they're holding up the game. They move into the Rovers supporters. A circular space clears for them cos people start freezing. Moving away. If you look across from the red side you'd see a hole in the terraces.

On the park Manchester United are hitting everything post, bar, arses, backs of heads. Wes Brown, Phil Neville, Michael Clegg and Alex Notman have all had good chances in two minutes.

It's only a matter of time. Brrr goes the Referee and we're into the second period of extra time. They change sides. Still one each.

Five minutes to go – Nick Culkin runs at an angle across the pitch – twenty yards out. A sudden back-heel to Michael Twiss and a rocket shot soars past everyone into Rovers' net. Manchester United fans go wild. Two–one. Rovers are dejected. Their heads are hung. The cold circle on the terraces gets wider. The Babes have lost their only route to Heaven. They try to re-enter the players but there's a block. The Man U fans are happy but the two widest grins in the stadium belong to Flannagin and Boyle. If they had their names hanging over the edge of the box you'd think the box belonged to a right dodgy solicitors' company. Or film producers. Flannagin and Boyle – Cunts Я-Us.

Flannagin lights up a cigar in glee. The smoke goes down instead of up. You can't tell if the strange air currents are due to the convection in the stadium or the despair of the Babes as they prepare to be sucked back into oblivion. For a million years maybe.

But the smoke snakes its way down. And there behind the Rovers goal is Benny. Sniff sniff he goes. And off he pops searching out Flannagin. Meanwhile the Rovers goal looks like it's going to give way any minute again.

As Benny pads across the ground sniffing Manchester United fans are singing victory. Rovers are pinned down.

Bang blam scud the ball's bouncing off
everything. It's a miracle it can't find its way through.

United are happy to have four snipers on the edge of the Rovers penalty box and every time the ball comes back out they're firing it back in like rockets. They're laughing. Every time a Rovers player tries to break free with the ball they take it off him like he's a wane. A wee bit of teasing to the oohs and aahs of the crowd. The Eight are as bad as they ever were now. But there's two players who've got a bit better.

One's Johnny Dillon. The only thing he does in the match. One thing. He lobs the ball over everybody's head cos he's spotted Jimbo making a run for it. Jimbo gets the ball. A Nicky Butt saunters over to flick it away from him. But fuckin whizz Jimbo's round him and away like a ferret. Two or three try but they can't take it off him. The crowd's on their feet. No one's saying a thing. It's not the time for shouting. Cos it's only Jimbo and the goalie. The whole place is silenced. Boyle nudges Flannagin cos he's leant back with his hands behind his head waiting for the final whistle and riches. And freedom from the threat of the Boss.

Come on Jeembo. Running runneen up the peetch – keek the ball een thee net Jeembo, Ingrid's shouting

He gets to the penalty box. A quick look behind and it's like the egg and spoon race coming at him. Every other man on the field is running up. Some dead set on stopping him and others dead set on helping him. He looks at the goalie.

The goalie's stayed on his line. Jimbo bangs it. It hits the bar. He bangs it again. It hits the post. He's watching the ball come curving back out off the post. That's how he doesn't see the goalie coming at him too. He knows the rest of the players must be nearly on him by now. He runs in to meet the ball. He's in the penalty box now. **Kerunch** – the goalie flattens him. **Penalty.** Jimbo's to take it.

Bailey Bloggs runs on the pitch and hugs him.

This is it son. Remember all the things I showed you. Pick your spot. Don't change it – it's picked and that's that. Keep over the ball and hit it hard and straight.

Jimbo looks round. Ingrid blows him the sexiest kiss ever. He gives her this nervous smile. It's him on nearly every telly in the world. And the whole world's behind him cos Rovers are the underdogs. The whole world's pressing for Jimbo to score. But there's some others that are wanting him to score even more than that. The Babes. They need him to score. Cos there's only thirty seconds left.

And what they do next only Mary Maglone can see. They morph into sheets of ultraviolet light. Well it's sub-ultra-violet really cos only Mary can see it. And they attach themselves onto the posts and the bar so there's a bigger striking area. So the ball will be funnelled into the goal if it's within four feet of the goalmouth. They just hope Jimbo can do it. Get it to within four feet.

The stadium is hushed. You'd think it was the preamble to a nuclear war. Flannagin's mouth's hanging open. His cigar's stuck to his bottom lip. Benny sniffs and turns with his ears up. The Babes – turned into secret sheet lightning – glow. Well it's secret apart from some people. But they're alright. They're on the right side. And there's somebody else knows what's happening. Sees a vague shimmer round the goal. It's Boyle. And right away he's into a spell to immobilise the Babes completely. He sets it up. But he's too late. Jimbo whacks it. It's two feet out but it seems to swerve at the last second and into the top right. The Babes sigh with relief in that split second silence you get after a penalty's scored.

THE ROAR OF THE CROWD

The Ref blows for the goal. The Rovers players mob Jimbo.

♪♪*Jim-bo Jim-bo when did you learn to kick the ball straight?* the Rovers fans are singing.

Underneath the roar Boyle's got the spell going. The Babes feel themselves getting dragged down under the weight of gravity. They're being drawn together into one energy. Benny moves with stealth through the ground sniffing out Flannagin. When the Ref gets the players to calm down Man U go to kick off again. But he blows the final whistle.

PENALTIES!

And none of the Rovers players can kick a ball.

The Babes don't know what to do. In a matter of minutes they could be interred in snow again. And another thing – the Rovers goalie is shite.

What the fuck are we going to do? Roger Byrne says.

Think everybody. Think!

They think. Mary Maglone comes over.

Hey here's Mary, Tommy Taylor says.

Frank Swift, shouts David Pegg – *Frank Swift!*

What about him? Duncan Edwards goes.

Well we can't get back into them so maybe Frank Swift . . .

But where is he?

I could get him, Mary says.

The Rovers goalie is walking towards the net. Mary pushes her arms into the mass of electric blue spirit.

Frank Swift calling Frank Swift. Can you help us.

I thought you'd never ask lass! says this striking figure in glowing sky colour.

The United player shoots to the goalie's right. The ball's on its way to the net. And Frank Swift thuds into the goalie's body. The ball's three feet from passing the line. Frank Swift dives and saves it. A wave of shock runs round the ground.

Rovers miss.

Frank saves.

Rovers miss.

Frank saves.

Rovers miss.

Frank saves.

Rovers miss.

Frank saves.

It's all up to the last kick of the ball. Jimbo steps up.

It's only the sound of his feet swishing over the grass. He stops. Not a sound. Nothing. The wind whistles over the top of the ball. He places the ball. Rolling round towards him

flick by tiny flick trying to get the right position. The right
way up. And there is a right way up for a ball. He finds it
and walks back. It's his heels on the grass this time you can
hear. A whistle starts from the Man U fans. First it's low and
it gathers volume and insistence and he walks backwards.
He stops to the deafening sound of a million snakes.

Bailey Bloggs's holding tight onto Mary. Bailey gives him
the thumbs up. Jimbo looks to Ingrid. Ingrid licks her lips
and blows him a kiss. The ghostly Babes can't look – they
shut their eyes. Their wily blue forms settle into one sphere
of energy. It's so alive some of the supporters start to see it.
But it's only out the side of their eyes. No trick of the light's
as important as this one kick of the ball. And the trajectory
it'll take after the kick. But the most important thing is where
it'll come to rest. Where it'll come to rest. And that's what
Jimbo's thinking as he runs at it. The cheer goes up in the
same curve as his run. Jimbo thuds the ball.

It travels.

The goalie moves. The wrong way first and then the right
way.

The crowd's silent.

It's Jimbo. The whole universe is Jimbo.

The Babes look on. Cos the whole of eternity's Jimbo.

The ball travels. The goalie's moving towards it.

The goalie's fingertips get to it but not enough.

Not enough.

Not enough.

Zip. The ball's in the back of the net. There's a stunned
silence in the ground before the roar goes up and the Padre
Pio song.

♪♪ *Padre Pio give us a goal give us a goal give us a goal*
Padre Pio give us a goal give us a goal give us a goal
Padre Pio give us a goal give us a goal give us a goal

Padre Pio give us a goal give us a goal give us a goal

Padre Pio give us a goal give us a goal give us a goal

Padre Pio give us a goal give us a goal give us a goal

Padre Pio give us a goal give us a goal give us a goal

Padre Pio give us a goal give us a goal give us a goal.

The noise is deafening. Man U are dejected. Rovers are going wild. Bailey and Mary and Ingrid flatten Jimbo before the rest of the players can get to him from the centre circle. It's chaos of the beautiful kind. Rovers fans invade the pitch. Frank Swift leaves George the bewildered goalie's body. The Babes mob Frank – their spirits passing through him turn by turn like breaths of fresh air.

No one notices the commotion in the box high above the terraces.

Benny bursts into the box. He looks at Boyle and growls, then Flannagin.

Get away get to fuck, Flannagin's going.

Benny stalks towards him.

Fuck off Mutley, he goes and swings a boot. Benny dodges. Flannagin leans over to pick up a Buckie Turbo bottle.

GNASHSHSH!! Benny sinks the teeth into his

leg. THUMP! Flannagin scuds the bottle over

Benny's head. *Yelp yelp*, goes Benny. The thud reverberates up Flannagin's hand and he lets it fall. It rolls to the edge of the box.

Boyle stuffs all the gear in his bag and makes off. Benny manages to dodge as Flannagin puts the boot in. He takes a couple on the ribs. But he whips round and gets Flannagin on the hand. Flannagin wrenches his hand away and takes two steps back. Benny rises and makes a dive for him.

Flannagin stands on the Buckie Turbo bottle.

YEARGH! he goes and flings his arm up in the air

as he tilts over the balcony.

Benny does a Mutley laugh, *Rassin Fassin. Rassin Fassin.*

Flannagin thuds onto the terrace. His arms hit the ground first and they're mangled and snapped by the weight of his body. He falls onto the gap left by the Rovers fans that have invaded the pitch. No one notices. There's too much going on over the other end.

The crowd's focused on the Wee Rovers. The World's focused on the Wee Rovers. Fascinated by the minnows that went all the way. All the way they went. All the fuckin way!

The teams shake hands and swap jerseys. Boyle sneaks out with his bag crushed shut under his arm.

The Babes are in the mix too. There's no instrument could measure their relief. They're milling about both teams.

Hey c'mere and see this, shouts Roger Byrne.

He's tugging at the Man U shorts on one player. The Babes are having a right old laugh at the state of their gear.

And that's when it happens. Eddie, Barney and Brian knew all about the possession but the other five players knew nothing. They just thought they were getting better all the time. Thought maybe the stuff about Padre Pio was true. Some divine intervention. That's what it was. What else could it be? But for a fleeting moment they're all stood there looking into the ghostly eyes of their counterpart. A surge of spiritual energy flows through them. And although time exists on earth it's a different time that exists elsewhere. In a moment the Rovers players know what's happened. And they smile the warmest smiles ever. Into the greatest love ever. The infinite things. It passes. They're confused as they walk towards their trophy. Glances and puzzled looks at each other.

As the Wee Rovers go up to collect the trophy the Busby Babes ascend on a stairway of clouds to Heaven's gates. Mary and Bailey can see it all clearly. They're holding hands. The big gates are plonked there on the clouds. And there's a man. It looks like a man. Surely it must be St Peter.

But that's not who it is. That's not who it is at all.

Des Dillon

At the gates Matt Busby is sitting on a rock. *Where the fuck have you lot been? I've been looking all over the place,* he goes, *all over the bloody place man.*

Roger Byrne shakes his head and flings his arms round him.

Good to see you Boss. Good to see you.

Jimbo holds the cup aloft to the riotous cheers of the fans.
George the goalie and John Dillon. Then it's the Eight to hold
the cup up one at a time. First they hold it to the crowds
below. There's the cheer. Then inexplicably they're moved to
hold it to the sky. And it's back again for that instant. The
understanding. The connection.

Brian Rogers holds the cup up.

Matt Busby pats Brian Rogers into Heaven.

Taylor Thomas holds it up.

Tommy Taylor runs up. *Good lad,* Matt says and pats him
through the gates.

Pegg Davidson up with the cup.

David Pegg's patted on the back at the gates. *Good lad
David. Good lad.*

Barney Wheelan blows his wife a kiss and holds the
trophy up.

Bill Whelan throws a couple of mock punches at Matt
Busby. *You're a lad and a half,* he goes. *C'mon get yourself in
there before it shuts.*

Cole Edwards – the same.

Good lad Edward. Great stuff. Pat on the back and in he
goes.

Jonesy Mark.

Mark Jones runs up to Matt. *Mark, Mark – you had a great
game son. You're in the starting line up next week.* Mark laughs.
But he's nervous when he looks at the gates. There's just this
amazing yellow light in there. But it doesn't hurt the eyes. It
doesn't hurt the eyes and yet it's the brightest light you've
ever seen. *C'mon in you go – it's OK.*

Brent Geogh goes up.

How do Boss.

C'mere you! Matt says and gives him a big hug. Brent's
reluctant to go in after he sees Jonesy **FﬁASHSHSZZZ**

into the light. *Get in there before I boot your arse.* In he goes.

Big Eddie holds the cup up. By now the crowd are delirious. A picture of Pat the Leg flashes in his mind. And the flowerball on his coffin. And his voice – Pat's voice – *Well done Eddie – well done son.*

Duncan Edwards runs to Matt. Matt can't say anything for a while. He holds onto Duncan and Duncan holds onto him. And they're crying. Both of them. And their tears are teeming with dolphins. Teeming.

You're all home now lad. All home.

Bill Wheelan's just inside the gate. Inside the light.

C'mon Boss, c'mon Eddie, he shouts.

Duncan and Matt, arms over each other's shoulders walk towards the light. But there's a voice. Somebody shouting.

Hey for fucksakes wait for me! They turn and there's Frank Swift legging it up the cloudy stairs. The two of them laugh and wait. Down below the Rovers goalie's watching with his mouth hanging open and the trophy in the air. The crowd's bewildered at him. They're nudging each other. The goalie still stares at the sky. Eventually the crowd fall silent. One by one they look up to the sky.

What they see is a bright bright light. And they see three figures walking into the light. And the shape of a gate. The shape of a gate closing. The yellow light turns blue. Then it bursts apart. There's two white blue figures standing on a cloud. But there's eight others. A high bell rings. Eight ghostly figures play the most beautiful football that'll ever be seen. The crowd's necks are stretched. But their souls are full. For a full minute they are awed by the display – and the most amazing music ever – voices singing in harmony – millions. The football stops. The spirit players join the other two figures in the light. The light crushes down to a pulsing star and shoots off into the sky. And then it's all wiped from their minds.

They shake their heads and start the Padre Pio song again. There's a procession round the ground with the mobile shrine. Priests, nuns, wheelchairs, nervous breakdowns, alkies, junkies, Jehovahs, the broken-hearted – all the needy. Film producers. Publishers. They're all there. And there's thousands of wee Padre Pio statues and candles lit.

Jimbo and Ingrid have found a wee quiet bit in the labyrinthine corridors of Wembley. They're shagging lumps out each other.

Mary Maglone's already bought and paid for her wedding dress. It's nothing too fancy considering her age. And they've been married before. But he doesn't know she's bought it. Bailey Bloggs doesn't know he's going to ask her. Doesn't know he's going to get caught up in the noise and party atmosphere and turn round shocking himself and say

Marry me Mary.

And then he's going to wonder what the fuck he's saying and then he's going to realise what he's saying. And he's going to hang his head and think of his dead wife for a second. But his head's going to come up smiling.

Aye – fuck it! he'll say. *Marry me Mary – will you?*

And she's going to jump on him and wrap her legs round him and they're going to spin in the middle of a sea of red and tangerine.

Flannagin's dead. His spirit soars and tumbles down a fiery tunnel into Hell. He's running and glancing behind cos he's getting chased. Chased and pursued by a pack of gnashing wide-jawed greyhounds. And there's red between their teeth. Blood. And they're big. As high as him and their jaws are big as crocodiles'.

Fat and red. Out of breath – he reaches a door. A wooden arch door. Like the kind you get on a castle with a portcullis. He can smell flowers. He looks back and the greyhounds are gaining on him. Coming round the last bend. A monstrous version of Benny's right at the front.

He looks for a handle. There's none. But up above the door it says:

He looks back at the advancing wide-mouthed greyhounds. He thunders his meaty fists on the door. Clunk clunk as locks are removed.

The greyhounds are closing in.

The door opens. A face peers round. He recognises the face. He doesn't remember where he recognises it from. But he's seen it somewhere before. It's the same feeling you get when you're trying to remember the name of a second-rate actor and what film you've seen him in.

But Flannagin's got no time for all that. The greyhounds are right on him. He barges past the figure. Goes in. Slams the door and slides the bolt. And as he slides the bolt he feels a similar bolt slide fast in his soul.

That's when he sees the flames. That's when he smells the burning flesh. That's when he hears the screams like screams he's never heard before. Ever. He sees another sign.

groaks - sproaks - zeelbebubs

Over in the distance in red ashes are these wee demons of all shapes and sizes. And they're smiling at him the way lassies do to a boy that's walking past himself. Just like that only multiplied by the size of the sun. He turns to the face that let him in. When he sees the man in full regalia he gasps.

Padre Pio says, *Yes my son?*

Are you real?

Yes. Look over there.

Flannagin looks over. There's two doors. And a figure outside each one.

One door goes into Death. And one returns you to Life. You only need to ask, Padre Pio says.

Fuck – and there's only one question? Flannagin asks.

Yes – how did you know my son? Have you been here before? Flannagin strides over. He says to one figure,

If I asked him there what's the doorway to life what would he say?

BUMP

Flannagin comes to on the floor of an ambulance speeding through London.
Hey George this guy's alive!

End

LILIAN FASCHINGER

Magdalena the Sinner

'Meet Magdalena Leitner, codename "the Sinner". She is a killer seven times over, clad in a second-skin, black leather motorcycle suit. She is Austrian – but not the yodelling type. Rather, she's bent on a singular, sinister mission: to force her confession upon the village priest she has kidnapped at gunpoint . . .

'As she tears through the European Union in search of love, liberty and in pursuit of happiness, Magdalena charges at the windmills of bourgeois mores, Church hypocrisy, nationalist instincts, and our selfish failure to listen to or care for others . . . Unfettered by moral scruples or social constraints, our leather-clad heroine acts out every woman's most subversive wish – and every man's – as she roars through conventions on her Puch . . .

'In the end, we, like the priest, are wholly in Magdalena's spell, and want this magical morality tale to go on and on and on' Cristina Odone, *Literary Review*

'Faschinger rings the changes with wit and ingenuity . . . Magdalena is a spellbinding raconteur' Margaret Walters, *The Sunday Times*

0 7472 5459 1

review

ISLA DEWAR

Giving Up on Ordinary

When Megs became a cleaner, she didn't realise that if people looked at her a cleaner would be all they saw. Megs has as full a life as the people she does for, Mrs Terribly Clean Pearson or Mrs Oh-Just-Keep-It-Above-The Dysentery-Line McGhee. She's the mother of three children and still mourning the death of a son; she enjoys a constant sparring match with her mother; she drinks away her troubles with Lorraine, her friend since Primary One; and she sings the blues in a local club.

Megs has been getting by. But somehow that's not enough any more. It's time Megs gave up on being ordinary ...

'Explosively funny and chokingly poignant ... extraordinary' *Scotland on Sunday*

'Observant and needle sharp ... entertainment with energy and attack' *The Times*

'A remarkably uplifting novel, sharp and funny' *Edinburgh Evening News*

0 7472 5550 4

review